A THING OF BLOOD

A Thing of Blood is the second title in the series of crime-caper novels set in 1940s Australia that feature William Power; it is preceded by *Good Murder*, and followed by *Amongst the Dead*. Robert Gott is also the author of *The Holiday Murders* and its sequel, *The Port Fairy Murders*.

For my parents, Maurene and Kevin. Always.

A THING of BLOOD

ROBERT GOTT

SCRIBE

Melbourne • London

Scribe Publications
18–20 Edward St, Brunswick, Victoria 3056, Australia
2 John St, Clerkenwell, London, WC1N 2ES, United Kingdom

First published by Scribe 2005
This edition published 2015

Edited by Margot Rosenbloom
Typeset in 10.5/15 pt Janson by the publisher

Printed and bound in Australia by Griffin Press

The paper this book is printed on is certified against
the Forest Stewardship Council® Standards.
Griffin Press holds FSC chain of custody certification
SGS-COC-005088. FSC promotes environmentally
responsible, socially beneficial and economically
viable management of the world's forests.

National Library of Australia Cataloguing-in-Publication data

Gott, Robert. / A Thing of Blood: a William Power mystery.

9781925321098 (paperback)
9781922072139 (e-book)

1. Murder–Fiction. I. Title.

A823.4

scribepublications.com.au
scribepublications.co.uk

This is entirely a work of fiction. All of the main characters are products of the author's imagination, and they bear no relation to anyone, living or dead. Only the streets they walk down are real.

CAST OF CHARACTERS

William Power
Brian Power
Mrs Agnes Power
Darlene Power
Peter Gilbert

Paul Clutterbuck
Gretel Beech
George Beech
Anna Capshaw
John Trezise
Ronnie Oakpate
Mr Crocker
Mr MacGregor
Mary Rose Shingle

Nigella Fowler
James Fowler
Mr Fowler
Mr Wilks

Detective Radcliff
Detective Strachan
Sergeant Wilkinson

Captain Spangler Brisket

CONTENTS

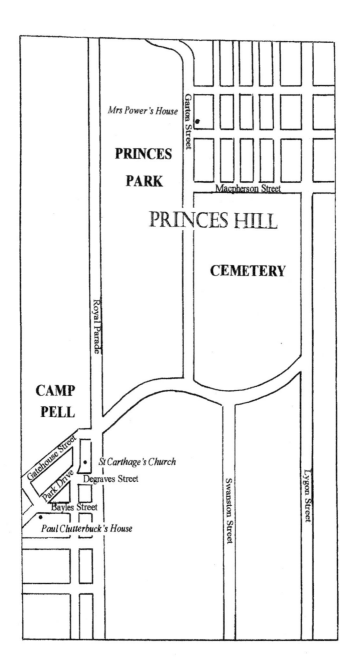

'… from face to foot
He was a thing of blood, whose every motion
Was timed with dying cries.'

Coriolanus, Act 2, Sc 2, Vs 110.

PART ONE

Chapter One

HOMEWARD BOUND

MY BODY WAS BRUISED. My ego was bruised. I was feeling, generally, a bit on the sensitive side — which is why my impatience with my brother's prurient questioning was beginning to show.

'Brian,' I said, my voice providing the thinnest of crusts against the emotional magma that threatened to break the surface. 'Brian, I am grateful that you travelled all this way to render assistance, but I really don't wish to discuss what happened in Maryborough any further.'

When I said these words, we were an hour into the train journey from Maryborough in Queensland to Melbourne, two thousand miles south. In 1942 this journey took four days, and the thought of going over and over the unpleasantness in which I had become embroiled was intolerable.

'All I'm saying, Will,' Brian said, characteristically indifferent to my mood, 'all I'm saying is that, even though I was only up here for a few days, it does seem odd that every woman you were involved with ended up dead. It just doesn't look good. I'd be reviewing my courtship strategies if I were you. This is all I'm saying.'

I leant forward. Between clenched teeth, and keeping my temper under admirable control, I told my smirking brother that we were now officially at the end of this conversation.

'And you needn't,' I added, 'think that I'm nursing a grieving or broken heart.'

'Oh, I didn't think for a minute that you were grieving or heartbroken,' he said, and somehow conveyed in this assurance his dubiousness as to my having a heart to grieve or to break.

'I'm going to find the dining car,' I said, and my tone made it unambiguously clear that I didn't want Brian to accompany me.

This first leg of our journey was to Brisbane, and as this was the night train the world outside sped by unseen. In any case the windows were shuttered against the unlikely event that the Japanese air force chose tonight to bomb the Queensland railway. The train was crowded, even though all civilians were required to obtain a permit before travel. We had had no difficulty getting a permit, and neither, apparently, had anybody else. I suppose any journey out of Maryborough would be looked upon as essential. We were travelling in what passed in these parts for style — a first-class sleeper — paid for by Brian who, in not making anything of this, subtly let me know that I was beholden to him. Is there anything more calculated than self-less generosity?

In the corridor of the second-class sit-up carriage I was told by a man — who smelled so strongly of horse that he must have been a stockman — that there was no dining car between Maryborough and Brisbane, but that one was attached for the Brisbane-to-Sydney leg.

'Broken arm,' he said, nodding in the direction of my ostentatiously slung left limb.

'Yes,' I said, in a manner that I hoped would discourage further conversation and indicate that I found his powers of observation unremarkable. He must have been brighter than he looked, or smelled, and didn't attempt further intercourse. He shrugged, muttered something that may have been 'arsehole', and pushed past me.

There was little to detain me in any of the carriages, so I returned to our first-class compartment.

'This train seems to be a special transport for the dull,' I said.

'So you won't stick out like a sore thumb then,' Brian said snippily.

'A few days away from those children you teach obviously isn't enough to rescue your wit.'

He folded his arms.

'At least I've got a job, Will. What are you going to do when we get back to Melbourne?'

'I'll see what's happening in the theatre, I suppose. That is my profession.'

'There's not much,' he said. 'A couple of plays. You might have to learn how to juggle. Get on the Tivoli circuit.'

'I don't do vaudeville, as you very well know.'

'Wirth's Circus is in town.'

'Very funny.'

'Well, it's a branch of show business, isn't it?'

'I'm not in show business, Brian. I'm a professional actor. I might start a new company.'

'They're looking for munitions workers. There are ads in the paper every day.'

I didn't dignify that with a response.

'Oh, by the way,' Brian said. 'I forgot to give you this. It was left on the bar at the hotel some time this afternoon.'

He reached into the pocket of his trousers and withdrew a sealed envelope. The name 'Power' flowed across its front in beautiful copperplate.

'It's nice that you eventually got around to giving it to me,' I said. I opened the envelope and pulled out a folded sheet of unlined paper. It smelled faintly of jasmine, as if it had come from a stationery box. In a script as elegantly and carefully formed as that used to write my name were the words, 'It's not over, you bastard. I'm on the train.'

I stared at it for a moment, willing it to make sense, and passed it to Brian.

'Charming,' he said. 'Any idea who it might be from?'

'Of course not,' I said.

'You know,' Brian said, 'it's amazing how you manage to rub people up the wrong way. You have a gift for making enemies. Darlene says that there's just something about you. You can't help yourself.'

'The thing about your wife, Brian, if you don't mind my saying so, is that she is very stupid.'

'The thing about my wife, Will, if you don't mind my saying so, is that she simply doesn't like you. That doesn't make her stupid. It makes her pretty normal. Now, if you'll excuse me, I have to use the dunny.'

He left the compartment and I didn't feel the slightest regret at having accurately diagnosed Darlene's stupidity. She was a harpy, with all the social graces of a wildebeest. Now pregnant, we would all be expected to bill and coo over her calf when it sensibly fought itself free from the mire of her womb.

When Brian returned we didn't speak further, but took to our bunks in sullen silence. I slept badly that night. The bunk was hideously uncomfortable, and I discovered something I didn't know about my brother — he babbled incomprehensibly in his sleep. Just after I'd managed to drift off I was awakened by Brian getting up to go to the lavatory. His bladder had always been the size of a peanut. He made no effort to minimise the noise he created. My irritation at his thoughtlessness prevented my return to Nod, but that irritation changed to puzzlement and then worry when he hadn't returned after half an hour.

I descended from my bunk, pulled on my trousers and opened the door into the corridor. I saw him immediately, lying on his stomach a few feet from the toilet door. Perhaps reprehensibly, my initial thought was that his termagant of a wife would blame me for whatever had happened to him.

As I walked towards him he began to move, and by the time I'd reached him he was on all fours and groaning. A small stream of blood was making its way down his neck towards the edge of his singlet.

'What happened?' I asked as I helped him to his feet. He seemed dazed and didn't immediately respond. 'You seem to have hit your head.'

This simple observation provoked a flurry of anger from him.

'I didn't hit my head. Someone hit it for me. I was on my way back from the dunny and someone obviously thought that I was you.'

'Well, I think that's a bit of a leap,' I said.

Brian became a bit short with me. Perhaps he was concussed.

'I'm twenty-seven years old and the only injury I've ever suffered is a shaving cut. I'm with you for a few days and someone tries to kill me.'

He shook off my support and we returned to the compartment.

Brian bled quite extravagantly from the scalp wound but, apart from a headache, he declared that he was unhurt. We agreed that my entry into the corridor must have prevented his assailant from finishing off the job, although I had seen no one.

'I suppose we should report this to the police when we get to Brisbane,' I said.

'Well, of course we should report it to the bloody police,' Brian snapped. 'Someone tried to kill me. That might be an everyday event for you, but I take a pretty dim view of it.'

Neither of us slept for the rest of the night and we kept a watchful eye on the door. We arrived in Brisbane without further molestation, but with Brian maintaining an uncommunicativeness that bordered on infantile self-indulgence.

In Brisbane we stayed in a hotel close to the station. There was no train to Sydney until the following morning, so this gave us plenty of time to inform the police about the assault on Brian. They were unhelpful, although their interest was aroused when I gave them a brief outline of recent, pertinent occurrences in Maryborough. News of that investigation had filtered through to them and they were mildly intrigued to meet me.

'Oh yeah,' said the overweight sergeant who was hearing our tale. 'We heard there was some actor or circus rouseabout — can't remember which — who got in everyone's way. So that was you, was it?'

'Yes, it was him,' Brian replied firmly, thereby denying me the opportunity of correcting this buffoon's absurd précis of my role. It transpired that the police were rather stretched at that time, what with all the Americans in town. They said that they would make a few inquiries, but that perhaps it was just a bungled robbery.

'After all,' the copper said, 'if he'd really wanted to do you in, I don't think you'd be sitting here telling me about it. But we'll look into it.'

This was most unsatisfactory, but it was as much as we were going to get. We returned to the hotel, drank in the bar, had a disgusting meal and kept to our room afterwards. Brian had become more and more jittery about his personal safety as the day had progressed.

The remainder of the trip to Melbourne was managed without incident. We stuck close together, never leaving our compartment separately. Over the three days the chill between us thawed slightly, but every look Brian gave me was inescapably imbued with his resentment at having been dragged into what he clearly considered was my sordid life. It was with some relief that we alighted at Spencer Street Station in Melbourne. Whoever had mistaken Brian for me had had no further opportunity to catch me unawares.

In the tram, on our way up to Mother's house in Princes Hill I was preoccupied by the impending meeting with the frightful and fertile Darlene, and with my mother, whose voracious appetite for gossip would brook no opposition. So I didn't consider the possibility that whoever had boarded the train in Maryborough with the intention of attacking me might well have disembarked in Melbourne, his intention geographically relocated but otherwise unchanged.

Chapter Two

CLUTTERBUCK

OUR MOTHER'S HOUSE in Garton Street sat opposite Princes Park and was rather grand. Unlike many of its neighbours it had not been subdivided into flats during the Depression. My father — who died when I was sixteen (his many absences meant that my memories of him were vague) — was a canny, and I suspect ruthless, banker. He picked up this double-storey Princes Hill mansion for a song, no doubt unsentimentally condemning its previous owners to a life of reduced circumstances in the process. Unlike my father, my mother, Agnes, looms in my childhood with the solidity of an impressive pinnacle. She is a striking woman. I get my looks from her. She is dark, and her hair has remained determinedly black throughout the vicissitudes of marriage and child rearing. It was a small shock to me to discover that its corvine splendour was protected by a proprietary dye.

'Hirohito himself might be perched in Spring Street,' she once said, 'but he won't have the satisfaction of seeing me with grey hair.'

The day of our arrival was, portentously perhaps, bleak. Rain was falling when we pushed open the front gate and climbed the few steps to the front door. There on the porch, despite the chill, was the gravid Darlene. Even from several feet away she exuded the smug self-assurance of the newly knocked up.

'Brian,' she said, her voice vibrating with solicitude, 'are you all right?', and she hurried to him. I couldn't help but notice that she'd put on rather a lot of weight since I'd last seen her, and it didn't suit her. If you don't have much in the way of a personality, a decent figure is advisable.

'Someone hit me on the head,' Brian said.

Darlene uttered a little squeal of horror and shot me an accusatory glance, as if that someone might have been me.

'He's fine,' I said, 'and so am I, you'll be relieved to hear.'

'Well, of course I'm relieved, Will. It must have been a dreadful experience for you. Mum and I have been just sick with worry.'

Among the vast catalogue of Darlene's unattractive features was her insistence on calling our mother 'Mum', as if marriage to my brother somehow entitled her to an extra parent. She leaned down and picked up my suitcase. This was an unnecessary gesture designed to elicit Brian's immediate intervention, and expressions of concern for her welfare and that of her unborn child. It was like observing the rebonding ritual of the albatross. In a miracle of transference I was, fantastically, being held responsible for endangering Darlene's health.

My mother was upstairs in her study, writing to my brother Fulton. Her correspondence with him was regular — much more regular than her correspondence with me. He was the youngest, after all, and being stationed in Darwin he was at far greater risk than I had been in Maryborough. He was also more assiduous in replying than I'd ever been over the course of my travels. Mother heard us come in and called from the top of the stairs.

'Is that you, Brian?' And with the awful thud of an afterthought, she added, 'And Will?'

'Brian was attacked,' Darlene called.

Mother gave an exclamation of fright and began her descent. Although I hadn't seen her in over a year, she'd somehow contrived to look younger than when I'd left to take my eponymous acting company to Queensland. She was tailored from head to foot, obviously diverting a considerable amount of her generous annuity into the coffers of a Collins Street seamstress. She never bought anything off the rack. It was a short step, she would say later, when the expression became current, from *prêt à porter* to *prêt à mourir*. With the example of our mother before him, how could Brian have settled for the drab fecundity of Darlene?

'I'm fine,' Brian said before Mother reached him. 'Just a blow on the head. Someone thought I was Will.'

She turned to me then, took in my broken arm and the cuts and bruises on my face, and said, 'Oh, Will,' but more in disappointment than sympathy.

'I have quite a story to tell,' I said quickly. She cheered up at that.

'I want to hear it all,' she said, laying her hand on my good arm. 'And don't spare me the gruesome details. Darlene, could you make us some tea? And perhaps you could sacrifice this week's fruitcake. I'm sure Brian and Will would love a piece. Darlene bakes a fruitcake each week,' she said to me, 'and sends it to the troops. It's awash with brandy, so whoever ends up with it will go into battle with a smile on his face.'

Darlene retreated to the kitchen and Mother steered us into

the front room — a room well furnished and dominated by its beautiful bay window. The window framed a view of Princes Park opposite, its surface scarred by wide trenches dug to provide residents with some form of protection should Japanese bombs begin raining down on Princes Hill. After the bombing of Darwin and the Jap subs in Sydney Harbour, this possibility didn't seem at all remote. I couldn't imagine my mother, though, hurling herself into a trench, a cork clamped between her teeth against the jarring shock waves produced by explosives. Nevertheless, a coat hung permanently near the front door, an object of clothing she referred to as her 'trench coat'.

'Now, Will,' she said, 'I'm cross that Brian had to get caught up in your affairs, but I am glad you're safe and well and able to tell me everything that happened. It sounds frightening and terribly interesting. And I don't want you to think that you can get away with leaving out the sex — unless there wasn't any, of course. It cost quite a bit of money getting Brian up to Maryborough and, frankly, I'm looking to get some value for it.'

I was used to my mother speaking like this, and so was Brian, so neither of us batted an eyelid. Indeed, I would have been shocked by any demonstration of discretion. While Darlene was still out of the room I rapidly sketched in the outlines of my recent history, confident that Mother would press for more and more details over the ensuing days. I didn't leach the colour out of the more lurid incidents. To do so would have been to agitate in my mother a suspicion that I was holding back, and this in turn would excite fierce questioning. I learned early in my childhood that my mother responded better to the embellished than to the undecorated truth. She liked, she said, a well-dressed story.

Darlene's fruitcake was, it pains me to say, excellent, although she looked at me as I was eating it as if I was depriving a soldier somewhere of his last meal. She didn't look at Brian in this way.

He was able to eat his slice under the benevolent assumption that it had been well earned — which, given that he shared Darlene's bed, I suppose it had.

After tea and more cake, both Mother and Darlene donned hats and gloves and set off for the city where Darlene was to be fitted for flattering (unlikely) maternity wear. I knew they wouldn't be purchasing anything made of the scratchy, government-approved cloth called 'shoddy'. Instead they would buy unconscionable silk and linen. Mother's seamstress had access to expensive reserves of pre-war material and, despite the papers railing against extravagance, my mother's philosophy not only accommodated such extravagance but insisted that it was, in fact, a sort of defiant patriotism.

After they left, Brian went upstairs to sleep, and I walked around Princes Park. Before I'd gone very far I'd determined that I would find alternative digs as soon as possible. I could not share a roof with Darlene for any longer than was strictly necessary.

On my way home I bought a copy of *The Age*, ignored the grim news on the front page about Stalingrad and an attack on Tobruk, and turned to the personal columns. My eye was drawn to a small advertisement for shared accommodation in Parkville, just a stone's throw from my mother's house:

'Bachelor (32) with furnished house and housekeeper. Parkville. Desires gentleman to share same. Apprx. cost £3 per week.'

The rent was steep, way above the twenty shillings I had been thinking of as my limit. But obviously this was a good house, and the bachelor, whoever he was, was probably wealthy and possibly well-connected. Poor people did not employ housekeepers. Even rich people had released most of their staff for war jobs. Perhaps I could negotiate a reduction in the rent somehow. I had access to some funds, my father having left money in trust for each of us. I had drained most of mine, but there remained more than enough to pay for several week's rent in advance to create an illusion in my landlord's mind of my having a comfortable income.

I telephoned The Age when I reached home, obtained the details that had been withheld from the advertisement and connected to the number I had been given. A woman answered and identified herself as Mr Clutterbuck's housekeeper. He wasn't at home, she told me, but would be back at six o'clock, when she was sure he would be pleased to see me. There had been no other callers, the three pounds rent acting as a natural filter against the hoi polloi.

I knocked on Clutterbuck's door at precisely six o'clock, punctuality being the courtesy of kings. The Edwardian house was very large (double-storeyed), and occupied the corner of Park Drive and Bayles Street. Its windows were disfigured by the ubiquitous anti-shatter precaution of cross-tape. The gate sat between two splendid square columns and it opened soundlessly, its hinges well oiled. Five steps led down to a tiled path that led, in turn, to the front door. The small garden had not been turned over to the growing of vegetables, despite the government's frequent exhortations that it was the duty of every citizen to eschew the frivolity of flowers and plant vegetables in their place.

Mr Clutterbuck's front garden was a formal grid of gorgeous blooms. So intent was I in admiring it (I had turned my back to the door to do so) that I didn't hear the door open. A voice at my elbow startled me by saying, 'The Yanks get drunk and piss in the front yards up and down the street. If you ever get invited to dinner at one of these places, don't eat the greens. The name's Paul Clutterbuck.'

He held out his hand and I shook it. I had him quickly tagged as the kind of man women find attractive, with his very short, tightly waved brown hair brushed back severely from a high forehead to reveal a discreet widow's peak. His eyes were blue-grey, but sufficiently deep in colour to escape that weird, unsettling look that very pale eyes give a face. I was suspicious of him at once. It has been my experience that people who look like Paul Clutterbuck have spent most of their lives getting away with things, and freely exercising the prerogative they think they have been given to treat lesser mortals with disdain. I found the carefully controlled wattage of his smile just a little too self-conscious to be entirely convincing.

'Why do Yanks piss in people's gardens?' I asked.

'Over there,' he said, waving towards Royal Park, the edge of which was visible from his corner. 'That's Camp Pell, the Yank army camp. There are still a lot of them there, even if MacArthur has gone to Brisbane.'

His tone indicated that perhaps I ought to have known this.

'I've been away,' I said, 'since before the Americans arrived. I've lost touch with what's been happening down here, apart from Leonski, of course. I know about him.'

Leonski, an American soldier, had killed three women in Melbourne and had thrown the city into a panic. The possibility that Melbourne had been nurturing its very own Jack the Ripper was sufficiently titillating to be carried in newspapers around the country. Leonski had been caught, tried and sentenced to death — a sentence that was due to be carried out quite soon. The Americans were obviously anxious to dispose of that particular public relations disaster as swiftly as possible.

'I met Leonski,' Paul Clutterbuck said. 'It was the night he killed his last victim in fact. He was at the Parkville Hotel. He was drunk. Nasty drunk. Belligerent. A blond punk. I didn't know it was him until afterwards, of course. He fell against me and I pushed him away. He wanted to argue about it, but he was in no condition to take me on. I left. He must have killed that woman a short time later. Apparently she met him in the street, by accident. Never seen him before. She rented a room a few houses down.'

'She was killed in this street?' I asked, with sudden dubiousness as to its desirability.

Clutterbuck laughed.

'No, not this street. She lived here, but she was killed around the corner.'

'Oh, that's all right then,' I said.

'You don't believe in ghosts, do you?'

'No. But I was looking for a quiet place.'

'You can't get much quieter than being dead,' he said. 'Come inside and we'll discuss the room.'

Inside Clutterbuck's house all was restrained and expensive good taste. The furnishings were sleek and new. I must have registered a reaction because he said, 'All this is my ex-wife's taste, not mine. I prefer decent armchairs. Furniture was just one of the things we disagreed about. The divorce documents fairly comprehensively catalogue the others.'

'I like it,' I said.

'It's awful to sit on, but I held on to it out of spite, and that's the ugly truth. I had a better lawyer than she had. She left with the clothes she stood up in, and that's about all.'

'I take it it wasn't an amicable divorce, then.'

Clutterbuck chortled.

'No. It was unpleasant and vicious, but as those are Anna's defining qualities, that's hardly a surprise. Whisky?'

Clutterbuck poured two generous, single-malt whiskies, and we sat opposite each other in elegant but uncomfortable seats.

'So, who are you?' he asked.

The question, so bluntly put, froze the delivery of the whisky to my mouth. I introduced myself, explained where I had been and what I did for a living. The conversation took an extraordinary turn when he asked me how I had broken my arm. I'd deduced from his own frank admissions that he wouldn't be alarmed by the truth, or some of it.

'I was involved in a murder investigation up in Maryborough. It came out of that. Indirectly.'

'Really? Were you being investigated?'

'Peripherally, but mostly because my own investigation crossed paths with the police investigation.'

'So you're what ... a sort of private inquiry agent as well as an actor? Is that your cover?'

Here, I should have disabused him. Instead, I put my foot on a very slippery slope and said, 'Yes. In a way, yes.'

'Are you licensed?'

'No. I'm afraid I'm rather dilettantish about it. It's more of a sideline.'

I thought Clutterbuck looked disappointed, so I added, 'But I've had a good deal of success. My instincts are good and I don't scare easily.'

He sipped his whisky, unleashed a magnificent smile, and said, 'You're perfect. The room is yours. Oh, and I've got a job for you.'

I should have left the house in Park Drive at that moment. Instead, without even looking at the room, I agreed to move in the following day, and left feeling elated that after only a few hours in Melbourne I had secured accommodation and a job. How could the future be other than rosy? How indeed.

Over dinner that night — a meal of vegetable curry, using mostly produce from the garden Brian and Darlene had planted, but introduced by smoked salmon which Mother had paid too much for at King and Godfree — I announced my immediate plans, omitting my acceptance of Clutterbuck's job offer. There were expressions of surprise at the speed with which I had moved, but no one howled me down or discouraged the shift.

'You're not offended?' I asked, giving each of them an opportunity to at least pretend that my absence might punch a small hole in the fabric of their daily lives.

'Oh, no dear,' Mother said. 'I'm sure you'd find living here far too humdrum. We have a quiet life.'

'At any rate,' I said, 'I'm not going far. Just across the park, so I'll call in regularly, of course.'

'Lovely,' Mother said, making a feint at sincerity and very nearly succeeding.

Over coffee and brandy I was given as much information as Mother had about my youngest brother, Fulton. Mail in and out of Darwin was irregular, and some of his letters had arrived with most of their contents excised, the military censor having decided that whatever he had written posed an unacceptable threat to national security. He was, Mother said, attached to some hush-hush unit up there, and her anxiety about him kept her awake at night.

'I write every day and send it off. I have no idea how many he actually gets, but it calms me down and makes me think that I'm talking to him. I told him all about your troubles, Will. I hope you don't mind.'

'Not at all,' I said. 'I'm sure it would cheer him up, take his mind off the bombs.'

'Yes,' she said. 'I tried to make it amusing.'

Only the fact that her eyes suddenly filled with tears prevented me from expressing my irritation that the most traumatic incidents of my life had been turned into comedy for the amusement of my little brother.

I retired to my old room. It had been repainted and redecorated, and there was no evidence that I had occupied this space until the age of twenty-two. I lay in the dark, but I couldn't sleep. Not unreasonably, I was troubled by the lie I had told Paul Clutterbuck regarding my credentials. He had hired me to investigate some matter on the understanding that I was in fact competent to do so. Well, I thought, how difficult can it be? Perhaps he wants me to follow someone. Any fool could do that. He was obviously a respectable man, so whatever it was I doubted it was criminal in nature. No. As I began to doze I settled on the idea that it was most likely to be of a delicate, personal nature. *Cherchez la femme* were the last words that ran through my mind before sleep finally overtook me.

The next sound I heard was the cliché of a piercing scream, followed by the inevitable crash of tumbling chinaware. Let me assure you, though, that the real thing can make your hair stand on end, cliché or not. I pitched into the darkness of the hall and heard Brian yelling from the top of the stairs, 'Darlene! Darlene!', and in such an hysterical, chilling manner that my heart almost stopped. I suddenly felt very cold. I followed him downstairs — he fell down them rather than ran down them — and entered the kitchen a few seconds behind him. I switched on the light. Brian was standing, wearing only his pyjama bottoms, his mouth agape. Broken plates and cups lay strewn on the floor and a smear of blood headed out the open back door. Mother came into the kitchen.

'What's happened?' she asked, her voice taut.

Brian numbly replied, 'Darlene came down to get some milk' — as if this explained anything.

I ran out the back door. There was very little moonlight but it was obvious that nobody was in the garden. The gate which gave access to the cobbled lane behind the house was ajar, but there was no sign of anyone to the left or right. I returned to the kitchen to find Brian sitting at the table, his head in his hands, and with our mother standing behind him. He looked at me, his face contorted by panic.

'Darlene's been kidnapped,' he said.

'Why would anyone kidnap Darlene?'

Brian, with despair yowling in every syllable, said, 'That letter you got on the train. It wasn't meant for you. It was meant for me.'

'You're fucking joking.'

'Please don't swear, Will,' my mother said.

Chapter Three

A FINE MESS

THE CLOSEST POLICE STATION was only a few blocks away in Fenwick Street, but after alerting the coppers to what had happened it was three quarters of an hour before an officer knocked on the door. While we were waiting, Mother and I heard a confession from a severely, almost catatonically, agitated Brian that was so bizarre and unexpected that I couldn't marry it with the brother I thought I knew. At first Brian sat in silence — not sullen silence, but stunned silence. I suppose that he was aware that when he began speaking nothing would ever be the same for him again.

'So the letter was meant for you,' I said.

He nodded.

'And the person who hit you? That wasn't a case of mistaken identity?'

He shook his head.

I folded my arms and allowed a small rush of self-righteousness to wash away the anxiety I should have been feeling about Darlene's safety. Just for a delicious moment. Our mother, with practised acuity, said, 'You had an affair with someone in Maryborough.'

Brian looked at her as if she were clairvoyant.

'Yes,' he said.

'Was it a man or a woman?'

Even from my mother, this struck me as an astonishing question. It jolted Brian out of the fug of his confused emotions.

'It was a woman, of course,' he said sharply.

'I've lived long enough to know that there's no such thing as "of course", Brian,' she said. 'If I'd asked you this morning whether you'd always been faithful to Darlene you would have said, "of course".'

'My God,' I said. 'You were only in Maryborough for a few days. Who was she?'

'Stop firing questions at me,' he said, 'I can't think.'

'All right,' Mother said. 'Take your time.'

'Her name is Sarah Goodenough. I went for a walk on the first night I arrived up there, just to clear my head. I ended up at the Royal Hotel. It's a nice place. I met a woman there. Sarah. We had an immediate connection. I can't explain it. It just took me over. We had a few drinks and it seemed perfectly natural that we should go up to her room. She was staying there. Her husband was in New Guinea. He was an officer in the militia, not one of the chocos.'

'What on earth is a choco?' asked Mother.

'You know, a conscript. A chocolate soldier. That's what they're called. It doesn't matter. I didn't mean to cheat on Darlene, but it was like the world outside that room didn't exist. When I was with Sarah there were no husbands, no wives, no betrayal. Just us. Intense. So intense. Fierce.'

'The intensity of madness,' Mother said.

Brian gave no indication that he'd heard her.

'I saw her twice after that. Only twice. It wasn't the same. There was something wrong between us. Sarah was highly strung. Nervy. I thought she might be worried about her husband, but she said she hated him and that she hoped the Japs would do her a favour and kill him. I found that a bit frightening. She said we could make a new life together. I'd told her I was married. I hadn't lied about that, but she sort of assumed, I think, that I felt about my wife the way she felt about her husband. The last time I saw her — the third time — there was a terrible scene. I told her that I was returning to Melbourne, to Darlene, that I loved my wife. She said — excuse the language, Mother — she said I fucked like someone who was glad to be doing it properly for a change.'

I hope, even under extreme emotional pressure, that I would have had the sense to omit such a hideous and telling detail. Mother, way ahead of me and unembarrassed by the revelation, said, 'If Darlene is boring in bed, Brian, that's your fault as much as hers.'

Suddenly, and mortifyingly, Brian began to cry.

'Sarah said that if only Darlene and Michael — that's her husband — were dead, we'd be happy. I told her I thought she was mad to say such things, and then I told her I thought we'd better not see each other again.'

'What do you know about this woman?' Mother asked.

'Nothing, really.'

'Is she a local Maryborough girl?'

'No. She's from Brisbane.'

'Let's assume that she followed you to Melbourne. Let's

assume that it was she who attacked and kidnapped Darlene. If she doesn't know Melbourne, what would she do with her?'

This line of questioning led to the ghastly consideration of the options available to the kidnapper. Would she imprison the living Darlene somewhere, or dispose of the dead Darlene?

Brian slumped, exhausted, in a chair.

Mother suggested that he go upstairs and put a shirt on.

'You must tell the police everything you told us,' she said, 'and you can't do it half naked. It all sounds so much worse somehow when one can see your nipples.'

Brian stood up and left the room.

'Honestly,' Mother said. 'I really do think the world would be a much better place without a single penis in it.'

When a policeman finally arrived it was after 3.00 a.m. I opened the door and admitted him. He was decked out in the absurd Gilbert and Sullivan uniform of the metropolitan police. On entering the hall, he removed the impractical helmet to reveal a head of grey, greasy hair. If there hadn't been a war on, I imagined he might have been retired by now.

Not wishing to hear Brian's story a second time, after giving my details to Sergeant Wilkinson — for that was his name — I decided to begin my career as a private investigator by wandering through the back lanes of Princes Hill. I hadn't done this since I was a child. Then, I'd felt a frisson of fear as I'd come upon the exotic offspring of poverty, playing or fighting on the filthy bluestone cobbles that paved the alleys behind their even filthier dwellings. I learned quite early, just by breathing in, that poverty is malodorous. Despite the privilege and security of my upbringing, I was aware of the putrescent breath of the poor being collectively exhaled in grim cul de sacs all over Carlton, just a few streets to the east of our house.

Now, the sinister air of these bluestone alleys was exaggerated by the possibility that I might come across Darlene's crumpled corpse or, even more alarmingly, her violent abductor, very much alive and not happy about being discovered. If dark nights and back streets were the natural haunt of the private inquiry agent I began to think I might not be ideally suited to the profession. I wasn't afraid of the dark, but I wasn't particularly fond of it when circumstances indicated that something nasty might be lurking under its cloak. I began to sing the 'thingummybob' song quietly to myself, imitating Arthur Aske's nasally voice as he assured us that it was the girl who makes the thing, that holds the oil that oils the ring, that works the thingummybob that was going to win the war.

I must have walked several miles. The only people I met were American servicemen, drunk, without being disorderly, on their way back to Camp Pell after a night in one of the sly-grog shops that provided liquor over and above the legal limit. Their presence was reassuring, despite the murderous Leonski having been one of their number.

When I returned to the house, Mother was sitting in the kitchen with Brian, and Sergeant Wilkinson was slurping tea from one of the cups she reserved for tradesmen. The detritus of many of the good cups still lay, shattered, on the kitchen floor. She had, however, lavished upon the good sergeant a generous slice of the absent Darlene's fruit cake. A stubborn crumb adhered to his rawly shaven jaw.

'I couldn't find her,' I said.

'That's a good sign,' said Sergeant Wilkinson.

Brian lifted his head.

'Why?'

'It means that whoever took her has still got her. If she'd been murdered the body would probably have been dumped.'

I suppose Sergeant Wilkinson thought he was being a comfort, but the confluence of "murdered" with "body" and "dumped" was not likely to provoke anything other than alarm.

'Thank you, Constable,' Mother said, ostentatiously demoting him, and she indicated by rising that she thought it was time he left.

'We won't touch anything, of course,' she said. 'I'm sure the detectives will want to check for prints and so forth when they arrive.'

She looked at the smear of blood on the floor.

'I suppose I shouldn't clean that up yet.'

'I'll have to stay,' said Sergeant Wilkinson. 'This is a crime scene. I'll have to wait for the detectives to do their stuff.'

'Given that this is a crime scene,' I said, 'perhaps having tea and cake in the middle of it isn't such a good idea.'

Sergeant Wilkinson blushed and coughed. Mother rescued him.

'Brian, you should try to get some sleep. You too, Will. I'm sure Constable Wilkinson will be quite comfortable down here for the next couple of hours.'

'I can't sleep,' said Brian.

'Darlene hath murdered sleep,' I said without thinking. Brian shot me a glance that conveyed the energy of outrage, even through his exhaustion.

'You really have inherited your father's gift for tact, Will,' Mother said.

'Are you saying that this Darlene murdered someone?' Sergeant Wilkinson said, suddenly alert. All three of us looked at him and knew that he would play no part in the solving of this crime.

I went upstairs to bed, and must have managed to sleep, because the next thing of which I was aware was Brian shaking me awake and saying, 'The detectives are here,' followed by the resentful *j'accuse* of, 'How could you sleep?'

It was early — 7.00 a.m. There were two detectives in the kitchen when I entered. If they were annoyed at such an early call, neither of them showed it. They were both in their early forties, I estimated, and both were lean and well groomed. Beside them, the bleary Sergeant Wilkinson looked like a very poor relation indeed. Good detectives create an unsettling impression that they are in possession of information that might be to one's disadvantage. The detectives in my mother's kitchen were adepts in this regard. I didn't like them one little bit, and immediately took refuge in the mildly satisfying fact that both of them were going bald, one more rapidly than the other. I knew when they turned their bland and disconcertingly neutral gaze upon me that they were considering me as a suspect as well as a witness, and I had just about had my fill of being suspected of crimes I didn't commit. Of course it was their job to believe the worst of everyone. A suspect's innocence would always be a disappointment to them.

Anxious to begin my move to Paul Clutterbuck's house, I answered their inquiries graciously, at least until one of them suggested, with a mock innocuousness that was insulting, that there was something odd about my search of the lanes.

'You say you left the house almost immediately.'

'Yes, to search the back yard.'

'And then later you wandered about the streets.'

'I didn't "wander" about the streets. I was looking for the person who had done this. Obviously.'

'Yes, obviously,' he said, but his tone suggested that for him the obviousness lay in an altogether different direction.

'I don't care for your tone,' I said.

'Oh dear. I guess that means we don't have a future together,' he said, with an ugly little sneer.

'What Detective Strachan is getting at,' said his companion, 'is that you might not have been hunting for the culprit, but checking on the success of an accomplice.'

'I am perfectly aware of what he is insinuating, and it is gratuitous and offensive.'

'So our visit here hasn't been a complete waste of time then,' said Detective Strachan.

At this point Mother came into the kitchen, and the demeanour of the detectives changed immediately. They weren't exactly charming — they couldn't draw on reserves of a quality they comprehensively lacked — but Mother has a way of encouraging the best in people or, at any rate, discouraging the worst. Her intervention meant that the rest of the interview went smoothly.

They had been in the house longer than I had thought. Before I'd come downstairs photographs had been taken, the room had been dusted for fingerprints, and a sample of the blood on the floor had been sent for analysis. They left an hour after my interview had been completed. After helping Brian and Mother clean up the kitchen, I took my suitcase and headed to Clutterbuck's house to take up residence there. It was a little more than a fifteen-minute walk across Princes Park, over Royal Parade and into Parkville. I knocked on his front door at 9.15 a.m., expecting his housekeeper to answer. There was no response, so I knocked again. I had turned and begun climbing the few steps up to the pavement, when the door opened and a woman's voice called, 'Paul thought it might be you. That is, if you're William Power.'

The woman who uttered these words was definitely not

Paul Clutterbuck's housekeeper. She was wrapped in a silk kimono, only just, and the unruly state of her glossy, hennaed hair indicated that she had come straight from bed to the door. Despite her dishevelled state, she was undoubtedly a beauty, and not at all what the Americans called a 'broad'. She was delicate, with pale skin and with lips so pink that lipstick would have sullied them. Her cheeks were faintly roseate, and there was something breathy in her voice that was irresistibly attractive. She hadn't been woken from sleep, I decided, but detached from sex.

'I'm sorry,' I said, unintentionally giving voice to this supposition.

'What on earth for?' she laughed.

'For waking you up,' I said. She came out of the house towards me.

'Oh, good heavens,' she said. 'We've been awake for hours. We've just been lolling. I'm Gretel Beech.'

I took the proffered hand, shook it, and followed her into the house.

'Paul's getting dressed,' she said, and left me in the living room while she repaired upstairs, presumably to get dressed also. I was struck even more forcefully than I had been the previous day by the fanatical neatness of the room. My suitcase made it seem untidy, and I was suddenly conscious that my clothes could have done with more careful pressing. I had the uncomfortable feeling that just by being there I was disrupting the general order. I was the human equivalent of a painting hanging askew.

'Will,' said Paul Clutterbuck.

I turned and was taken aback by the sight of him; his hands on his hips, and wearing a crisp, well-cut American army uniform. His tie was tucked into the shirt below the third button, and a forage cap sat jauntily on his head.

'I'll show you the house,' he said, clearly feeling no need to explain why he was dressed as he was. 'And then we'll talk about the little job I want you to do for me.'

I picked up my suitcase, self-conscious now about its scuffed corners, and followed him upstairs.

'Your room first,' he said.

The room he took me to was at the back of the house, but it was no servant's room. It had the handsome proportions of a master bedroom, and next to it was a bathroom.

'That's your bathroom,' he said. 'You can't share a bathroom *and* call yourself a civilised human being. Can you?'

He explained that his housekeeper, Mrs Castleton, washed the bed linen twice a week, Mondays and Thursdays, so I shouldn't leave anything too personal lying about.

'She's discreet, but she does have a rather Edwardian capacity to disapprove.'

Mrs Castleton, he told me, was a treasure, and that one of the most awful and under-appreciated consequences of the war was the limitation on the hours domestic help could be employed.

'Did you know about that?' he asked. 'It's supposed to free up the servants for war work. The idea of Mrs Castleton stuffing bullets into ammunition belts is ludicrous — although they'd be the neatest belts in the line. Mrs Castleton has a thing about order, and that's why I have a thing about Mrs Castleton. She takes hair left on soap very personally, as of course do all reasonable people.'

I felt compelled to agree with him on this point. I certainly didn't want to give the impression that I was careless in this department, separate bathrooms notwithstanding. Mrs Castleton would find no fault with my bath soap.

By the time I'd seen the rest of the house, I'd realised that although Paul Clutterbuck must have had a good deal of money, he couldn't afford its upkeep without the relief provided by a tenant's rent. Of the six rooms upstairs, two were unfurnished, and the air in them had the uncirculated dullness of the air in rooms that are never visited.

When we returned to the living room Miss Gretel Beech was there, dressed and poised for departure. With her hair brushed into place and wearing a dress that flattered her figure, but which had seen better days — I was surprised to see that the seam at one of the shoulders had begun to come away — she was, somehow, diminished. She now seemed merely pretty. When I'd first seen her I had thought her beautiful. I wondered which incarnation the obsessively neat Paul Clutterbuck preferred. Perhaps ungroomed women were a violation of his ordered life which he found exciting. The few seconds it took for these thoughts to race through my mind were sufficient to stir in me sensations of delightful lust.

'Will I see you at the show tonight?' she asked Paul.

'Yes,' he said, and turning to me he added, 'Will you come, Will? To hear Gretel sing?'

'Of course,' I replied, and knew even as I did so that I should be spending the evening with Brian, supporting my brother in his anxious wait for news of Darlene. Looking at Gretel Beech, however, familial obligation evaporated, and I found myself hoping that my evening would not be ruined by the inconvenient discovery of Darlene's corpse and the ensuing necessity of being on hand to offer condolences.

'Of course,' I reiterated. 'I'd love to hear you sing.'

'Paul says you're an actor,' she said. 'I hope you won't think I'm an amateur.'

She kissed Paul lightly on the cheek and he crassly cupped one of her breasts in his hand. She seemed unconcerned by this public intimacy.

'I'll see you tonight then,' she said.

When she had gone, Paul Clutterbuck sat in one of the uncomfortable chairs and indicated that I should do the same.

'Is your room OK?'

'Oh, yes,' I said. 'It's a generous size.'

'And you can manage three pounds?'

'Oh, yes,' I lied.

'You'll like Mrs Castleton. She works miracles with tired shirts and trousers. What do you think of Gretel?'

'She's lovely,' I said. 'She's a singer. Is that what she does for a living?'

'Oh, she does a bit of this, a bit of that, and a bit of the other, you know.'

'Is she any good?'

'She's OK at this, better at that, and superb at the other.' He laughed and stood up suddenly. 'What do you think?' he asked and smoothed down the front of his dark green army shirt. 'Gretel says women can't take their eyes off the Yanks' groins. It's the zipper, see. No chunky buttons. She says you can't beat the zipper for ease of access. And, I have to say, she's right.'

'I've never had a pair of trousers with a zipper,' I said.

'As a private inquiry agent, aren't you wondering why I'm wearing the uniform of our over-paid allies? It's not exactly legal to impersonate a soldier.'

I seized the opportunity to demonstrate my natural, instinctive skills in this area.

'Asking obvious questions almost always leads to hearing obvious lies,' I said. 'The truth has a tendency to leak rather than spill.'

He considered that for a moment and sat down.

'I'm glad I hired you,' he said.

'Have you hired me?' I asked.

'Two week's rent,' he said. 'Six pounds to do the job. It's

straightforward and it's not dangerous.'

I nodded acceptance, relieved that I'd been given a stay with regard to my precarious finances.

'But first,' I said. 'Why are you wearing that uniform?'

'Ah,' he said. 'It's ridiculously simple. I'm afraid I've become addicted to tinned cream and coffee, and both of those are found only in the American PX. Australian soldiers, and certainly civilians, are not allowed into those G.I. canteens. I do a passable Yank accent — sort of mid-Atlantic rather than regional — and the PX at Camp Pell is just around the corner. I haven't been challenged yet. Do you smoke?'

'No,' I said.

'Pity. A packet of twenty is only sixpence. That's less than half what you'd pay normally. It's enough to make you want to take it up, isn't it? The uniform is good for sex, too. Shop girls love it. You'll find them any night of the week at the Australia Hotel. It's like shooting fish in a barrel, as the Americans say. Lots of Yanks, lots of girls. It's almost impossible to find an unoccupied doorway after closing time.'

'Sex in a doorway doesn't sound very edifying.'

'You're not a Puritan, are you? Or a moralist?'

'No, of course not. I was thinking about comfort.'

'I think you'd be pleasantly surprised at the amenity offered by a narrow doorway. And the thrill of discovery doubles the pleasure and doubles the fun.'

'No wonder our blokes can't stand Yanks.'

'Let me tell you something about our boys, Will. Their uniform is ugly, they don't know how to shave properly, they smell, and most of them have their teeth ripped out for free when they join up. Dentures are no match for a good, clean set of American teeth. Do you have your own teeth?'

'Yes,' I said. 'And my mother's still got all hers, and she's in her sixties.'

'Ah, you must have had money.'

He ran his tongue over his front teeth.

'I've got all mine, too. No girl would believe I was a Yank if I had dentures. A few sweeps of the tongue and I'd be found out.'

He seemed so pleased with this vulgarity that he laughed.

'Now,' he said. 'To business. Are you able to do something for me this afternoon?'

I nodded, and was filled with trepidation.

'I want you to find out who my ex-wife is fucking.'

I didn't betray any emotion. I impassively took this direction in, but it did seem extraordinary, given his own priapic tendencies, that he should be concerned about the sexual gymnastics of a woman from whom he was now permanently disengaged. Knowing that discretion is a private inquiry agent's most important characteristic, I forbore to ask him 'Why?', settling for the more professional and detached 'Where?' and 'When?'. The address he gave me wasn't a private house, but a bookshop in Little Collins Street, in the centre of town, called 'Leonardo.' He said that his ex-wife would be in the bookshop at 2.00 p.m. He didn't tell me how he knew this.

'Her name,' he said, 'is Anna Capshaw, formerly Clutterbuck, of course. She'll be meeting a man there. I want you to find out where they go.'

'But how will I know her?'

'She'll be the most beautiful woman in the shop. You'll know her. You won't be able to take your eyes off her. Are you up to this job?'

'Of course,' I said, thereby committing myself to a series of events that were to make my recent troubles in Maryborough look like a mild comedy of manners.

Chapter Four

POOR DECISIONS

HAVING UNPACKED MY MEAGRE WARDROBE of clothes — most of them with the dust of Maryborough still on them, and all of them smelling faintly of the kitchen of the George Hotel where we'd been staying — I stretched out on the bed and considered the last few crowded hours. Darlene's kidnapping began to assume the strange dimensions of a dream.

A madwoman rising out of the darkness and snatching a pregnant woman from the safety of her own house: this was bizarre. Even more bizarre was the notion that this madwoman had become so besotted with my brother that she had followed him all the way from Maryborough to Melbourne. What kind of woman was this? Knocking Darlene to the ground would be like felling a bullock. Sarah Goodenough would have to be of

Amazonian proportions to overpower Darlene and drag her from the house. It occurred to me that Brian had not described her, and it was suddenly obvious that heft was of some importance.

With a few hours to spare before my 2.00 p.m. stalk, I decided to return to Mother's house. I wanted to ask Brian a few questions. He was on the front porch and he saw me coming across Princes Park. He hurried over and met me beneath a large Canary Island palm. His eyes were red-rimmed from lack of sleep, he was unshaven, and his breath smelled of tea and fruitcake. He leaned in close to me and almost whispered, 'The coppers think I had something to do with it.'

'They think that about me too, Brian. That's what coppers do. It's why they've got no friends.'

He clutched my arm.

'I had nothing to do with it.' There was panic in his voice.

'Of course you didn't,' I said. 'You need to get some sleep. You're not thinking straight.'

We went into Mother's house and found her upstairs in her study, writing her daily letter to Fulton.

'I haven't told him about Darlene,' she said. 'I don't want to worry him until we know what's really happened.'

I thought this was an odd expression, but didn't comment on it. I knew that Mother loved gossip, but I also knew that she held firmly to the view that events could not be dressed neatly as anecdotes in the presence of grief. She put down her pen and asked, 'Brian, is this Sarah person a big woman?'

This was precisely what I had intended to ask.

'No,' he said. 'She's small, petite. Smaller than Darlene. The coppers asked me the same thing. I told them that she was mad, and that mad people are very strong.'

'Yes,' Mother said, 'when they're in a frenzy. But this was planned. She must have had help.'

'Yeah. And they think I'm the one who helped her.'

'Well, of course they do, darling. They're not entirely sure that I'm innocent either. We just have to get on and let them do their work. There's no point taking it personally.'

'If I could just turn the clock back,' Brian said and began expressing his profound regret over his affair with Sarah Goodenough. Mother listened patiently, but I left them and went downstairs, and helped myself to a slice of Darlene's ever-diminishing fruit cake. While I was in the kitchen, I realised Mother was right — Sarah Goodenough must have had an accomplice, and the accomplice must have been a man. He probably came with her from Maryborough. If I wanted to go any way towards finding Darlene, I would have to telephone Sergeant Peter Topaz in Maryborough, and this was something I really didn't want to do.

My relationship with Peter Topaz was less than cordial. I acknowledge that I had made one or two understandable errors of judgement in my efforts to clear my name, but he'd been wrong about me, and that should have evened the score. He hadn't quite seen it that way. Nevertheless, finding Darlene, apart from being the first feather in my PI agent's cap, was more important than my feelings about a country-town walloper who harboured a grudge. I rang the exchange and booked a call to the Maryborough police station. I would be connected, I was told, in half an hour.

While I was waiting, I flicked through that day's copy of *The Age*. There was very little in the way of professional theatre in town. 'The Mikado' was playing at His Majesty's — nothing for me there. Singing is not among my accomplishments, although I can carry a tune well enough. 'Robert's Wife' was on at The Comedy. Lowbrow fare. Apart from that, there was the Tivoli, and I wasn't prepared to prostitute my talent by donning a pair of roller skates and performing a vulgar dance surrounded by half-naked women. I don't consider dancing on roller skates to be a skill. It is simply a failure of the imagination.

My acting career might have to be rested. Indeed, I saw no reason why I couldn't combine acting with investigating, should a suitable part come along. The certainty that one did not preclude the other, and the equal certainty that I had a talent for both, filled me with a sense of optimism and excitement. My reverie was interrupted by the clang of the telephone. My person-to-person call to Peter Topaz was now ready. I thanked the operator and waited for the sound of Topaz's voice.

'Well, well, well. Will,' he drawled, and I reminded myself that those elongated vowels didn't reflect any lassitude in his thinking.

'Peter,' I said, and tried to sound as though all that had passed between us was now of no consequence. 'How are you?'

'Is this just an expensive personal health inquiry, Will?'

I pretended I thought this was funny and laughed.

'And how's the Company? How are they getting on?'

'Since you left? Never better, Will. Never better.'

'OK,' I said. 'Let's drop the pretence that this is a social call.'

'No pretence at this end, Will. I imagine you want something.'

'I need your help,' I said, and let this startling admission sink in.

'All right,' he said, 'but the only reason I'm listening is that you're two thousand miles away. So whatever it is, I won't be tempted to thump you.'

'It's about my brother Brian,' I said, and told him all that had happened. He wasn't in any way censorious about Brian's having had an affair, but he said Sarah Goodenough wasn't the ideal choice of mistress.

'Given who he's related to, that's hardly a surprise though, is it?' he said.

He told me that Sarah Goodenough was known to the Maryborough police, although she had never been charged with anything. The owner of the Royal Hotel had had suspicions that she had been using her room there as a brothel. It was true that she entertained a lot of men, but there had been no evidence that money had changed hands.

'There's no law against giving it away for free,' Topaz said, 'so you might like to tell your brother that he'd been cultivating a well-ploughed furrow, and that if Sarah Goodenough told him she loved him she was lying.'

Topaz said he'd do some checking, but that any information would be passed to the Melbourne police, who would, he assumed, be contacting the Maryborough police in due course, if they hadn't already done so. He would, however, ring later that afternoon and tell me anything he thought was relevant as long as it didn't compromise the investigation. I gave him Paul Clutterbuck's number and said that I would be there about 5.00 p.m.

'I liked your brother, Will. I'm doing this to help him. I still think you're a complete dill.'

'Give my regards to everyone,' I said.

'Now why would I want to ruin their day?' he said, and hung up.

I congratulated myself on not having risen to any of Topaz's childish taunts, and was pleased to admit a little rush of professional superiority. I felt I had passed some sort of test. Private inquiry agents don't allow their emotions to run away with them.

The Leonardo bookshop sat at the eastern end of Little Collins Street in an area that was favoured by a louche crowd who thought themselves modern. Here one could see men in corduroy trousers, (I recalled my mother's advice that corduroy was always a mistake), and with beards, and with the self-conscious swagger of the determined and committed outsider. Artists and writers and communists gathered here, but I wasn't interested in what they painted or what they wrote. I am not, I hasten to add, a philistine, but I don't believe that verses penned by badly dressed, scrofulous comrades pose a serious threat to the sonnets of Mr William Shakespeare. It seemed to me that the only thing these people had in common with the Bard was facial hair.

I wasn't entirely comfortable in this part of town but, drawing on my acting skills, I affected an appropriate slouch and entered the bookshop at a quarter to two. It was an odd place. There was no counter at the front. Instead, the man who I took to be the proprietor sat behind a table in a far corner. He nodded when I came in, and went back to reading his book.

I began browsing casually: there was a table in the centre of the room and I picked up one of the titles that lay upon it. It was a collection of poetry written by someone with an unpronounceable name and translated by someone else with an equally unpronounceable name. I read the opening line of the opening poem and recognised the words as being English, but could force no sense from them. I put it down and browsed through a volume of photographs. There were some rather beautiful nudes among the pretentious still lifes and brooding landscapes, and I was surprised that such a book had not been seized by the police. I could see that the Leonardo catered for a literary crowd that differed markedly from book-buyers in Melbourne's more staid establishments. I imagined that material of a particularly racy nature could be obtained under the counter from the corpulent owner.

There was one other customer in the Leonardo when I

entered. He was a man who looked to be in his early forties, and was clean-shaven, though sporting a neat, Ronald Colman moustache. He was wearing a Dedman suit, the austere lines of which had been softened by its being made from expensive material. This compromise made me think that he might work in a government position where adhering to the clothing regulations would be expected. Perhaps he'd come down from Parliament House, which huddled behind sandbags just a few minutes' walk away. He looked up expectantly when a woman came in, but returned his eyes to the page as soon as he'd seen her. This shabbily dressed creature was unmistakably a comrade. Her hair, dragged back from her plain face, was ragged from the rigours of self-cutting.

'Gino,' I heard her say, and she kissed the proprietor on both cheeks.

As she did so, a second woman came into the Leonardo, and this, without a doubt, was Anna Capshaw. Clutterbuck had exaggerated her beauty, but she was rather remarkable nonetheless. If she had been impoverished by her divorce it didn't show in her appearance. Her dark hair was parted in the middle and fell in carefully regulated waves to her shoulders. No penny-pinching Victory Bob for Anna Capshaw. When I saw her face in full light I couldn't help but notice that she bore an arresting resemblance to Hedy Lamarr.

Anna Capshaw went over to the man with the neat moustache and they touched each other lightly on their respective forearms. I found the gesture peculiarly intimate, more intimate than a social kiss. There was something furtive about the touch, something deliberately restrained which nevertheless revealed that their relationship was sexual and illicit. They left immediately and I followed them.

In Little Collins Street they headed uphill towards

Parliament House, but ducked into a café on the way. It was called the Petrushka, and as soon as I went inside I realised that I had entered a grim ventricle of Melbourne's bohemian heart. Heads were raised when I came in and lowered when people had reassured themselves that I was neither a literary enemy nor the police. The café was noisy, and if the food was as poisonous as the place smelled I didn't think its patrons could look forward to a long life. Anna Capshaw and her male companion were sitting at a table at the back of the café. I caught her eye unintentionally, but it seemed to be of no more consequence to her than if she had caught the eye of anyone else in the room. I sat down and a waiter asked, 'Wine?' This was such a singular question to be asked in a café that I automatically replied, 'Yes.' A chipped mug was placed before me containing a liquid that was wine only if that term is expanded to include sump oil. I took a small sip, and felt that if I had any more my teeth would dissolve.

I couldn't hear anything of what passed between my quarries, and couldn't get any closer, but they were deep in conversation and, from the looks on their faces, this wasn't chit-chat. They left at exactly two thirty. This is noteworthy only because Anna Capshaw arrived at the Leonardo at exactly two. She seemed to be running to a timetable.

Once outside, they began to walk briskly towards Parliament House again but before they reached the top of Little Collins Street, they turned down an alley which cut through to Collins Street. This was the sort of narrow space where American servicemen took their dates for a quick exchange of fluids. I followed warily. If one of them had turned around he or she would have formed the inescapable impression that they were being tailed. Fortunately this didn't happen, and I emerged in Collins Street undetected. I kept them in view until they disappeared into the foyer of the Menzies Hotel. By the time I'd stepped through its doors, they were nowhere to be seen — they must have hurried upstairs.

At this point I became acutely conscious of my inexperience in matters of pursuit. Bribing the concierge was out of the question, not only because the idea of doing so was mortifying, but also because I had no money. I thought I had nothing to lose by asking him a simple question.

'Oh, yes,' he replied. 'Mr and Mrs Cunningham.'

'That's right,' I said. 'I've just forgotten what room they're in.'

'I'm sorry, sir,' he said. 'I'll be happy to let them know you're here, but I can't tell you their room number. Hotel policy. I'm sure you understand.'

'Of course,' I said. 'I understand completely. I'll catch up with them later.'

'Do you wish to leave a message?'

'No, no,' I said. 'I'm seeing them this evening.'

At least I now had a name. Clutterbuck should be happy about that at any rate. I assumed that Anna Capshaw and her companion had gone upstairs to make love, and I wasn't going to hang about waiting for them to re-emerge. Besides, I needed to be back at Clutterbuck's to take Topaz's phone call.

When I got back to Clutterbuck's, or my place, as I would have to get used to saying, it was empty. I went up to my room and was immediately aware that someone had been there. It only took a moment, though, to deduce that it had been Mrs Castleton. My clothes had been pressed and my socks, underwear and handkerchiefs had been arranged in neat rows in their drawers. The socks, which I had rolled into a ball, had been pulled apart and folded flat. This had the unfortunate effect of drawing attention to their ragged condition. I would have to sacrifice some clothing coupons and do something about my wardrobe.

In an attempt to feel more comfortable in my digs I explored the house from top to bottom, although I didn't poke about in cupboards or drawers. It was absurdly big for two people. How on earth had Clutterbuck come to own such a place? There were no clues anywhere. There wasn't a single photograph to be seen. I thought this odd, but then perhaps they had been put away in order not to compromise the rigid formality of each room's design. Clearly there was no place for sentimentality when decorative integrity was at issue. When I entered the living room, I was struck forcibly by the sense that space had been disciplined and maintained by a brutal hand. Mrs Castleton must be a formidable woman, I thought.

The telephone rang at 5.00 p.m. precisely, and the operator said that she was connecting me to Sergeant Peter Topaz of the Maryborough police in Queensland. Without niceties of any kind, Topaz said, 'Sarah Goodenough got on the train at Maryborough at the same time you did, but she got off at Brisbane, and she's still in Brisbane, staying with her sister, and that's been confirmed.'

'Well, that just doesn't make any sense,' I said.

'It makes perfect sense to me, Will. She got on at Maryborough. She got off at Brisbane. Doesn't seem too complicated. That's all I can tell you. The police down there know what they're doing, so I suggest you stay well out of it and let them do their job.'

It didn't seem politic to tell him that I was making it my job now as well.

'So she's got an accomplice,' I said.

'Just let the police handle it, Will,' he said, and without so much as a cursory farewell hung up.

Topaz hadn't said whether or not Sarah Goodenough had been questioned, but I supposed that she had. Had she denied writing the note? Had she also denied striking Brian?

I picked up the phone, gave the operator Mother's number, and wondered whether it was really such a good idea to give this information to Brian. He answered the phone, and before I had a chance to speak, said, 'Those detectives were here this arvo. Sarah's in Brisbane. They wouldn't tell me what she told the Brisbane coppers, but they looked at me in a funny way, and one of them, Strachan, sort of shook his head and said, "Quite a story", like he was accusing me of something.'

'Don't get agitated, Brian. Sarah Goodenough probably said that it wasn't over between you, and that you'd promised to leave your wife.'

Brian was stricken.

'Why would she say that?'

'That's a question that doesn't need answering, Brian. You know perfectly well why she'd say something like that. Firstly, she's nuts and, secondly, if she really does hate you it would be a good way of making things difficult for you. Hell hath no fury and so forth.'

There was silence on the line, then he said quietly, 'Fuck.'

'The problem now is that the police don't have any suspects — except for those of us who were conveniently on the premises at the time that Darlene was abducted. Believe me, the longer it takes to find the culprit, the more impertinent and aggressive the dicks will become.'

The front door opened and closed.

'I have to go,' I said. 'I'll talk to you later.'

'I have to go back to work tomorrow,' he said irrelevantly.

'I'll call tomorrow night, if not before.'

I hung up.

Paul Clutterbuck came down the corridor to the small alcove that housed the telephone.

'Ah, there you are,' he said, as though he had been searching for me. 'Come upstairs while I change, and tell me what you found out.'

Clutterbuck was no longer wearing his American army uniform, but a beautifully cut suit with cuffs, pockets and buttons. It would have given the Austerity Committee conniptions. As I followed him up the stairs, wafts of cigar smoke and alcohol drifted from his clothing. In the bedroom he took off his shoes and placed them at the foot of the bed. He took off his coat, socks, tie, shirt and trousers, laying each item carefully on the counterpane. In his vest and underwear he went into the adjoining bathroom and ran a bath. He came back into the bedroom and opened the door to a large, custom-made wardrobe. I had never seen anything like it before. His shirts — and there were dozens of them — were grouped according to colour, and within each colour group they were graded from dark to light. Each shirt was separated from its neighbour by a stay on the rack on which they hung, so that no hanger could slide into the one beside it.

Clutterbuck selected a shirt. He pulled out a narrow drawer, not unlike a map drawer which was segmented into many small compartments so that it resembled a specimen case of some kind. In each wooden square a single pair of socks rested. He selected a pair. The drawer beneath was pulled out, and from it he retrieved a pair of underpants, each of which, like the socks, occupied a single square. I wasn't sure if it was admirable or disturbing that someone would go to so much trouble to curtail the disorderly tendencies of socks and underwear.

'The trousers,' he said, 'are in the other wardrobe.'

A wardrobe of identical design stood on the opposite side of the bedroom. He crossed to it and chose trousers from the rack within. He draped all of these items onto a chair, took off his vest and stepped out of his underwear. I wasn't in the least perturbed by his lack of modesty. As an actor, I had abandoned my own a long time ago. There is no room for coyness when quick changes have to be made in cramped wings.

Clutterbuck went into the bathroom, turned off the tap and climbed into the tub.

'Now,' he said. 'Tell me what happened.'

I sat in a comfortable armchair in his bedroom and called through the half-opened bathroom door.

'Your former wife arrived just when you said she would and she met a man there. Well dressed. Well heeled, I'd say. Moustache. About forty-two or forty-three. They went to a café called the Petrushka.'

'I know it,' he said. 'Commies, queers and Jews go there,' and he gave each word an equal weighting of contempt. The venom in his voice made my heart sink. Was Clutterbuck some sort of fascist? Had I foolishly moved in with a black shirt? A sudden burst of laughter from Clutterbuck assuaged my fears somewhat. Perhaps he hadn't been serious, but had wanted to shock me, to test my response to his remarks.

'Not a salubrious place for a tryst,' he said.

'They went to the Menzies Hotel after that, and took a room. They're there under the name of Mr and Mrs Cunningham.'

'Good,' he said. 'But that's not six pounds worth, is it? I want you to find out who this Cunningham is. Has he got a wife? That sort of thing.'

A bitter little acid drop of bile rose to my throat. Was Clutterbuck planning on blackmailing this man? I walked to the bathroom door and leaned against the jamb. Clutterbuck had a washer across his eyes and didn't see me.

'This isn't about blackmail, is it?' I asked.

He didn't flinch at the sudden closeness of my voice, but took the washer away from his eyes.

'No, Will,' he said. 'This isn't about blackmail. It most certainly is not. I'm in no position to blackmail other people about their sex lives, and when I get dressed we'll have a drink and I'll tell you why. I'll see you downstairs in ten minutes.'

As he was paying me I suppose he had a right to dismiss me in this way, but I didn't like it.

When Clutterbuck joined me in the living room the first thing he did was apologise.

'I'm sorry if I sounded officious,' he said. 'I'm told it's one of my least attractive qualities.'

Then he smiled, confident that his charm would be sufficient to repair my opinion of him. After the first, large single malt, I was reassured, but I now knew I would have to remain wary of Paul Clutterbuck.

'While you were out tracking Anna and this Cunningham,' he said, 'I was having lunch at the Melbourne Club. I'm not a member. I was a guest. My fiancée's father is a member.'

'Gretel's father is a member of the Melbourne Club?'

I was surprised in spite of myself. Clutterbuck looked at me for a moment, then produced a sputter that escalated into a laugh.

'I'm not sure Gretel even knows who her father is but, whoever he is, I'm sure the closest he's ever come to being a pillar of the community is in propping up a bar somewhere. No, Will, Gretel Beech isn't my fiancée. That honour goes to Miss Nigella Fowler. Her father is big in banking; I'm not sure what he does exactly, but whatever it is he makes a lot of money out of it, and his daughter is keen on me. I'm certainly keen to marry her. My funds aren't what they were before the war. So you see, Will, I'm in no position to blackmail anybody. My former wife knows about my little dalliances, and I don't want to give her any reason to start blathering about them. Fowler isn't entirely happy as it is with the fact that I'm divorced. If word got back to him about anything else, there'd be no wedding, I can assure you. And I'll tell you quite frankly, Will, that this is all about money, not love — not on my side anyway. As far as I'm concerned this is a financial arrangement, and I fully intend to fulfil all statutory requirements in relation to sex and procreation. Nigella is not unattractive, and it will be no sacrifice to consummate our union when the time comes. Are you appalled?'

I couldn't make up my mind whether there was something admirable about Clutterbuck's frankness, or whether it pointed to a serious deficiency in his understanding of the limits of social intimacy. At least he was consistent in his amorality. His well-oiled smile was good camouflage, and even that wasn't intended to disguise so much as to excuse. I could imagine that if Anna Capshaw had started out loving this man, it wouldn't have taken too long for her feelings to curdle into hatred. Miss Nigella Fowler stood in peril of ruining her life, but this was none of my business. I was, at any rate, relieved to know that I wasn't being paid to procure a blackmail victim for Paul Clutterbuck.

'You can meet Nigella here tomorrow,' he said. 'She'll be over in the afternoon. We're having tea and cake. Very civilised. Her father will be here too, and her brother, who is a pill. So, will you join us?'

'Yes,' I said. 'And I'll see what I can find out about Cunningham in the morning.'

He exposed his perfect teeth in a grin and made a little snapping noise with them which sounded unnervingly like the tumblers of a lock falling into place.

Clutterbuck had told me that we would be going with Gretel Beech to hear her singing at a place in Carlton called Ma Maguire's — a speakeasy that had been lubricating customers since the 1920s. Ma Maguire was long dead, and the place was now run by shady businessmen with, Clutterbuck insisted, the full cooperation of the police. Gretel performed irregularly, usually when someone was indisposed — a term I took to mean off having an abortion. Tonight she would perform two shows, one early in the evening and the other much later, after midnight.

'We'll come back here between sets,' he said. 'I'm not going to pour money into the pockets of those crooks, and besides, only the beer is worth drinking.'

I went upstairs and changed into my freshly pressed clothes. I heard Gretel arrive and came downstairs. She was wearing her stage outfit. At least I presumed the assemblage was her costume: she was draped in filmy scarves and wrapped in cloth that evoked a bizarre meld of Classical Greece and Hollywood vamp. With her bee-stung lips and heavily kohled eyes, she looked like a throwback to Theda Bara. She seemed melancholy to me, but I think this had less to do with how she was feeling than with my own response to the recollection of Theda Bara.

When I was the vulnerable age of ten, it was Theda Bara who shattered my faith in movies. I had believed in the man-eating vamp, born in the shadow of the Sphinx, her name a mysterious anagram of 'Arab Death'. So I was devastated to discover that Theda Bara was really plain old Theodosia Goodman, born in Cincinnati and not weaned on serpent's blood after all. From that point on, the realisation grew that life was little more than the slow dismantling of illusions, one by agonising one. It was these progressive revelations that sharpened my observational skills and made me less gullible than I might otherwise have been.

'Are we ready?' Gretel said, and twirled so that her scarves drifted around her like smoke.

We walked to Ma Maguire's. It was a double-storey terrace just a stone's throw from the police station in Carlton. Gretel left us as soon as we arrived. Clutterbuck knew his way around and he took me to a room where a dozen American soldiers were laughing, smoking and drinking. There were a few women there, but they didn't look at ease; it was as if the twilight reined in their carnal desires, which would assert themselves more freely later under cover of darkness and dim bulbs. Clutterbuck disappeared and came back with two beers.

'She'll be on in ten minutes,' he said. 'Meanwhile, I'll tell you why I want you to find out about Cunningham.'

He had to lean into my ear to be heard over the babble of American voices.

'When I divorced Anna she said she would find a way to get even, to get back what she reckons she's entitled to. It was ugly. To do that she'll need a lawyer, and I happen to know that she has no way of paying one. But I also happen to know that she's not above fucking her way to success. This Cunningham has to be a lawyer, and if he's going to start poking around in my affairs, I want to have the jump on him.'

'So all you want me to do is find out what Cunningham's job is.'

'Exactly. I want you to find out who he's working for and what kind of reputation he has.'

The people in the room reacted to a signal that I'd missed, and began heading upstairs. We followed them into a large, front room, stripped of all furniture except for rows of seats. In one corner a man, who couldn't have been more than twenty, sat at a piano. His youth, and the absence of any obvious physical defects, indicated to me that the reason for his not being in the armed forces lay in the probability that he was a member of the criminal class. I had heard that many of his kind had enlisted early, but that they had been dishonourably discharged after exploiting opportunities for violence and theft.

Gretel Beech leaned languidly against the piano; startlingly, she was completely naked. The audience took their seats, and whistled and foot stomped, and yelled obscenities. Everyone's proximity to Gretel made it shockingly intimate. She pushed herself away from the piano and assumed a defiant stance, hands on hips, feet apart. Her eyes roamed over the audience, but I doubt she found the eyes of many in return. Their gaze was firmly locked on her breasts and her pudendum. The piano player struck a chord, and then another, and the audience began to quieten down. With swagger, assurance, and considerable skill, Gretel began to sing, and as she sang she began a reverse strip-tease, gradually re-clothing herself with all the sensual gestures of that craft, until by the time she delivered the final line of the song she was seated in a chair, fully dressed, but with her legs splayed obscenely. She sang:

If you're a young man, or older,
I don't mind, you're a soldier,
And you're willing to fight so we can be free.
I've a soft spot for privates,
And for sergeants I'll sigh,
But they all stand to attention when they come home with me.
I ain't scared of your guns, be they small ones or bigger,
And I know when to stay well away from the trigger.
You're safe with me, boys,
Don't run helter-skelter.
Come home with me, boys.
I've got room in my shelter.

'So what did you think?' she asked me on our way back to Clutterbuck's house.

'You have a fine voice,' I said, being unsure how to address the most prominent features of her act. Clutterbuck laughed and put his arms around Gretel's shoulders.

'Gretel has more talent in her little finger than Gladys Moncrieff has in her whole body — and I don't think many people would pay to see Our Glad do what Gretel does.'

When we reached the house Gretel said that she'd like a bath before the next show, which was still a few hours away. Clutterbuck went upstairs with her, and I took the opportunity to ring Mother. She said that there'd been no progress in the search for Darlene, and described how Brian was becoming more and more agitated about the attitude of the police towards him.

'What I'm much more concerned about,' she said, 'is whether or not Darlene's kidnapper intends to strike again, especially now that we know that we're not dealing with a slightly built woman, but with a brute of unknown dimensions.'

'Would you feel safer if I came home?'

'Good heavens no, dear. I know you've only been gone one day, but we're managing quite well. I'm worried about Fulton, too. I was sure a letter from him would come today.'

I said a few comforting words and hung up. When I walked into the living room, Clutterbuck was there, pouring himself a drink. He automatically poured one for me.

'Gretel wants to soak for a while,' he said.

'Does Gretel know about your fiancée?' I asked.

'Of course,' he said. 'She makes no claims on me at all. She's the original libertine. Mine isn't the only bed she sleeps in, and I have never demanded fidelity. I'm sure you couldn't help but notice from her performance that she's not exactly a nun.'

'She has talent,' I said.

'She's also rather lovely, isn't she?'

'Yes, she is.'

'I'm very attached to her. Giving her up isn't going to be easy.'

An expression of some sort must have crossed my face because he shook his finger at me.

'Don't make the mistake of thinking that she's waiting for someone to rescue her,' he said. 'That's sentimental tosh. She knows exactly what she's doing, and it suits her to do it.'

I had to agree that there was nothing reticent about Gretel's stage persona.

'Let's go for a walk,' he said. 'I'm bored sitting here.'

'Fine,' I said.

In the hallway he called up the stairs to Gretel.

'Will and I are going out.'

'OK,' she called back.

'Do you want us to come back, or will we meet you there?'

She turned on the tap and called over its noise, 'I'll meet you there. I'm on at twelve-thirty.'

In the street outside, the weird and chilling yawn of a lion reached us from nearby Melbourne Zoo. We walked aimlessly for a while, and Clutterbuck sang to himself a few bars of 'Praise the Lord and pass the ammunition'.

'I wouldn't have picked you as a propaganda peddler', I said.

'That's Nigella's influence. She works for that crowd. Have you seen that hideous short that's on before every film?'

He raised his voice a few octaves and minced in imitation of a woman: 'I found the WAAF in many important respects just as vital as the RAAF. There's so much a girl learns in the air force. It's given me a new interest in life. An entirely different outlook, and has supplied the answer to a question. It's a haunting question, you know.' He paused dramatically. 'Are you in a war job? Are you?'

He snorted.

'That's one Nigella had a hand in. Frightful, isn't it? Needless to say I told her I loved it, and, if it comes up in conversation tomorrow, don't be surprised if I dragoon you into expressing admiration for it, too.'

'But I haven't seen it.'

'What you just saw is better than the original, so that should be enough to carry any expressions of awe you are required to make.'

We slowly wended our way towards Ma Maguire's, and Clutterbuck began asking questions about my background. I told him as much as I thought he needed to know. As we crossed Princes Park he asked me to recite something from Shakespeare. Confident of my skill, I did not demur, but produced a sound, if subdued, reading of a passage from *The Tempest*. I threw in a few lines of Caliban's, just to demonstrate my range. He seemed genuinely impressed, which was pleasing, and he nodded and said, 'Yes' and 'Yes' again as if to reinforce that his affirmation was well considered.

We walked on in silence after that, until we reached Ma Maguire's. The entrance to this establishment was through a lane at the rear, and as soon as the door was pushed open the heat and noise that hit us indicated a crowded house. Gretel would have a large audience for her late performance, and from the raucous sounds coming from deep in the house, most of them were already drunk.

Clutterbuck left me to my own devices, and I was soon approached by a woman who said she was on her way to the dunny outside. She paused long enough to observe that she thought I looked like 'somebody.'

'Don't know who,' she said, 'but somebody in the movies.'

She meant, of course, Tyrone Power, to whom I bore more

than a passing resemblance. This made the coincidence of our surnames remarkable.

'People say Tyrone Power,' I said.

She was quite drunk, and slurred, 'No. Not someone good looking. But someone in the movies. Definitely.' She stumbled away towards her date with a toilet bowl.

Twelve-thirty came and went, and when Gretel still hadn't arrived at one-thirty Clutterbuck said that she must have fallen asleep, and that we should go and wake her up. There was still time for her to perform. There would be a crowd at Ma Maguire's until the early morning.

We half-walked, half-ran back to Clutterbuck's house. Inside it was dark and quiet, so I assumed Gretel must indeed have fallen asleep. A few moments after our arrival, Clutterbuck came out of his bedroom and said that Gretel wasn't there. He shrugged.

'Maybe she just decided she had better things to do. She's not the most reliable girl in the world. They'll be pissed off at Maguire's, but all she'll have to do is expose her breasts to the manager, and maybe give him a feel, and she'll be sweet. I'm turning in. Goodnight.'

He produced an elaborate yawn and closed his bedroom door.

In my bedroom I felt obliged to fold my clothes neatly and not just toss them in a heap. Knowing that there was no one else in the house, there was no reason to wrap a towel around my waist in order to walk to the bathroom next door. I switched on the dim light and saw in its pale, yellow glow that Gretel Beech was lying on her back in the bathtub, her face submerged beneath the water, her eyes open and glassy. Simply because I didn't know what else to do, and perhaps because I thought she might sit up at any moment and hoot with laughter at the fright she'd given me, I approached the tub and put my hand in the water. It was cold. I forced myself to look into Gretel's face, and I saw, with sickening dread, that there was a tie wrapped so tightly around her throat that it bit deeply into her skin. I only owned one tie, and this was unmistakably it.

I stood back from the bath and was pleased to discover that I hadn't descended into an irrational panic. I was clear-headed and relatively calm. If the bath water was anything to go by, Gretel Beech had been dead for quite a while, which meant that whoever had strangled her had done so while Paul Clutterbuck and I had been waiting for her at Maguire's.

The first thing that I had to do was to tell Clutterbuck that his girlfriend had been murdered in his own house. I didn't expect him to take her death hard. He had demonstrated by his general behaviour that hysterical displays of grief were probably outside his emotional range, but I didn't know exactly how he would react. I put on a pair of trousers and knocked on his bedroom door.

'Come in,' he called.

He was in bed, and sounded as if he had been on the brink of falling asleep. I could think of no subtle way to inform him of the horror that was lying in my bath.

'Gretel has been murdered,' I said, and wished that there might perhaps have been a gentler way of saying it. He sat up in bed and was silent, probably considering whether what he had heard was real or part of a vivid dream. He leaned across and switched on a lamp.

'What did you say?'

'Gretel Beech's body is lying in my bathtub. I think she's been strangled.'

Clutterbuck slowly got out of bed. I couldn't tell what effect my words had had on him. He seemed calm, but his stillness might have been shock. Without speaking, he pushed past me and went into my bathroom. When he emerged his face was unreadably impassive.

'Did you kill her?' he asked.

I was so stunned by this question that I gasped.

'Of course not. She's been dead for hours. You can see that. Someone must have done it while we were at Maguire's.'

'I'm sorry,' he said. 'I'm not thinking clearly. I need a drink.'

Downstairs, Clutterbuck poured each of us an enormous whisky.

'We should call the police,' I said.

'Should we?'

He looked at me over the top of his glass. There was a wariness in his eyes, as if he was gauging my reaction to this challenge to common sense.

'Gretel's been murdered,' I said quietly. 'We don't have any choice.'

'It's, what, two in the morning. Who'd be on duty at this hour?'

It wasn't really a question, but more like an expression of disbelief that there were people in the world who had organised their lives so poorly that they could be required to work at uncivilised times. I knew exactly who would be on duty. It would be Sergeant Wilkinson, and he would doubtless be surprised to find me at two different crime scenes within the short space of twenty-four hours. Despite the awful conclusions such a ghastly coincidence must provoke, there was no question but that we should contact the police, and I told Clutterbuck this.

'No,' he said sharply. 'Let me think, let me think.'

'There's nothing to think about. There's the body upstairs, of a girl you were having some kind of a relationship with.'

'That's precisely the problem.' His voice was now edgy. 'She can't be found here. The Fowlers can't know about her. Nigella mustn't find out about her.'

'You're not serious,' I said, feeling quite certain that he was very serious indeed.

'This is a set-up,' he said suddenly. 'This is to stop me marrying Nigella Fowler.'

'Who would want to do that? And why?' I asked.

Clutterbuck put his drink down and rubbed his eyes with the heels of his hands.

'Will, you've known me for two days. You have no idea how complicated my life is. I can think of half-a-dozen people who would stop at nothing to destroy me. Murdering some tart, and leaving her body where it causes the greatest inconvenience, would be no problem at all. And maybe it isn't even about the Fowlers, but it sure as hell is about destroying me. If the coppers get a hold of this, how would you rate my chances of joining the Melbourne Club?'

He began to work himself up into an indignant fury.

'Those pricks are not going to get away with this. It's going to take more than a trollop's corpse to shut me down.'

'Paul,' I said, 'who are you talking about? Who are these people?'

He looked at me squarely.

'Communists. My former wife. A jealous husband. I don't know. Take your pick.'

'But you have an alibi. You weren't here when she was killed. Dozens of people can attest to that, and Gretel was alive when we left the house. I can attest to that.'

'I don't know how much you've had to do with the coppers, Will, but they'll find out we left Maguire's with Gretel and came back without her. Your word won't be worth shit to them. In fact, when they find out it's your bathtub she's in, they might be even more interested in you than in me.'

'That tie around her neck is mine,' I said flatly.

Clutterbuck said nothing for a moment.

'How do I know she's been dead for hours and not minutes?' he asked.

I knew what he was doing. He was trying to put me in the uncomfortable position of having to defend myself against an absurd, but devastating, allegation. And he succeeded. I couldn't hold back the awkward bleating of my innocence, and it sounded desperate and unconvincing. He stopped me before I'd gone very far.

'Listen, Will. I know you didn't do this. I can't explain why she was strangled with your tie and dumped in your bath. I imagine the half-wit who did it just got it all wrong. But you've got to admit, it looks bad for both of us.'

There was no disputing this.

'There is a way out,' he said.

I began to feel ill.

'You're a PI. You could find out who did this and present the information to the police at the right time. What do a couple of days matter? No one's going to miss Gretel for a while. What have we got to lose?'

'This is murder, Paul. Somebody has to be told that Gretel Beech is dead.'

'It doesn't make any difference to her whether it's today, or tomorrow or the next day. I can't afford to have the police crawling all over my house. Christ! The Fowlers are coming for afternoon tea.'

'Paul, tea with the Fowlers is not more important than Gretel's death.'

'Yes it is, Will,' he said fiercely. 'Yes it is! All we're talking about here is doing the coppers' work for them. I'm not saying we don't report it. I'm saying we don't report it yet. That's all. You're a PI, for Christ's sake. Why should the police get the credit here? You can fix this. And I'll pay you.'

This last was thrown casually into the mix. I wasn't seduced by his flattering confidence in my untried abilities, but I began, God help me, to see the situation from his point of view. What, after all, was wrong with paying Gretel the compliment of finding out who had killed her?

'If we don't have these people, or the person, in two days' time,' I said, 'do you agree that you'll come with me to the police?'

'Of course,' he said hurriedly. 'Of course I do. But we will find them.'

'All right then,' I said.

Clutterbuck looked so relieved I thought he might embrace me.

'We'll have to move the body,' he said.

I hadn't considered this, and his words fell on my ears like blows. I was suddenly dizzy, and could do nothing to prevent myself from falling forward in a faint. I woke on the floor, with whisky running down my chest and with Clutterbuck looking down at me — the expression on his face must have been concern, but my swoon distorted it so that it resembled laughter.

Chapter Five

BEARING UP

CLUTTERBUCK LAID A SHEET on the floor beside the bath, and we lifted Gretel's naked body onto it. All my sensibilities were outraged by what we were doing. It wasn't just irregular. It was illegal, immoral, imperilling, and ill-conceived. And yet ... And yet, I went along with it and carried Gretel's body downstairs and into the back garden, at the bottom of which sat a small garage. Until Clutterbuck opened the garage door, I hadn't known that he owned a car — a Studebaker that was at least ten years old, but looked well maintained. We manoeuvred the corpse into the back seat. Clutterbuck took a shovel from the corner of the garage and laid it across Gretel's body.

'Where are we going?' I asked.

'We don't want the coppers to find the body until you've sorted out who did this.'

'Then what? We can't retrieve it and plonk it back in the house.'

'It's too late to worry about that now.'

Clutterbuck started the engine and pulled out into the lane behind his house.

'Where's the best place to hide a body, Will?'

'I have no idea.'

'If you wanted to hide a specific marble, where would you put it?'

'This isn't a parlour game, Paul.'

'Where would you hide the marble, Will?'

Giving him what he wanted I stated the obvious. 'In a bag of marbles.'

'Exactly, so I hope you're not afraid of goblins or ghouls.'

Clutterbuck stopped his car outside the back entrance to the Melbourne cemetery, in MacPherson Street. No light seeped from the edges of the blackouts in the houses that faced the perimeter. This was hardly surprising, given the hour. The gate was shut and locked, presumably to protect the dead from the living and not the other way around. The fence wasn't too difficult to negotiate, although heaving eight stone of uncooperative flesh over it took some ingenuity, especially with the handicap of my broken arm. I managed it by imagining that my actions were part of a performance — that I was Hamlet, lugging 'the guts into the neighbour room' and that once accomplished the curtain would fall and the 'guts' would spring to life to be lugged another day.

Once inside the cemetery, our task, Clutterbuck said, was to find a recently dug grave, preferably one that had been excavated and filled that very afternoon with the earth still loose in preparation for the pounding down and the stonemason's craft. To give Clutterbuck his due, I had to acknowledge that as a place to conceal a corpse a cemetery was an inspired choice. We were obliged to leave the body unattended while we sought out a new grave. It took us twenty minutes, but a tarpaulin stretched over a rising in the ground indicated that there had indeed been a burial there that day. We collected Gretel Beech and began to dig into the recently turned earth. It was surprisingly easy, and in a very short time we'd made a depression sufficient to accommodate the body. In the great tradition of such matters, it was a shallow grave; neither one of us wishing to dig to the depth of the already buried coffin. When we'd finished and remounded the soil and replaced the tarpaulin, the scene looked much as we had found it. Later, in my bedroom, I remembered that I hadn't removed my tie from around Gretel's neck. That it was my tie, there could be no doubt — I had sewn my name onto its back to prevent my losing it when travelling.

Despite not having been able to sleep until almost 5.00 a.m., I was awake and dressed at eight. I was surprised that Clutterbuck too was awake and I found him in the kitchen, making coffee. On the bench there was a tin of the cream he had purchased from the American PX.

'Try it,' he said. 'You'll like it.'

'Where do we go from here?' I asked.

'You're the PI, Will. You do realise that there's every chance now that Gretel's body will never be found, and that means that if you don't find her murderer, he'll get away with it.'

'We're going to the police in two days, right?'

Clutterbuck shrugged.

'It seemed like a good idea at the time, but now that I think about it, unless you hand over the culprit the police are going to respond poorly to an unauthorised burial. No. This is entirely in your hands, and I have no doubt, Will that you can protect us both — and we both need protecting. I'm placing my trust in you.'

In the few seconds it took for Clutterbuck to speak these words, my emotions lurched from furious resentment to reluctant acceptance, and settled on that vaguely satisfying sensation that expressions of trust arouse in me. The situation in which Clutterbuck and I found ourselves was a long way from the ordinary, so I had to expect that the rules and regulations that govern the ordinary would be suspended. I drank Clutterbuck's coffee with Clutterbuck's cream in it and I knew that from that point on I stood apart from legislated behaviour. It was strangely liberating and frightening in equal measure.

'You're right to trust me, Paul. I'll find who killed Gretel.'

'Good,' he said. 'So life goes on. Nigella and her father and brother will be here at three o'clock. Mrs Castleton will prepare afternoon tea and I'll ask her to include you in her baking. I want you to meet these people. I also still want you to find out as much as you can about Cunningham and Anna. You might get lucky and kill two birds with one stone, as it were. I wouldn't be in the least surprised if Anna paid someone to set me up.'

This seemed ludicrous to me. I wasn't completely discounting the possibility that the purpose of Gretel's murder was to undermine Clutterbuck's reputation, but there were other scenarios. Gretel had lived among a dissolute crowd. She'd mixed with criminals and strip-tease artistes and God knows who else. It was among this crowd that I thought her killer lurked and it was this crowd that I would need to infiltrate.

'How much do you know about Gretel Beech?' I asked.

'Practically nothing. I met her at Maguire's a few months ago and we enjoyed each other's company. I never met any of her friends and I never went to her place — she had a room in a boarding house in St Kilda, I believe. I don't think she was from here. She mentioned some family connection in Horsham, or somewhere in the bush. There was something of the country girl about her, wasn't there?'

'Well, no,' I said. 'Although I didn't know her as well as you did obviously, stripping in a speakeasy isn't my idea of rural manners.'

'It's what happens sometimes when country girls get lost in the big city.'

'Where are her clothes?'

'I've bundled them up. I intend to burn them.'

'I want to look through them. I might find something that will help me locate somebody who knew her.'

Clutterbuck looked sceptical, but led me upstairs to a chest in one of the unoccupied rooms where he'd placed her clothes.

'They were stuffed into my wardrobe,' he said, 'and were obviously meant to be found there by the basset noses of the constabulary.'

Gretel's garments smelled of perfume and were slightly acrid with sweat. There were no pockets, but a small, beaded purse was caught up in the folds of one of her scarves. It was empty except for a torn piece of paper on which was scribbled an address in East Melbourne, a time, and a date. Gretel's rendezvous was later that morning, and I immediately determined to turn up in her place.

'This isn't where she was staying?' I asked.

Clutterbuck looked at the scrap of paper.

'Heavens no. That's a good address.'

I didn't mention my plan to Clutterbuck. He was more forthcoming about his plans for me.

'I don't want to tell you how to run your business,' he said, 'but it might be relevant that Anna likes to have a late breakfast. So if you hurry you'll probably catch her and her lover in the dining room of the Menzies Hotel. She isn't the kind of woman who would pass up a free feed.'

ℒ

Clutterbuck was right about his ex-wife. I entered the dining room at the Menzies Hotel at nine-thirty, and saw Anna and Cunningham seated at a table, the detritus of a recently eaten meal before them. They gave every appearance of being a respectable couple, and didn't betray by expression or gesture that there was anything illicit about their relationship. The same couldn't be said of the several US Army officers who clutched the hands of the women opposite them with proprietorial and post-coital vulgarity. There were no Australian Army uniforms in the room.

I sat in the foyer reading the paper and hoped that they would leave the hotel soon. Gretel's meeting was for eleven o'clock. I couldn't form a plan beyond that until I had ascertained the nature of the appointment. I suspected it might be sexual, in which case her client would be unwilling to help me. The important thing was not to give away the hideous fact of her death. I would have to think on my feet.

As I was half-reading the paper and half-pondering how I would approach Gretel's assignation, Anna Capshaw and Cunningham came into the foyer and passed outside into Collins Street. On the pavement they said a few words and went in different directions. I followed Cunningham. He began to half run, half walk as if he was late for an appointment. At Spring Street he turned left and increased his pace so that in a few minutes he had reached St Patrick's Cathedral. He moved quickly up its steps to the entrance and disappeared inside. There was so little alteration in his stride that I formed the impression that this monolithic, intimidating edifice was a familiar haunt. I didn't enjoy the same familiarity; despite having grown up in Melbourne, I'd had no occasion to enter this earthly manifestation of Catholic power. I did so now with some trepidation.

The soaring Gothic space was obviously designed to diminish the congregation, rather than celebrate God, and the odorous silence, broken only by the echoey footfall of someone hidden in its depths, frankly gave me the creeps. I saw Cunningham kneeling in a pew outside what I presumed were the confessionals. I sat several pews behind him and waited for something to happen. A person emerged from one of the cubicles and knelt to pray. I wondered what tawdry little sins she had divested herself of. Cunningham took her place. He would probably unburden himself of the terrible sin of fornication. I didn't know yet whether or not he was married, but I supposed that the virgin priest listening to his tale of lust would take a pretty dim view of the transgression. Three Hail Marys as penance certainly wouldn't cover it. He was in there for a very long time and when he came out he didn't kneel to begin his penance but headed for a side door. Before he reached it a voice called, shockingly loud in the respectful silence:

'Mr Trezise!'

Cunningham turned and met a priest who was coming towards him. He smiled and held out his hand. The priest shook it, and they walked together behind the enormous altar. By the time I got there they'd gone, but it was impossible to discover where. The cathedral seemed to me to be a rabbit warren of mysterious doors and side chapels.

So Cunningham was really named Trezise. I wasn't surprised that he'd given a false name at the hotel; no doubt he was married. Now I could begin the real work of finding out the information that Clutterbuck needed.

With Cunningham, or more correctly, Trezise, occupied with the priest, I decided to make my way towards the address scribbled on Gretel Beech's scrap of paper. It was a house in East Melbourne. With an hour to spare, I thought I'd walk the distance rather than spend money on a Red Top taxi or a tram. The walk would clear my head, and give me time to think about Gretel's murder and Darlene's kidnapping. I couldn't shake the notion that there was something amiss there. Having just disposed of a body myself, I realised how difficult it would have been to have snatched Darlene and effectively made her vanish in only a few minutes. This was surely more than a single person was capable of achieving. Could an embittered woman thousands of miles north organise a gang of thugees to do her bidding in punishing the man who threw her over? It seemed unlikely.

Perhaps it was Darlene's life that needed to be examined, but this was too absurd. She was socially inept certainly, but not to the point of provoking someone to take her out of circulation by abduction. She was too drab and boring to attract the attention of professional ransom-raisers, if such people existed outside cheap Hollywood programmers. There had been no demands for a ransom thus far. If squeezing money from her nearest and dearest had been the intention, I imagined that her kidnappers would have been filled with despair when they spoke to her, or saw her in the harsh light of day. If I'd been one of them I would have argued for an immediate reduction in the asking price; realistically, I would have realised that, far from expecting payment, the kidnapping gang could possibly be held liable for cartage costs.

I smiled to myself as my ruminations became more extravagant and unseemly, and arrived at my destination just before 11.00 a.m. It was a large house, double-storeyed, with a beautiful cast-iron railing around the upper veranda. It was, without doubt, a good address, and an unlikely rendezvous point, at this hour of the day, for a prostitute and her client. I rang the bell. The woman who answered the door was obviously the help. She wasn't wearing a uniform, but the lady of this house would not have been seen dead in such ill-fitting attire, made entirely of shoddy.

'I'm here on behalf of Miss Gretel Beech,' I said.

'Wait in the hall,' she said. 'Mr Wilks won't be happy.'

She climbed a broad staircase and entered a room off the upper landing. A babble of voices escaped when she did so. A man in his fifties emerged and came down the stairs towards me. He was wearing a ridiculous beret and a pleated smock. All that was missing was a carefully trimmed moustache and a French accent, and the cliché would have been complete.

'Not again,' he said in broad Australian vowels, which immediately mollified the effect of his costume. 'Gretel is so unreliable. This is the second time she's done this and she swore solemnly it would never happen again. The ladies will be so disappointed. They were looking forward to a woman this week. We had a bloke last week.'

I had no idea what he was talking about but it seemed wise to behave as if I sympathised with whatever inconvenience Gretel's absence had caused him.

'Yes,' I said. 'I'm sorry, but Gretel isn't the most reliable girl in the world.'

As soon as I'd said this, I realised I was quoting Paul Clutterbuck.

'But she sent me instead.'

Mr Wilks sighed. 'Well, you'd better come up and get ready.'

He stood back and looked me up and down.

'You've got a broken arm. I suppose that might be quite interesting. You're not fat, which is a pity. It would be so much easier for them if you were fat.'

I thought it strange that he hadn't formally introduced himself, and he hadn't yet asked my name. I followed him up the stairs and into the room from which he had emerged. There were eight ladies there, each seated behind an easel and each wearing the loose clothing of the amateur artist. One of them had tied a scarf around her head in what I presume she thought approximated fascinating bohemianism. It was evident from the perfume that hung in the air and from the various pieces of jewellery I glimpsed that none of these women was so poor or unconnected that they would need to consider the grim possibility of taking on a war job.

'Our model has done a bunk,' Mr Wilks said. There was a collective groan. 'She has, however, done us the courtesy of sending a replacement. It wasn't what we were hoping for, but what is art without sacrifice, struggle, and disappointment? I'm sure Mr ... I'm sorry,' he said, turning to me, 'What is your name?'

'Power,' I said. 'William Power.'

'I'm sure Mr William Power will provide us with enough dramatic poses to get our creative juices flowing. If you would like to step behind that screen, Mr Power, and prepare yourself, we will begin.'

It was with some relief that I now understood the nature of Gretel's work here. These ladies were gathered for a weekly drawing class, for which Mr Wilks no doubt overcharged them. It was almost quaint. They had obviously progressed from the tedium of still lifes to the discipline of the figure. Whatever costumes were waiting for me behind the Japanese screen would have been chosen with a female model in mind, but I knew I could adjust them into something resembling a toga or a tunic. I imagined that the standard modelling outfit for a woman was a shapeless but diaphanous bolt of cloth designed to be wrapped about the body in simulation of a figure on a frieze somewhere. I would have to make do, and think of this as a performance piece with gestures, but no words. When I ducked behind the screen, there was nothing there but a chair. I poked my head around and said, 'There's just a chair here.'

'Do you need a second chair?' Mr Wilks asked.

'Well, no, but the … the costumes. There's no costume.'

'Why would you need a costume, Mr Power? You have done this sort of work before, haven't you?'

'Of course,' I said. 'I thought Gretel mentioned a costume, that's all.'

'Oh, yes,' he said. 'We did that once early on with Gretel, but we draw the body now. You can't draw the clothed figure properly unless you know how the body is moving beneath. As I'm sure you are aware.'

My eyes circuited the room. The eight ladies, the oldest of whom looked to be approaching sixty, and the youngest barely in her twenties, were watching me expectantly, but not lewdly. They each had the carefully studied look of the professional artist, even though they probably were no more than bored socialites indulging in a daring hobby.

'Are there any particular poses you would like me to strike?' I asked Mr Wilks.

'We'll decide as we go along. If you could get ready now please,' he said, a little testily.

I began undressing and draping my clothes over the chair. I took a deep breath and stepped out from behind the screen.

'I wonder if you would mind taking your socks off, Mr Power. They are distracting and we need to see your feet.'

I peeled off my socks and stood before the half-circle of easels, physically naked, but mentally armed.

'The first pose will be ten minutes. If you would strike an attitude, Mr Power?'

I placed the hand with the cast on it on my hip and raised the other towards heaven, like a languid Grecian athlete. If it had been carved in marble, it might have been labelled 'After Praxiteles.' The ladies began to concentrate and there was a scratching of charcoal on paper. Mr Wilks walked among them, scrutinising their lines and scrutinising me to determine the discrepancies. After ten minutes he said, 'Next pose please. Another ten minutes.'

I turned my body as if throwing a discus. This proved uncomfortable after only a few minutes and I took my hat off to the chap who must have modelled for Myron in Ancient Greece. Two more ten-minute poses — one of which had to be changed when I was asked if I could not, on this occasion, bend over in quite that way — and two twenty-minute poses followed, and suddenly it was all over. The ladies packed away their charcoals, I got dressed, and Mr Wilks pressed ten shillings upon me saying that he hoped Gretel wouldn't let him down again the following week.

I made a noncommittal movement of the shoulders, and said, 'Is this your place?'

'Of course not,' he snorted. 'I take drawing classes here because Lady Bailey pays me to do so. It's her house. She's a widow and I'm teaching her how to draw. She invites her circle and it's her ten shillings in your pocket. Very generous, wouldn't you say?'

I had to admit that, after the initial awkwardness, the work wasn't very demanding. It didn't require skill, just immodesty. I wondered if Mr Wilks wasn't hopeful of Lady Bailey's patronage, or matronage, extending beyond its current generosity. It may have already done so for all I knew.

Mr Wilks took off his beret and his smock.

'I hate these,' he said. 'Lady Bailey thinks I should look the part.'

'Was she there at that session?'

'Of course. She was the oldest of them. On the end. The oldest and the least talented. Not that any of them have any real talent, except for Nigella Fowler. She's got something. She's good at likenesses and she can draw hands and feet.'

It took a moment for the name to register with me.

'Nigella Fowler was one of the students?'

'Do you know her?'

'No. I've heard the name, that's all. I don't know where.'

'Well, there's talent there, but she'll waste it. She's got herself engaged to some bloke no one knows anything about. Her father isn't happy about it apparently — so Lady Bailey told me at any rate, and she should know. She's in with all that crowd. Her husband was a cousin of Nigella's father. I think that's right.'

I couldn't figure out what relation this made Nigella to the widow Bailey, something with 'once removed' appended to it probably, and I never understood what that was all about. It made no difference to my situation. I was due to have afternoon tea with a young lady who had spent the morning staring hard at my naked body. This discombobulating thought made me determined to get the information I had come for.

'How did you meet Gretel?' I asked.

'At the National Gallery School. She was modelling there for a class I was teaching. I haven't seen you there. Have you done work for them?'

'I don't do this sort of thing for a living, Mr Wilks. I'm an actor.'

'I see. Between engagements, as they say.'

'I've just returned from engagements interstate.'

'If you need the work, I can fix you up with a few jobs at the Gallery School. They're a bit prudish there. You'd have to wear a posing pouch. And it doesn't pay as well as Lady Bailey does.'

'May I be frank with you, Mr Wilks?'

'Is there something you need to be frank about, Mr Power?'

'It's about Gretel Beech. It's a sensitive matter.'

He stopped gathering up bits of broken charcoal and looked at me.

'Miss Beech isn't suggesting that she has been the victim of inappropriate behaviour while under my tutelage, is she?'

'No,' I said, and knew instinctively that something intimate had occurred between Gretel and Mr Wilks. I didn't for a moment think that it had been forced intimacy.

'No. Certainly not,' I said. 'I actually don't (I almost said *didn't*) know Gretel very well, but she spoke highly of your classes.'

This didn't sound like anything Gretel would ever say, but I was making it up as I went along. He raised his eyebrows when I said it, and I knew that he'd detected my slight miscalculation.

'She owes me money,' I said. 'She's been avoiding me for the last couple of days. I was hoping that you might know where she meets her friends. That sort of thing.'

From the expression on his face I knew that I had hit upon something that he recognised as being a likely consequence of knowing Gretel.

'So she owes you money,' he said. 'I think you'll find that there are quite a few people with a prior claim. How much?'

'Only two pounds, but still, I don't have two pounds to spare.'

He laughed.

'You're way down the pecking order, Mr Power. Forget your two pounds. As to where she might be …? You might find her in the Petrushka café, or the Alexander Hotel. The Australia Hotel might be worth a look, too. I think she does quite well out of the Yanks.'

'You don't know the names of any of her friends?'

'I wasn't on social terms with Miss Beech. I can tell you that the fellow she sent along in her place last week was named George. He didn't give a last name. Just George. He had a very large penis, if that helps with your identification further down the track. I'm sure if you asked at the Petrushka for George with the big cock somebody would be able to help you. It's that sort of place.'

With nothing more to be learned from Mr Wilks, I thanked him and made to leave.

'As I said, if you ever need work, contact me. We're always looking for models.'

It was too late to do any further investigation into Trezise and his connections. I wanted to call into Mother's place to check on the situation there before joining Clutterbuck and the Fowlers for afternoon tea. I suppressed any consideration of how I'd greet Nigella Fowler, given that she already knew more about me than I was ever likely to know about her.

Brian wasn't at home, having been obliged to return to teaching, misplaced wife or no misplaced wife. Mother's eyes were red from weeping.

'Don't mind me, dear,' she said. 'I always cry when the postman fails to bring a letter from Fulton. It's how I manage. It's a sort of ritual.'

'He's fine, I'm sure. If something had happened you would have been told by now.'

'It depends where he is though. If he's out in the sticks somewhere there mightn't be a way of getting a message through.

I went to Darwin once, you know. With your father. Before you were born. It was an awful, awful trip and when we got there it was hideous. There was practically nothing there and I had never been so hot and uncomfortable in my entire life.'

Mother had never mentioned this little autobiographical detail before.

'What on earth were you doing up there?'

'Your father had business interests there. In Broome, too. We must have spent the best part of a year in Broome and in Darwin. If I hadn't been young and in love I would have high-tailed it out of there, I can tell you, even if I'd had to walk through the Tanami Desert to do it. I really can't abide the tropics. One never looks one's best. The humidity does dreadful things to one's hair. I'm sure I've told you about our year of heat. I'm sure I have. You probably weren't listening, darling. When you were growing up you never actually listened to what you were being told. It was one of your most annoying qualities.'

I let that pass. My mother had not told me the story of what she'd called her 'year of heat', despite her claims to the contrary. This wasn't the moment to contradict her.

'Perhaps you could tell me about it again some time, and next time I'll give you my full attention.'

'Yes dear,' she said, 'but I'm sure you'll be far more interested in the news one of those detectives brought me today. They have the results of the blood they analysed and they're rather puzzling. It isn't human blood.'

'Hardly surprising,' I said. 'It is Darlene we're talking about after all.'

'Don't be catty. The blood is bullock's blood.'

I lifted my eyebrows to indicate that I had always known that Darlene was more bullock than beauty, but allowed this satisfyingly amusing reflection to persist for only a moment.

'Do the police have a theory?' I asked.

'If they do, Will, they didn't share it with me.'

'Why would someone kidnap Darlene and splash bullock's blood around the kitchen?'

'Well, *I* have a theory,' Mother said. 'I think Darlene is still alive. Whoever took her has no plans to kill her. Yet. The blood — they must have known it would be analysed — is a sort of warning on the one hand, and a reassurance on the other.'

'But why haven't we been contacted?'

'Yes, I'm worried about that. I have a bad feeling that something has gone wrong. Maybe Darlene lost the baby and she's ill and they've panicked and left her somewhere. If they're amateurs they might have bitten off more than they can chew, and just walked away from it.'

'It's certainly very strange. I can't see that it's all being directed by this creature Brian had an affair with. I wonder if he's told us everything about his activities in Maryborough.'

'I've been wondering if this has anything to do with Brian at all. What if the person who took Darlene, wanted Darlene?'

The possibility that Darlene could be of such interest to somebody as to prompt an abduction struck me as ludicrous. I had never really thought of her as having a life away from Brian, or as having had an existence prior to Brian. I reluctantly admitted to myself that she had as much right to a biography as anybody else.

'That little detective, Strachan, was asking questions about Darlene's friends,' Mother said, 'and I was embarrassed to have to admit that I knew very little about her. As far as I know she doesn't have any close women friends. No one calls here for her and she has never invited anyone. Her life is very bound up with Brian. The police are coming back to ask him some more questions this evening.'

'They'll want to speak to me again, no doubt. Strachan took an instant dislike to me. Did you notice that?'

'Well, dear, perhaps you were rude to the poor man.'

'Oh, Mother. Don't take his side. Poor man indeed. Don't trust the police to find the truth. They'll settle for a quick solution and they won't care too much who gets hurt along the way. I know. Believe me.'

'Yes, dear.'

'No, seriously Mother, I think you have too much faith in these detectives. They don't find evidence and work out who's guilty from that. They decide who's guilty and then select evidence and make it fit.'

'Don't be silly, Will. They are professional policemen and they know what they're doing. Of course we're under suspicion and of course it's an unpleasant feeling, but I don't believe for a minute that the jails are filled with innocent men, locked up on the basis of manufactured evidence. It's too absurd. I think your experience in Queensland has given you a jaundiced view of things.'

'I won't argue with you, Mother. All I'm saying is that you and Brian should be careful what you tell that Strachan character.'

I left Mother's house feeling agitated by our conversation. I hadn't expected her to be quite so naïve about the motivations of investigating officers. Like most people, she believed they were moved to solve crimes out of some sort of moral outrage, as if the solving of the crimes somehow made the world a cleaner place. She seemed to think they were like priests, dedicated to tipping the balance in favour of all that was good and decent, and banishing evildoers into the outer darkness of the prison or the hangman's drop. I had no doubt that what actually motivated them was the scramble for advancement in their careers.

As I was walking across Princes Park towards Clutterbuck's

house, the awful reality of Gretel Beech's death hit me forcefully and I was obliged to sit down on a bench for a moment. It was imperative that I find the well-endowed George. After tea and cakes with the Fowlers, I would return to the Petrushka and begin my sleuthing in earnest. As I stood to continue on my way, I became suddenly dizzy and had to sit down again. I was overwhelmed by the events of the past three days: I'd been back in Melbourne such a short time, and already I found myself grappling with the stress of an abduction, a murder, moving house, and the demands of a new and uncertain career. I almost envied Brian the monotonous safety of daily teaching.

The Fowlers and Clutterbuck were already drinking tea and nibbling at Mrs Castleton's cakes when I arrived. There was an unbearable *froideur* in the room and I didn't have the sense that I'd interrupted a lively conversation, but rather that I could provide a welcome relief from awkward silence. I was introduced to Nigella Fowler first. She betrayed by only the slightest smile that she recognised me as the person whose body she had spent the morning drawing. I guessed that her discretion had to do with the probability that her father wasn't aware of his daughter's artistic ambitions. She was no great beauty, and she didn't reveal the evidence of her father's wealth in her dress, the cut of her hair or her *maquillage*. She was determinedly dressed down, and unselfconsciously plain. For all that, there was something about her that was immediately and strongly attractive to me.

Individually, none of her features was remarkable, but she emanated a quality that hinted at great reserves of kindness and sympathy. When I shook her hand, her smile ignited in me a profound desire to remove her from Clutterbuck's influence. His frankness about his intentions and his feelings, while admirable in its way, now seemed cruel.

Mr Fowler, who shook my hand, but who didn't rise from his chair to do so, was pear-shaped. His tweed trousers were secured around a tautly rounded belly and curved down so tightly that there was no doubt at all that he dressed to the left. He was bald, except for sparse, reddish remnants that were slicked wetly above each ear. His most prominent feature was his mouth, which was fleshy, with a glistening under-lip that was almost repellent. He was not a handsome man, and the fact that he was not happy at this moment did nothing to soften his features. I didn't like Clutterbuck's chances of winning this man's approval.

James Fowler, the son, was a slimmer, much better-looking version of his father, with thin, glossy hair of a vulpine shade. He looked younger than his sister, and there was something wry and detached about him, as if all this was amusing, but of no consequence — the amusement deriving from his father's obvious discomfort.

Clutterbuck was unexpectedly jittery, his normally suave demeanour was clearly unsettled by Mr Fowler's antagonism and its potential to dash his hopes of marriage to Nigella.

'Will is an actor,' he announced to the room.

Nigella raised an eyebrow.

'Would I have seen you recently?' she asked with mischievous ambiguity.

'I've been in Queensland with my company, bringing Shakespeare to the barbarians.'

'Shakespeare won't win the war,' Mr Fowler said dismissively, 'unless you're going to bore the Japs to death.'

'Dad has a narrow view of combat tactics,' his son said. 'He's not too keen on my profession either.'

Mr Fowler snorted.

'Patting boongs on the head,' he said.

'What my father means is that I work in the department that looks after the Native Policy for Mandated Territories. He'd rather I shot them than found them work. The fact that I'm not in uniform is something of a disappointment to him.'

'Damned right,' Mr Fowler said quietly.

I could see that Clutterbuck's civilian status would seriously besmirch his prospects as a son-in-law. My being an actor would only have confirmed Mr Fowler's no doubt bleak view that he was surrounded by shirkers and cowards. Afternoon tea must have been a torture for Fowler senior, and his sullen silence was a testament to this fact.

'You're in propaganda?' I said to Nigella, in an attempt to begin a conversation.

'Yes, I write scripts for cinema shorts. *The Diary of Diana*. That's one of mine. Have you seen it? It's on at the moment.'

'Yes,' I lied. 'I liked it.'

Nigella laughed.

'Nonsense,' she said. 'It's not the kind of thing you like. It's what you endure to get to the feature.'

Her brother James launched into a recitation from the short, just as Clutterbuck had done.

' "Are you in a war job? Are you? It's a haunting question you know." '

Nigella laughed again, and my desire to remove her from Clutterbuck's influence quickened.

'There's a new short just out,' she said.

'Let's go tonight,' said Clutterbuck. 'What film's on?'

He looked at me as if my being an actor meant that I would be up to date with cinema programming.

'There's *Suspicion* on at the Regent,' said Nigella. 'Yes, let's do that. Will? You'll come?'

Without confirming by a glance at Clutterbuck whether this was all right by him, I agreed.

The conversation, after this, moved in fits and starts. Mr Fowler ate more than his share of Mrs Castleton's cakes, contributing little to the conversation apart from wondering where she had procured the butter for her sponge, and suggesting that his son, James, was too facetious for his own good. He also added that his daughter was naïve if she really thought the Japanese would be marching up Swanston Street any time soon.

'Not long ago,' he said, 'your people were telling us that the Japs were short-sighted and didn't fight at night. Now you're telling us that they want to make us all slaves.'

Nigella calmly turned to her father and said, 'Fear is much more effective than ridicule in rallying people.'

It was clear to everyone in the room that she wasn't just talking about propaganda, but the complete absence of emotion in her voice gave her father no cause to leap to his own defence, to fuel old fires of familial discontent. It felt as if whatever had transpired between Mr Fowler and his children had been regulated by time into a dull acceptance of a mismanaged childhood. Where was Mrs Fowler in all this? No mention had been made of her; and knowing that Mr Fowler disapproved of divorce, I suspected that he had long been widowed.

'These chairs are bloody uncomfortable, Clutterbuck,' he said.

Clutterbuck looked as though he was about to lay the blame for the furniture at his ex-wife's door, but thought better of drawing attention to his late marriage.

'They are a triumph of design over common sense,' he said lightly.

Nigella laughed, but Mr Fowler shot Clutterbuck a look that eloquently diagnosed him as a damned fool. I could almost hear him thinking that if Clutterbuck didn't have enough sense to own a chair he could sit on, the demands of being his son-in-law would tax him beyond his abilities. It was clear why Clutterbuck wanted me to be present at this awkward little tiffin. Whatever personal questions Mr Fowler might want to ask could not be asked in the presence of a stranger. Despite his born-to-rule demeanour, Mr Fowler conformed, on this occasion, to social niceties, of a sort.

The grim festivities broke up with Mr Fowler declaring that he couldn't sit about all day drinking tea. He departed with his son, while Nigella stayed on. She and Clutterbuck decided that they would walk into town for an early dinner, and meet me afterwards at the cinema. Clutterbuck and I went upstairs. He wanted to fetch a coat and I wanted to take a bath, my first since the discovery of Gretel's corpse. There was a faint odour of carbolic in the bathroom — Mrs Castleton must have been instructed to scrub and disinfect the tub — and while I was glad that she'd done so, I couldn't help but wonder whether she now thought that I was suffering from some sort of infectious disease.

My initial distaste on slipping into the bath gave way to pleasure under the soporific influence of the hot water. Even though I had by then become so used to the cast on my arm that I barely noticed it, its removal in four days time would end the annoyance of having to keep the wretched thing dry. Thankfully, my body was recovering well from the various traumas visited upon it in Maryborough. The only scar I carried was the bullet wound just above my collar bone. I wondered if Nigella had noticed it when she had drawn me that morning. I also wondered what I should do next. The picture didn't begin until ten to eight, which left me a few hours in which to either continue my surveillance of Anna Capshaw and Mr Trezise, pursue the generously endowed man named George, or attempt further to unravel the kidnapping of my sister-in-law.

I settled on visiting Brian, certain that I would winkle useful information out of him by subtle questioning. I closed my eyes and luxuriated in the steaming water. Clutterbuck seemed to have no shortage of wood with which to fuel his hot water service, or his stove, or his open fires. While the rest of Melbourne's citizens bathed themselves in a mean five inches of tepid water — firewood was in desperately short supply — the house in Bayles Street appeared untouched by the dead hand of austerity, restrictions or shortages. I knew he couldn't have secured his luxuries, let alone what in peacetime were considered necessities, without recourse to the black market, but I was in no position (up to my neck in hot water) to cast moral aspersions his way.

I was turning such matters over in my mind, and drifting into a half sleep, when a footfall in the corridor outside gave me a little rush of anxiety. Whoever was out there was moving with the stealth of an intruder. With a mixture of annoyance and trepidation, I clambered as quietly as possible out of the bath, wrapped a towel around my waist, and opened the door just sufficiently to see into the hallway. There was no one there. While I was considering my next move, I heard what must have been Clutterbuck's bedroom door open. When I reached it, it was ajar and someone was moving about inside. I pushed it slightly and saw a man bent over the open drawers of Clutterbuck's wardrobe. His search was careful, almost finicky; he was lifting each item to see if anything lay beneath it, and replacing things with great deliberation. He was kidding himself if he thought Clutterbuck wouldn't detect his disciplined rummaging. Clutterbuck's fiercely obsessive eye would detect the smallest alteration as a seismic shift.

When this figure turned his head slightly, I was astonished to see that it was James Fowler. My instincts told me not to give myself away, so I withdrew and let him complete his search in the mistaken belief that he was unobserved.

I returned to my room, dressed hurriedly, and emerged in time to see James Fowler's back disappearing down the stairs. The opening and closing of the front door indicated that he had left the house. I checked downstairs but there was no sign that anything had been searched or taken. The tea things were where we had left them, waiting for Mrs Castleton to clean them up, and everything else looked to be in unviolated order.

Fowler had revealed little of himself during afternoon tea. He'd been polite, amusing and detached. Clutterbuck had said, prior to my meeting him, that he thought he was a bit of a pill, although he hadn't expanded on how or why he'd come to this conclusion. I could now add to this portrait the unsettling touches that he was a snoop, and possibly a thief. I couldn't believe that James Fowler had been deputised by his father to check on Clutterbuck's suitability as a husband for his daughter. I didn't suppose that Clutterbuck's eligibility, or otherwise, would be discovered in the spaces beneath his socks and underwear. No. There was more to this trespass than that. Much more. I added what James Fowler was hunting for to my growing list of private inquiries.

At my mother's house I found Brian having a cup of tea with her in the living room. He looked haggard and exhausted; as much from his daily toils to reach unreachable adolescents as from concern about his missing wife. At least, that's the interpretation I put on his strained expression. I'm afraid my imagination failed me when it came to attaching enervating grief to the absent Darlene.

'It makes no sense,' he said as I sat down. 'This business with the blood. It makes no sense.'

'It makes dramatic sense,' I said. 'And I think Mother's right that it probably tells us that Darlene is still alive.'

Brian grasped at this eagerly.

'So neither of you thinks she's …'

'No Brian,' I said, 'neither of us thinks she's …' I filled the unsayable pause with a suitable hand gesture. 'But we are mystified by the silence.'

'It's only been one day,' Brian said. 'Perhaps the ransom note has just been posted.'

'If I were a kidnapper, Brian, I don't think I'd be trusting my demands to the PMG. I'd find a more certain way.'

'Still, it's only been one day.'

A knock at the door signalled the arrival of the two detectives. They didn't think it was necessary to question me or Mother further, and requested a private audience with Brian. We withdrew upstairs, and I was relieved that I was not going to be subjected to Detective Strachan's impertinence. I told Mother about my afternoon tea with the Fowlers, thinking that she might perhaps have known, or heard of, Mr Fowler.

'Your father was a successful man, Will, but he was not one of Melbourne's Brahmins. He was a country boy who made good. He didn't mix with the Melbourne Club set and didn't aspire to. If he ever met Mr Fowler, he didn't mention him to me, and I'm sure Mr Fowler would have said something if he'd recognised your name.'

As I was agreeing to the truth of this, the sound of a piece of furniture being turned over, and a gallimaufry of raised, excited voices, reached us.

Mother and I entered the living room to the spectacle of Brian lying face down on the floor, pinned there by Detective Strachan's knee. Handcuffs were securely in place, and all three combatants were panting. The detective who was standing — whose name I didn't yet know — said flatly, 'Brian Power has been arrested on suspicion of murder. We have reason to believe that he has killed his wife and done away with her body.'

Brian was dragged to his feet and it was clear from the paralysis of his features that he'd gone into a kind of shock.

'My son is a schoolteacher,' Mother said strangely, as if the occupation precluded violent behaviour of any kind; as if, although we have all wanted to kill a teacher at some time in our lives, no one ever expects to be killed by one of them.

'That's what he does during the day,' Detective Strachan said. 'It's the stuff that's not on his curriculum that we're interested in.'

'Where will you take him?' I asked with cool professionalism. I knew expressions of outrage at the injustice before us would achieve nothing, so I behaved as though the arrest of my brother was a technical triviality that would be processed rapidly and corrected. This was a sensible reaction my mother neither understood nor appreciated, as she freely expressed after the silent Brian had been bundled out the door, on his way to the lock-up in Russell Street.

'How could you just stand there and allow that to happen?' she asked. 'You did nothing. You said nothing and did nothing.'

'He was under arrest, Mother. What was I supposed to do? You're the one who said we should let the police go about their business. Well, they've certainly gone about their business.'

'You might have shown Brian some sort of support. A word. Something.'

I paid Mother the courtesy of not pointing out that her own contribution to Brian's situation had been confined to telling him something he already knew — that he was a teacher. She had been as dumbfounded as Brian, and now was not the time to score points against her, despite the fact that she had no qualms about dressing me down.

'Brian felt abandoned. I'm sure he did. He was waiting for you to make a demand, to express some sort of anger at the effrontery of the detectives.'

She became overwhelmed by the awfulness of the scene she had witnessed and tears welled into her eyes.

'I'll go down there,' I said, 'and try to see him. They won't hold him for long. They have no evidence. The whole thing is absurd, but I hope it shakes your faith in the police force. They flail about. There's nothing precise in what they do or the way they go about doing it.'

With repeated assurances that Brian wouldn't be detained for long, and that his experience wouldn't scar him for life, I managed to calm her a little.

At Russell Street police station I discovered that, far from obstructing me, the functionaries there were quite helpful. I was guided into a neat office, and asked if I needed a cup of tea. I declined. The detective who was Detective Strachan's companion came in.

'I don't think we've been introduced,' he said. 'I'm Detective Michael Radcliff.'

'William Power. You've arrested the wrong man. You do know that, don't you?'

'If I had a guinea for every time I've been told that, Mr Power, I'd be a rich man. As it is, I don't think our jails echo to the weeping and teeth gnashing of suffering innocents.'

His turn of phrase was extravagant for a copper, but it was delivered without emotion. Clearly, he was not an excitable man.

'Your brother has, of course, denied any involvement in his wife's disappearance. We, however, have information to the contrary, and it is sufficiently compelling to require us to hang onto him for the moment.'

He wasn't watching me in any obvious way when he said this; he was skilled at feigning indifference to the effect his words might have had. But he was, I knew, acutely sensitive to my reactions, and he must have detected the involuntary jump of surprise that caused my eyes to open fractionally wider.

'I was there,' I said. 'I was right behind Brian from the top of the stairs until we reached the kitchen, and Darlene was nowhere to be seen.'

Detective Radcliff enjoyed an infuriatingly indulgent smile. In a more animated face, it might have been a smirk.

'I think we can agree on that, Mr Power. Darlene was nowhere to be seen and Brian did nothing to her ...' he paused, before adding, 'at that time.'

There was silence for a full minute as the implications of that three word addendum sank in.

'Are you suggesting that Brian had killed Darlene at some time earlier in the evening?'

'You're a quick study, Mr Power. I was half expecting that I would have to cross the t's and dot the i's for you. I've spoken at length with Sergeant Peter Topaz in Maryborough, and the picture he painted of you was not a flattering one.'

I didn't engage with this gratuitous insult.

'There was a scream in the kitchen. I heard it. Darlene was alive and screaming at the same time that I was with Brian on the stairs.'

'Let me lay this out for you Mr Power, and I'm doing this because I'm convinced that you're not involved in any way. You don't have to be concerned that your recent experience in Maryborough is going to be repeated here. You're under no suspicion whatsoever. What we want you to do is listen to what we think happened, and talk to your brother. It would save us all a lot of time if he came clean, and cooperation will work in his favour when this comes to trial.'

I thought about interrupting this ludicrous stream of police babble, but assented to hearing Radcliff out, conscious as I was that one of the best tools at a PI's disposal is his ability to listen — and not just to what's being said, but to what's not being said as well.

Radcliff took a notebook from his pocket and consulted it before he began.

'There are, of course, a few unanswered questions. Until Brian talks to us we can't know the whole story. Let's start with Sarah Goodenough. You know your brother had an affair with her in Maryborough.'

I nodded, and felt compelled to add, 'I wouldn't call a few fucks an affair, would you?'

'If the terminology is important to you, let's just say that he committed adultery, and leave it at that.'

I had to silently acknowledge that 'affair' sounded much more palatable than its biblical alternative.

'I don't know how much Brian told you about his relationship with this woman, but her version differs from Brian's.'

'Well, it would, wouldn't it.'

'Indeed. Our job is to decide whose interests the differences serve. Sarah Goodenough has been interviewed by Brisbane detectives and they found her to be a credible witness, and yes, they were fully informed about her reputation in Maryborough. She agrees that she met Brian at the Royal Hotel, and that there was an immediate mutual attraction, and this is where the accounts diverge. Sarah insists that her relationship with Brian was no different from the other promiscuous contacts she had engaged in; she is ashamed of this behaviour but claims that she was maddened by grief and worry about her absent husband.'

I snorted.

'Well, Mr Power, I'm just repeating what she said. I'm not a psychiatrist, and whether she's just rationalising bad behaviour or not isn't relevant. What is relevant is that she says Brian became obsessed with her and he frightened her. She told him that she had no intention of leaving her husband, and consequently Brian threatened her. She said he took it back almost immediately, and started blubbering about how much he loved her. He became so distraught that he told her things he'd never told anyone else. One of these little intimations was how he'd cheated on his wife in Melbourne more than once, and that just before he'd come to Maryborough he'd planned to tell her that the marriage was over.'

'Detective Radcliff, if you'll pardon the interruption, this story is almost comical. If any part of it is even remotely true then Ned Kelly was a gentleman.'

'I haven't finished Mr Power. Its plausibility improves I assure you. Apparently, your brother told Sarah that he would do whatever was necessary to disentangle himself from Darlene. In the light of recent events, Sarah now takes this to mean that he meant murder. She recalled that he had a wild look in his eye when he said it.'

He held up his hand to prevent my speaking.

'I admit that this interpretation wouldn't hold up in court. However, after Brian had made these remarks she did something extraordinary, something that helps corroborate the bare facts of her version, if not its extravagant emotional content. She rang Darlene and told her everything.'

'And you believe her?'

'There is, I'm afraid, a record of the call. She placed it and Darlene took it. They spoke for ten minutes during which, Sarah says, she told Darlene about her dalliance with Brian and warned her that he intended to leave her as soon as he got back to Melbourne. Darlene, of course, didn't believe any of it, couldn't believe her, but was obliged to when Sarah described Brian's penis.'

Detective Radcliff paused for a moment to allow that bizarre little detail to sink in. Feigning nonchalance, I said, 'Surely one penis looks very much like another.'

'You might think that if the only one you ever see is your own. Women like Sarah Goodenough know differently, and her description was sufficiently exact to convince Darlene that she had at least got close enough to see it, and not just in repose.'

This was such an avalanche of information that for the moment I could make no sense of it.

'I would have noticed that something was wrong between them,' I said. 'Darlene was happy to see Brian.'

'If what Sergeant Topaz says about you is true, your observational skills are not exactly Holmesian.'

I let that go. I'm sure he and Topaz had had a lovely time assassinating my character.

'My mother would certainly have noticed something.'

'Your mother is a charming and sensible woman, but if you'll excuse the liberty, what Sergeant Topaz called your 'epic self-absorption' might be partly inherited.'

I was not, as a matter of fact, prepared to excuse that liberty, and I stood up with every intention of slamming my fist into Radcliff's thin, complacent face. He must have been ready for this, waiting patiently for his goading to have an effect, because he was out of his chair and had my unencumbered arm twisted behind my back before I was aware of what had happened.

'Calm down,' he said in my ear. 'Calm down or I'll help you calm down.'

'I am calm,' I hissed.

With one hand on my shoulder and the other still painfully pressing my arm, he pushed me back down into the seat.

'I have to say, Mr Power, that your priorities are a little askew if what provokes you is a suggestion about your mother's ego rather than your brother's proximity to the hangman's noose.'

'If you knew my brother you'd know that these Machiavellian manoeuvres are beyond him. My god, he fell in love with Darlene, and, believe me, that should tell you all you need to know about his imagination. You don't grow dissatisfied with Darlene by degrees. It's something that happens on the spot — unless you're my brother, in which case you make the macabre decision to shackle yourself to her.'

'He did cheat on her.'

'Yes, and all I can say is that it was completely and inexplicably out of character.'

Radcliff had by this time returned to his seat.

'Given all the information that we have gathered over the last twenty-four hours I can safely say that at least you are behaving in ways that Sergeant Topaz would recognise as absolutely characteristic. You're not seeing what is staring you in the face.'

'The only thing staring me in the face is a detective who doesn't know his arse from his elbow.'

Radcliff maintained the impassive demeanour of a man used to being proved right in the end.

'Have you filled him in?'

Detective Strachan had entered the office unannounced, and with oily stealth.

'Pretty much,' Radcliff said.

'The other one's not being helpful. He's putting on a good show of being scared witless — I almost feel sorry for him. Is this bloke going to talk to him?'

'This bloke,' I said, and did a first rate imitation of Strachan's voice, 'isn't too impressed with the case you've constructed. I heard Darlene scream. That fact alone makes a nonsense of the idea that Brian had killed her earlier.'

'Detective Radcliff obviously hasn't told you what we think happened.'

'I was getting to it,' Radcliff said. 'I was just extracting a little of Mr Power's bile first.'

'Well, I'll hurry things along,' Strachan sat on the edge of Radcliff's desk and crossed one leg over the other, exposing a blackly hairy ankle.

'Miss Goodenough has given your brother a poor character reference, and we have no reason to disbelieve her when she says that he was unfaithful to his wife prior to his arrival in Maryborough. You say you heard a scream coming from the kitchen and the sound of breaking china. We don't dispute that. Your mother confirms it. Your assumption that it was Darlene screaming is what we dispute. We believe that this is a classic case of misdirection. We think that the woman in the kitchen was Brian's Melbourne mistress and that the two of them cooked up this performance. Hence the speed with which the so-called kidnapper vanished and the silly splashing about of bullock's blood. We don't know whether your brother approved this flourish. We doubt it. He's smart enough to realise that it would be analysed and distract us from the simple storyline he had set up.'

As Strachan was unfolding the police version of what had happened the previous day, my resistance to its logic began to weaken. It was neat and hideously possible. The only stumbling block was that I could not imagine Brian coolly planning and then carrying out so callous a crime. Of course, if I hadn't heard from his own lips that he had had a sexual relationship with Sarah Goodenough, I wouldn't have thought that likely either.

'Can I see him?' I asked.

Radcliff indicated the door and I followed him. I thought Brian would be across the road in the cells, but I was led into an interview room where he sat slumped behind a table. He looked hollowed out. A uniformed officer sat in a corner.

'Your brother hasn't been formally charged as yet,' Radcliff said. 'I'll leave you alone — apart from the officer there.'

Brian's face was puffy from crying, and from fear, and from the devastation wrought by the internal bomb blast of having his life brutally altered. I knew as soon as I saw him that the police story was absurd. Brian simply didn't possess the qualities required for serial adultery, murder and concealment. He breathed shakily.

'You know what they think?' he said, and his voice was thin, stripped of its confidence by the humiliation he was suffering.

'Yes, but they don't actually have a case, just a theory, and it's all based on the word of a madwoman.'

'How could they think these things?'

'I understand what it feels like to be where you are now.'

He nodded.

'Now listen to me, Brian. If I'm going to help you I need to know everything there is to know.'

'How can you help me? What do you mean? You're an actor.'

'I'm not just an actor anymore. I'm a private inquiry agent, too.'

This was meant to reassure him; instead, even through the fog of his now thoroughly obscured normal life, he laughed.

'You're kidding me.'

'No Brian, I'm not kidding you, and you're not my first job either. As a matter of fact I'm working on a couple of things.'

'But Will, you couldn't detect your arse if it wasn't always in the same place.'

'Only last year they hanged someone in Victoria for murder.

Now probably isn't the time for smart-aleck remarks. Whatever you think of my skills, I don't see a queue of people lining up to defend you.'

'Mother will get a good lawyer.'

'Lawyers don't investigate. I don't care how good he is, if this goes the wrong way the best he might be able to do is get your sentence commuted.'

A new wave of fear broke over Brian, and he was immediately more compliant.

'All right. All right.'

'You have to tell me everything, however sordid.'

He inclined his head.

'Was Sarah Goodenough really the first woman you cheated with, or were there others here in Melbourne?'

The look on his face was one of disbelief that such a question needed to be asked. He calmly said, 'Sarah Goodenough was the first and only one. There was nobody in Melbourne. Nobody.'

'So everything that Sarah told the police is a frighteningly convincing lie?'

'Everything.'

'There's no one I need to speak to? No one who can provide me with any information?'

Rallying for a moment, Brain declared angrily, 'Will, there *is* no information to provide.'

All I could offer at this point was an assurance that I would do my best to find Darlene's kidnappers.

'I'm not going to spend the night in jail, am I?'

'I don't see how that can be avoided, but you'll be out tomorrow, I promise you.'

The look of unmitigated horror that flooded Brian's face as he suddenly realised that he would be spending at least one night in a cell was heartbreaking. As I left I told Radcliff that Brian had emphatically denied all allegations against him, and that they would be hearing from our lawyer almost immediately.

'We've already heard from him,' Radcliff said, 'while you were in with your brother. Your mother organised it.'

I had no idea who Mother had hired or how she even knew who to ring. As I walked down the steps of the police headquarters in Russell Street I thought that there was a great deal about my mother that I didn't know.

Chapter Six

BY GEORGE

IT WAS SEVEN-THIRTY by the time I had crossed Russell Street and walked past the lumpish conglomerate of the Magistrates' Court. The picture was due to start in twenty minutes, so I could easily make it to the Regent Theatre in Collins Street in time. There were a lot of people on the streets, most of them American servicemen squiring women to the lounges of hotels.

The local boys couldn't afford to do this. Bars, many of which ran out of beer regularly, were obliged to close at five-thirty and thereafter alcohol could only be bought in the lounge — and the prices in the lounge were prohibitively high. A beer that cost seven pence in the bar at twenty-five minutes past five cost one shilling in the lounge ten minutes later. The price of spirits was even more inflated. This didn't put too much pressure on the doughboys' pay packets, and for underpaid shop girls or exploited

WAAFs turning down the offer of a few two- shilling gins was a sacrifice they weren't prepared to make. I can't say I blamed them, returning as they would be to unheated houses and five lousy inches of tepid bathwater. I wondered if the emperor of Japan had any idea of the effect his belligerent expansionism was having on the sex and social lives of Melbourne's bourgeoisie.

Very quickly I found myself in Little Collins Street passing the Petrushka café. It was open and busy, and I decided, on the spur of the moment, to duck in and make an enquiry about George, the fellow who could possibly tell me something about Gretel Beech. I pushed open the door and was hit by a fug of human heat and cigarette smoke. Melbourne's bearded, corduroy crowd was here in force. Surprisingly, there were a couple of Yanks as well. At the counter I raised my voice above the surrounding babble, and asked whether a man named George was in the café tonight. The woman shrugged. 'George who?'

'I don't know his last name,' I said, and summoned the courage to nonchalantly add, 'All I know is that he's very well endowed.'

'You're a pervert,' she said. 'Get out before I get someone to throw you out.'

Mr Wilks had overstated the *laissez-faire* virtues of the Petrushka café. Anything did not go, after all.

I turned away from the counter and was preparing to move among the tables, to ask discreetly whether this or that person was George, when four policemen burst through the door and began blowing their whistles hysterically. Three of them hurried to the rear of the café and the fourth stood by the entrance. Two suited men, who had come in after them, surveyed the crowd, who had gone quiet, and one of them said loudly: 'Everyone stay where you are. We're Manpower officials and we're here to check your papers. Please get them ready and we'll get this over with as quickly as possible.'

I found this an extraordinary situation, but the patrons of the Petrushka seemed resigned to the interruption — so obedient were they that this couldn't have been the first time a Manpower raid had been conducted on the premises. I'd heard about them and thought it bizarre. A Manpower official had the authority to redirect anyone not working in a designated war job into such a job. If you had the misfortune to be scratching a living in an inessential industry, such as hairdressing or shop assisting, or any of the thousands of other occupations deemed frivolous, you might find yourself ordered to report for work at a munitions factory. We were all supposed to carry ID cards showing the name and address of our employer. If you weren't employed, someone from Manpower would helpfully find you something ghastly to do. I was in the fortunate position of holding a card that indicated that I was in a reserved occupation — entertainers being regarded as essential to the morale of the general populace — so I had nothing to fear from the little Napoleons of the Manpower unit. When my papers were examined the odious man looked down his vein-webbed nose at me, as if I was one of the loathsome deserters on the home front who was not pulling his weight, but there was nothing he could do. He made no attempt to hide his disappointment at his inability to transfer me to a dully repetitive factory job.

The raid was over in a few minutes. I don't know if any orders were issued. I'd be surprised if everyone in the Petrushka that night was making a critical contribution to defeating Japan, but perhaps many of them were sufficiently well connected to carry convincing, if not necessarily accurate, identification papers. The patrons of the café didn't strike me as being members of an underclass. Their politics were, I suspected, as susceptible to fashion as their outfits.

The arrival of the Manpower people had distracted the

woman behind the counter from her intention of having me thrown out. The clamour of conversation reasserted itself as I began to look for George. I approached table after table and said, 'I'm looking for a man named George. I know this sounds odd, but I have a message for him from Gretel.' I didn't risk mentioning George's most distinguishing feature again. At a table of four men, carefully, artfully shabby in their attire, I interrupted a boisterous argument about the merits of an artist whose name was unfamiliar to me. It didn't appear to be a particularly friendly exchange of views, and when I asked my question a dark-haired young man said, 'Yeah. I'm George. What's she want?'

He didn't look at me when he spoke, his attention still commanded by the man opposite him, and his mind yet engaged on some combustible point about modernism.

'It's a private matter,' I said. 'Could we speak outside?'

'Nothing's private here, mate. If Gretel's got something to tell me, she should tell me herself, not send a message boy. So what is it?'

He looked at me finally, and in his pale, Irish face I read that the dominant emotion in his life would be anger. He was handsome enough to draw a woman like Gretel Beech to him, but there wasn't a skerrick of humour in his eyes. Life, for George, was a very serious business indeed.

His three companions were now waiting for me to deliver Gretel's nonexistent message. It occurred to me suddenly that any one of them could be Gretel's killer. It's a rare victim who doesn't know her murderer, and the way to find this culprit was to assemble those people who knew Gretel and eliminate them as suspects by careful questioning and intelligent reasoning. I'd eliminated Clutterbuck already — I'd been with him the night Gretel died — and I now had in front of me several people who might move my inquiries forward. I didn't think Detectives Strachan and Radcliff could have done any better, and I certainly couldn't see either of them being prepared to stand naked in a roomful of women in the service of an investigation.

'The first thing I need to know,' I said, 'is if you're the right George.'

'I'm George Beech. Gretel's husband. How many other Georges would Gretel be sending a message to? Who the hell are you anyway, and where's Gretel? Is she shacked up with you or what?'

The ugly tone of these questions was no different from the ugly tone of all George Beech's utterances, and it wasn't driven by anger particular to the possibility that I was sleeping with his wife. Uxoriousness was not a quality George Beech could be congratulated upon possessing. They had, I surmised, an open marriage. I thought I'd show him how open I could be, too.

'You're the George I'm looking for only if you have a larger-than-average penis.'

This was met with silence, until George Beech stood up, said, 'You tell me,' undid his flies and produced what any sensible person would describe as a larger-than-average penis. This didn't go unnoticed by people at other tables, but it happened so quickly that there wasn't time for anyone to register a shocked response before the impressive appendage had been re-housed.

The three other men with George turned to me, and one of them, a slightly overweight, sandy-haired chap with ink-stained fingers asked, 'Right George do you think?'

'The evidence for that seems pretty good,' I said.

'So what's the message?' George asked.

How was I going to play this? I had to assume, until proven otherwise, that Gretel's death was unknown to her husband. What was the etiquette?

'May I join you?' I asked.

'No,' he said flatly. 'You may not. Just tell me the message and piss off back to Gretel with a message from me. My message is, "Fuck you". Got that? "Fuck you".'

I wasn't going to tell him that Gretel was past caring about her estranged husband's obscenities — a fact, I had to remind myself, that he may already have known. With little else to go on, I would have to accept that the obvious rift between them might be a motive for murder.

'To tell you the truth, George, there is no message. I haven't seen Gretel for quite a while, and I can assure you that there was nothing at all between us. I didn't even know she was married. A Mr Wilks, who teaches drawing, suggested you might know where she was because you modelled for him a few weeks ago when Gretel couldn't make it. This is embarrassing, but she owes me some money, just a couple of pounds, and I'm a bit short and need it. And that's all there is to it.'

'Let me tell you something Mr whoever-you-are. I wouldn't care if Gretel owed you several million pounds. If you're silly enough to lend her money, that's your lookout. I suppose you were hoping for other favours.'

I didn't much like being portrayed as a fool who has been parted from his money, especially as the story was spurious.

'I just need to find her,' I said, and tried to inject a little note of desperation, designed to elicit sympathy, into my voice.

One of his companions jumped in at this point.

'Why don't you quit while you're ahead, mate? You can see George isn't interested in answering your bloody questions, so maybe now would be a good time to piss off.'

The hostility around the table was palpable and I saw no advantage to myself in pursuing the matter any further, so I decided that I would wait outside and follow George Beech home. I would have to forgo meeting Nigella and Clutterbuck and not see Katharine Hepburn. The latter was hardly a sacrifice. As an actress I had always found her so unappealingly equine that I suspected a centaur in her family tree.

Outside the Petrushka there was nowhere close by that was suitable for dawdling unseen. I found a doorway on the opposite side of the street, and some way up from the café, and leaned in it as inconspicuously as I could. An American soldier, slightly drunk, passed, returned and passed again, before stopping and making an obscene inquiry as to what I charged. He was disgruntled when I set him straight. I thought perhaps Manpower needed to do a sweep of Melbourne's doorways, unless of course the government considered prostitution an essential service. After half an hour and another approach — I could have earned a few quid that night — I was so catatonically bored and uncomfortable that I abandoned my plan to wait for George Beech to emerge. The fact that Mother was alone at home, and no doubt anxious to hear how my meeting had gone with Brian, began to nag at me. I would return to the Petrushka in a few hours when there was a chance that I would find Beech still ensconced there, a good deal drunker and less guarded.

I had never seen my mother so frantic. She'd always been dependably unruffleable, almost unshakeably languid. To find her distracted and agitated was shocking to me.

'We will have to get Brian out of there,' she said. 'He won't manage. He isn't strong enough for all this.'

'He's doing all right, Mother. Really.'

'Oh, Will, you don't know your brother very well. He's much more highly strung than you think, and he's fragile and naïve and lovely, and this shouldn't be happening to him.'

She broke into tears. I wasn't quite sure how Brian's lurid affair with Sarah Goodenough might be accommodated into his fragility, naivety and loveliness, but it wasn't the moment to make inquiries on that point.

'I was told that you've hired a lawyer.'

'Peter Gilbert. Yes. He was an associate of your father's and he's a good man. We've been friends for many years.'

When Mother had calmed down she told me that this Gilbert fellow would go through the coppers like a dose of salts, and that he would have Brian home as soon as was legally possible — even if it meant posting a large bail. I wondered how Brian's arrest would affect his job. Would the Ministry of Education approve of bailed murder suspects teaching the nation's youth, even in this time of severe teacher shortage?

I made a cup of tea and outlined the police case against Brian. Mother listened and, unexpectedly, acknowledged its awful plausibility — from the police point of view. But she insisted it wouldn't be sustained among people who knew Brian. While we were discussing these matters, Peter Gilbert arrived. He was a man in his early sixties; neat, almost dapper, and with a build still sufficiently athletic to ensure that his face had not begun its melt into jowliness. He was uncommonly solicitous, I thought, of Mother's welfare and sat close by her, holding her hand in startling intimacy and paying scant attention to my presence. After the briefest of introductions his concern was entirely for Mother.

I was clearly supernumerary to Mother's immediate needs, so I made my farewells and headed for Royal Parade, where I caught a tram into the city. Having been away from Melbourne for a while, the sight of a female conductor was still disconcerting, although this one wasn't the best advertisement for the innovation. She was a surly hulk of barely contained rage, and she seemed to hold each of the passengers personally responsible for whatever grim depths to which her life had descended. She took my money and issued the ticket and the change with such ill-grace that you'd think I had just confiscated her soul.

I disembarked at Collins Street and walked quickly in the direction of the Regent Theatre. By now the picture would be over, and before returning to the Petrushka I might be lucky and catch Clutterbuck and Nigella as they came out. I could make some excuse for missing the movie, but it wouldn't involve telling them about my brother's incarceration. I identified this reluctance to tell the truth with an unsettling swelling in my attraction to Nigella Fowler. When I thought of her I considered what it might be like to be alone with her, and more and more I thought it incumbent upon me to step between her and Clutterbuck. I knew that relationship could only end in tears, and the tears would be Nigella's. I hadn't seen much evidence of Clutterbuck's lachrymose leanings.

There was a small crowd outside the Regent Theatre — the rump of that evening's audience — and Nigella and Clutterbuck were not among them. I was disappointed, and found myself indulging in an inconvenient rush of jealousy. Just how far had Nigella licensed Clutterbuck's roving hands? This was none of my business, but the knowledge that the only part of my own body she had yet to discover was the forearm hidden beneath the plaster cast somehow made me feel proprietorial towards her, as if the intimacy was already mutual.

Clutterbuck had money and this gave him an advantage, although Nigella didn't strike me as a gold digger. In all probability she had her own fortune — her father was a wealthy man — so Clutterbuck's attractiveness must have been other than his cash. If it was his looks, this was puzzling. He was good looking but he didn't, as I did, bear a striking resemblance to Tyrone Power.

Nigella must see that Clutterbuck was driven by self-interest, and that she couldn't hope to curb his adulterous fornications once they were married. It was while I was turning these matters over in my mind that a hand fell on my shoulder and I was spun around entirely against my will. I found myself facing Paul Clutterbuck, grinning in the dimmed lights of Melbourne's brownout. It took me a moment to recover from a natural abhorrence at being so casually manhandled.

'Where were you?' he asked. I could smell whisky on his breath. Its source was revealed when he reached into his voluminous and beautiful coat and produced a flask, which he pushed towards me. Knowing that his whisky was reliably good and not the vile hooch that sometimes found its way into reclaimed bottles with undamaged 'Bottled in Scotland' labels on them, I took it and enjoyed a decent swig.

'I got caught up,' I said. 'I found Gretel's husband.'

'Didn't know she had one. To be fair, I didn't ever ask. Is he our man?'

'He's a possibility, but there are three other blokes who are of interest as well.'

I was pleased with how professional this sounded and from the surprised look on Clutterbuck's face I could see that his confidence in my abilities had been given a boost.

'Four suspects already,' he said. 'That's good going.'

'Where's Nigella?'

'She went home.'

'I thought she'd stay over.'

Clutterbuck laughed.

'God no. Nigella's not that sort of girl. It's all very proper. No hanky-panky before the wedding night.'

This was an enormous relief, and it fixed my determination to step between Clutterbuck and Nigella. I would have to take things slowly though. He was employing me after all, and the accommodation he offered was luxurious. I was also welded to him for the moment by our experience with poor Gretel Beech's body. The sooner I solved that crime the better. I didn't know Clutterbuck sufficiently well to be able to predict with confidence how he might react to losing Nigella, and I was hideously conscious of the fact that Gretel Beech was lying under a few feet of earth in the Carlton Cemetery with my tie around her neck. This was as good as a signed confession, and an enraged Clutterbuck might well deliver it to the police. With a newly fierce determination to find out as much as I could about my chief suspect, George Beech, I said, 'I'm on George Beech's tail. That's where I'm headed. Beech knew that his wife was cheating on him. I just need to find out how he knew it was you. He definitely has a motive.'

Clutterbuck screwed the cap back on the flask and returned it to the folds of his coat.

'Fine. But don't forget Cunningham. I need to know about him, and soon.'

With cool professionalism I told him that Cunningham was really a man named Trezise, and that he'd popped into confession quite soon after his most recent ejaculation. Clutterbuck was duly impressed.

'Good man,' he said and took another swig from his flask. 'I'll wait up for you and you can fill in the details then. You know, Will, I'm glad you're working for me. You're bloody good at your job.'

I'm as susceptible to praise and affirmation as the next man, and Clutterbuck's words, along with the whisky, made me flush with warmth. He turned then in his beautiful coat and walked away. I remained firm in my intention to rescue Nigella from the horrible mistake of marrying him.

The Petrushka café was still open, and even busier than it had been earlier. The noise and smoke were intolerable. Beech was still there, but only one of his companions remained with him, and they were both so bleary-eyed with drink that they didn't register my entrance. There were no available tables, so I leaned against the counter, performing nonchalance rather that feeling it.

'I warned you earlier,' said the woman behind the counter. Almost simultaneously I felt a firm grip on my unplastered arm and before I had time to think I found myself propelled into Little Collins Street. The thug who'd tossed me into the street yelled, 'This is a café not a brothel, arsehole!' His extraordinary supposition, based on my earlier inquiry I presumed, didn't go unnoticed by patrons about to enter. As a PI's enemy is exposure, I thought it wise not to attempt to correct my assailant, and slipped discreetly into the surrounding darkness. The nearest doorway was occupied. I couldn't see who was fondling whom, but I heard the squeal and giggle of a woman and smelled the sickly odour of American aftershave.

This was a most unsatisfactory situation. I wasn't keen on lurking in Little Collins Street and was reassessing my options when George Beech staggered through the door of the Petrushka. He was alone, and set off in the direction of Parliament House. Following him undetected was straightforward. His inebriated mutterings allowed me to keep a bead on him even though the darkness was absolute. If he moved more than a few feet ahead of me he became an indistinct shape. He crossed Spring Street and walked into the deep almost physical darkness of the Treasury Gardens, and must have put on quite a burst of speed, because one minute I could discern his silhouette and the next he'd vanished. There were no lights; not even the occasional dim, hooded ones that were to be found in other public parks. The government clearly thought that the palest pinpoint of light in the vicinity might lead to bombs raining down on Treasury.

Keeping to the path I felt rather than saw before me, I walked carefully forward — carefully because I didn't want to stray from it and tumble into one of the air raid ditches that criss-crossed the open ground. I was suddenly aware of a sinister silence and stopped to listen for the reassuring night sounds of American soldiers rutting local girls. There was nothing — only the unexpected, instinctive rush of panic in my ears as I became aware that I was in danger. I swung around, and became immediately disoriented by fear. If I moved now I had no way of knowing whether I was heading deeper into the gardens or back the way I had come. I stood stock still, hearing my breath coming in little, desperate pants, sounding to my ears like a terrible parody of mounting physical pleasure.

When the blow came it fell across my shoulders with the awful heft of a heavy length of wood, wielded in a wide swing, and probably aimed at my head. The darkness in this respect was my friend. I pitched forward and fell face first into the abrasive embrace of the rough, gravelly path. I remained on the ground and drew my legs up to offer some protection against the kicking which would surely begin. Shoes and trouser bottoms appeared so close to my face that I could smell the leather and see enough to note that the wearer was at least doing his bit for the war by not having cuffs. The figure crouched down and revealed itself to be George Beech. A sharp, nasty little kick to the buttocks indicated the presence of a second person.

'Who are you?' Beech said. 'You're a copper, aren't you.'

If I hadn't been in quite so much pain I might have found this amusing. Beech grabbed my hair and pulled my head off the ground.

'This is a warning, copper. I don't give a fuck who you are, stay out of my business. If I catch you hanging around the Petrushka or following me, the next time you see your teeth, you'll be picking them out of your shit.'

He pushed my gravel-rashed face back into the dirt. There was nothing to be gained by arguing with him, so I didn't disabuse him of his misidentification. He straightened up and I relaxed, which is why my ribs took the full force of his savage kick. The fact that he settled for one was proof enough of the gratuitous nature of his violence.

I lay very still, feeling sick, and with a sharp pain in my chest which I visualised as a shard of jagged rib tearing at my lungs. When I was certain that I was alone I forced myself upright and was gingerly pressing against my ribcage when the narrow beams of two partially masked torches made me wince.

'Jesus mate, you look terrible.'

'Well, that certainly tallies with how I feel.'

'You've been assaulted,' said an observant second voice.

The owners of the torches introduced themselves as Constables Kelty and Burke, presumably on patrol in the gardens to defend the nation against lewd and immoral acts. They were sympathetic until I said that even though I'd been attacked I'd be unable to identify my attackers, (the last thing I wanted was the police crossing my investigative path), and that therefore it would be best if we let the matter rest.

'So you don't want to make any report at all,' Constable Kelty said.

'That's right.'

They thought about this for a moment and concluded that I might have been guilty of just the sort of lewdness they were deputised to uncover and prosecute.

'Were you here to make sexual contact with another man?' asked Constable Burke, with ludicrous formality.

'Gentlemen,' I said slowly. 'I have been assaulted, not fucked. Perhaps your training has not prepared you for the difference.'

Constable Kelty snorted.

'We meet lots of your kind who like it rough, or maybe you just picked the wrong bloke tonight.'

Even through my discomfort I found his suggestion impertinent and offensive. With exemplary calm I said,' I was not soliciting for sex- not with a man and not with a woman and not with a possum. I was simply walking.'

To hurry things along I produced my identification, waited while they examined it, and requested that I be allowed to go on my way.

'You're an entertainer, Mr Power,' said Constable Kelty, and in a tone that indicated that he thought this was, in and of itself, half-way to proving a charge of buggery.

'William Power,' said Constable Burke. 'Never heard of you.'

'Well, constable, I don't roller skate through lines of half-naked women while singing *There'll Always Be An England*, which is no doubt your sort of theatre experience. I perform the plays of Shakespeare.'

Constable Burke was all for taking me in, the mention of Shakespeare having confirmed my probable deviancy, but Constable Kelty was by this time bored, and I suspected he wanted to move on, hopeful of discovering a couple *in flagrante delicto*.

'You can go, Romeo,' he said, and chortled at his witticism. Constable Burke, clearly the beta male, chortled sycophantically, and probably spent the rest of the evening wondering who Romeo was.

I walked all the way back to Clutterbuck's house, and as I did so the pain in my ribcage declined to a dull ache, replaced in intensity by the sting in my face. So nothing had been broken at any rate, although I could expect extensive bruising. I was glad I'd got the life modelling out of the way. The class would have thought they were drawing someone recently pulled from a train wreck.

There were no lights on downstairs when I entered Clutterbuck's house, and upstairs was similarly unilluminated. It was late, so I assumed he was asleep. I went into my bathroom and began to pick small pieces of gravel out of my cheek. I looked terrible and I was furious with George Beech. A private inquiry agent should blend into the background, not draw attention to himself by looking like the victim of some ghastly, temporarily disfiguring accident. I gritted my teeth and splashed a dilute solution of peroxide onto the angry skin. It hurt so much I gave free rein to a yowl of pain and listened guiltily for evidence of having wakened Clutterbuck. The house didn't stir, and the silence, perhaps because it reminded me of the silence just before George Beech jumped me, made me suddenly edgy. There was something amiss. I knew so little about Clutterbuck that I didn't know whether I would find him asleep in his room, or still out somewhere. His routines were unknown to me. I had to check on him and put my mind at ease.

I switched the light on in the hallway and approached his bedroom door. If he was in fact asleep, there was nothing to be gained by waking him, so I didn't knock. Instead, I turned the doorknob carefully and pushed the door gently. It gave, but met resistance after a few inches. My heart began to race and I pushed harder, believing that it was Clutterbuck's corpse that lay slumped on the other side of the door. Fortunately my instincts, usually so reliable, were wrong, and the door easily dislodged the impediment. This, however, was singular, because I couldn't imagine Clutterbuck sleeping happily in a room where something had been carelessly discarded onto the floor.

The light from the hallway was enough to show me that something was very, very wrong. I snapped on Clutterbuck's bedroom light, certain that he wasn't there, and was greeted by a scene of utter chaos. Every drawer of every wardrobe was pulled open and its contents hurled into the room. Someone had gone through Clutterbuck's belongings with the concentrated destructiveness of a highly localised cyclone. His bed had been stripped and the mattress turned over. His shirts, trousers, socks and underwear were spread in violent disarray and the gaping, empty compartments in which they had lain made this look all the more shocking. His bathroom had been similarly turned upside down. Bottles of aftershave and cologne tumbled from the cabinet, and towels were thrown willy-nilly into the bath. Surprisingly, there was nothing broken. This had been a search, not a burglary.

I came back into his bedroom and stood among his clothes, like Ruth amid the alien corn. Clutterbuck was leaning in the doorway.

'You've been busy,' he said calmly. 'Find anything?'

Initially his words made no sense to me, but my mouth fell open when I grasped his meaning.

'I didn't do this,' I said, and, caught completely off-guard, blurted out, 'I think it was James Fowler.'

Clutterbuck coolly raised an eyebrow.

'No, Paul, really. What reason could I possibly have for turning your room upside down? It was definitely James Fowler.'

I was relieved when he nodded and said, 'I told you he was a pill.'

'But why, Paul? Why would Nigella's brother do something like this? What's he looking for?'

'Let's not jump to conclusions, Will. Why are you so sure it was James?'

'I didn't want to tell you, but this afternoon, after you and Nigella had left, I caught James snooping around your room. He didn't see me. He was being pretty careful though. I wouldn't have expected this.'

Clutterbuck remained impressively composed; his innately disciplined nature overcoming what must have been outrage at the state of his room.

'You might want to think about whether Fowler had something to do with Gretel's death.'

'Surely your fiancée's brother wouldn't be so opposed to the marriage that he'd kill someone to stop it.'

'The person who did this,' Clutterbuck said, sweeping his hand over the room, 'would not find murder too much of a stretch.'

Although I couldn't equate untidiness with a tendency to kill, I had to admit to myself that James Fowler was now, as a coroner might say, a person of interest.

Chapter Seven

CHURCH GOING

I SLEPT BADLY. Every time I turned my cheek to the pillow I woke with a stinging pain. In the morning the pillow was speckled with blood. What must Mrs Castleton have thought of me? — carbolic in the bath, blood on the pillow. Her impression of Mr Clutterbuck's new tenant would surely be a grim one.

I began to shave but abandoned it. The razor being drawn across raw skin was more than I could tolerate. By the light of day my face bore spectacular witness to George Beech's attack. It looked as if someone had taken a cheese grater and rubbed it up and down my right cheek.

I'd told Clutterbuck what had happened in the Treasury Gardens, and although he acknowledged that I was earning my keep, the state of his room had prevented him from offering a more sympathetic response. I'd noticed, indeed, that his reaction to any departure from the norm was a nervous, uncomfortable little smile. It would be easy for the unobservant to misinterpret this. The smile on his face when he examined my injury wasn't one of pleasure, but an involuntary expression of a little-boy belief that a smile might make it better. I saw it as a charming idiosyncrasy in his otherwise formidable, cool self-assurance.

I left early, before Clutterbuck made an appearance. I wasn't sure where he'd slept — in one of the spare rooms probably. I couldn't imagine him dozing in his own bedroom. The mess would have created a storm of noise in his head. As I walked towards Mother's house, nursing tender ribs which sat beneath skin the colour of monsoon clouds, I determined that by the end of the day I would know all that there was to know about Mr Trezise, and that I would have discovered who killed Gretel Beech and why. How I was going to accomplish this wasn't yet clear, but I was buoyed by the amount of information I had accumulated in only two days.

As far as Gretel Beech's killer was concerned, I was now quite sure that he was either George Beech or James Fowler. Beech seemed more likely, especially given the ease with which he felled me. He was no stranger to violence. James Fowler, a late entry, was an outside chance. Even though Clutterbuck was suspicious of him — and he was certainly up to something — I couldn't see him strangling anybody. No one cares that deeply about whom his sister marries. He and his father were doubtless less than happy about Nigella's choice, but the Melbourne Club, however unpleasant its members, didn't use murder to control its intake.

It was 7.30 a.m. when I knocked on Mother's door. I was surprised when it was opened by Brian. He looked much better, certainly much better than I did, as evidenced by the expression on his face when he saw me.

'My God, what happened to you?'

I was about to lie and say that I'd tripped in the brownout, but remembering his jibe about my being a PI, I said, 'I was doing some work for a client and it turned nasty. I'd appreciate it if you'd keep this under your hat and let Mother think that I simply tripped and fell. How did you get out of jail?'

'I never went to jail,' he said, as we went down to the kitchen. 'The police let me go late last night. Mother's solicitor reckons they're playing a game of cat and mouse. They show their hand, let me know that they think I did it, apply pressure, then release me to see what I do. They don't have any evidence, only a theory, and their best chance is to hope that I make a mistake. That's what Peter Gilbert says.'

'God knows how anything gets solved. I thought they'd arrested you.'

'They let me think they were going to, and then changed their minds.'

'That doesn't sound exactly legal. What does this Gilbert say about that?'

Brian shrugged. 'Tactics. He says it's just tactics.'

He was a different man from the badly shaken suspect I'd seen last night. He'd rallied with admirable speed.

'My only worry,' he said over a cup of tea, 'is that, while they're concentrating on me, Darlene is out there somewhere.'

I was about to make Brian the rash promise that I would find Darlene, and that I would do it before the day was over, when Mother appeared and prevented this absurdly optimistic statement being uttered. I was sitting with my back to her, so I told her before she saw my face that I had had an accident and that it looked worse than it actually was. She lavished a small cluck of sympathy on me before inquiring with real solicitude about Brian's health. She must have spoken to him when he returned the night before, so why she would expect a deterioration in his health to occur over the ensuing few hours was beyond me.

'I'm fine,' Brian said, 'but I've made a decision. I'm going to resign from school rather than wait to be suspended from duty or dismissed, and, even if Darlene is found and is safe, I'm not going back to teaching. I'm the only man there as it is, and anyway, I've had enough.'

'You've got flat feet,' said Mother. 'Like Will. You can't join up.'

'I'll get a job of some kind. Manpower will put me somewhere. I don't care where.'

This was certainly a surprising decision, but I could see Brian's point about jumping before being pushed. If he did stay, the word would soon filter down to his students that Mr Power was suspected of having done away with his wife. This would make the maintenance of classroom discipline a challenge. Being taught by a murderer would unleash the natural anarchy in the most docile of boys.

I warned Brian that the police might pick him up for another round of questioning during the day, and that he shouldn't give them the satisfaction of being upset by it.

'That Strachan character will be pissed off to find you bemused rather than frightened.'

Mother agreed, but hoped that Brian's bemusement would be more attractive than my own expressions of this emotion. I let the remark go, firstly because I had no idea what she was talking about, and secondly because I recognised that it was the kind of observation generated by the stress and worry that she was experiencing.

I caught an uncomfortably overburdened tram down Lygon Street. It was so crowded that it made me claustrophobic, and I disembarked well before I'd intended to. With no clear idea of what I should do I simply headed in the direction of St Patrick's spires, emboldened enough by what I had so far achieved to believe, like Mr Micawber, that something would turn up.

The cathedral was filled with the smell of floor wax, stale incense, and the sound of beautiful voices. It must have been a choir rehearsal, because the music stopped abruptly and was followed by the incongruous sound of an instruction in German. The singing recommenced, was halted, and another, sharper instruction rang out, again in German. Curious, I moved up the aisle and sat where I could see the choir and its master. They were singing in English, but it was a clipped, careful, slightly accented English.

'It's the Vienna Boys' Choir,' a voice behind me said. 'They got stuck here when the war broke out.'

I'd heard that the choir had been unable to leave, but I'd never given it enough thought to wonder what had become of them. I turned to thank my informant and found myself face to face with Trezise. My immediate fear that he might have recognised me was justified.

'Why have you been following me?' he asked coolly. There was something nasty behind the coolness though, and its expression in this supposedly hallowed place sharpened its edge.

'You must be mistaken,' I said, and turned away from him. A moment later his arm was around my neck, pressing uncomfortably on my windpipe and preventing me from producing a sound more coherent than an indignant gurgle. The Vienna Boys' Choir had stopped singing and was riveted by the spectacle. I resisted the urge to kick and scrabble. It seemed wildly inappropriate to wrestle in a cathedral setting. I'm not a religious man, but I hope I appreciate the difference between a boxing ring and a House of God. Mr Trezise didn't share my sensitivity on this point and tightened his grip.

'You've been following me since Wednesday. I spotted you in the bookshop, right off. If someone's paying you, you're crap. Now, what's it all about?'

He loosened his grip sufficiently to enable me to splutter that perhaps it was time for us to talk like civilised men. He stood up, grabbed a handful of cloth at my shoulder and tugged at it to indicate that I too should rise. The choirmaster issued another order in the Axis tongue, and the boys stiffened and prepared to sing. With his arm firmly through mine Trezise led me into the dark recesses of the cathedral and knocked on a door — one of many situated in different, shadowy corners. It was opened by a priest and we were shown into a small room furnished with a desk, a picture of a martyr being disembowelled, and a rack of vestments. It was stuffy and gloomy and too small for three people.

The priest was tall and had something of Cassius' lean and hungry look, with hollow cheeks, charcoal with freshly and closely shaved stubble. When he spoke his voice retained a slight Irish burr not yet dislodged by rubbing up against his colonial congregation.

'Who have we here, Mr Trezise?'

He smiled with all the beatific warmth of a wolf.

'He's been following me and I want to know why. His Grace warned me that there'd be people who'd want to stop the Movement.'

The look on my face was one of unequivocal puzzlement, and the priest saw that I genuinely had no idea what Trezise was talking about. I didn't have to act at all when I asked, 'Who's His Grace? What Movement? You really have got the wrong man. I haven't a clue what you're on about.'

'His Grace,' said the priest with the patronising patience of a man who believed he was my moral superior, 'is Archbishop Mannix.'

'Oh,' I said. 'I've heard of him. A tall man.'

'He towers above us all in every way,' said Trezise, and there was the tremor of the zealot in his voice.

'The Movement,' said the priest, 'is the Catholic Social Studies Movement. There is nothing sinister about it. We are determined to stop the evil of communism from infecting our society. You're not a communist, are you, Mr ...? I don't know your name.'

The priest's words had had the effect of calming Trezise down, and I, too, felt more at ease. I was in no danger. I wasn't going to end up sprawled on the steps of the altar like Thomas à Becket. I decided that I would adopt the strategy of telling the truth, and present Trezise and his priest with the evidence of Trezise's infidelity. He might then be amenable to backing off, and withdrawing his support for whatever Anna Capshaw had in mind for Clutterbuck.

'My name is William Power.' I was immediately conscious that my tone was too grand for the room, too 'Call me Ishmael' for the circumstances. 'I'm a private inquiry agent and I've been retained by Mr Paul Clutterbuck to protect his interests in relation to his ex-wife, Anna Capshaw. Mr Trezise is currently engaged in an affair with Miss Capshaw and is advising her on the best way to exact revenge on my client who won rather more than she did in the divorce settlement. I think that just about sums it up. This other business — the Movement and Mannix ...'

'His Grace,' Trezise said sharply.

'This other business is of no interest to me. Movements and communists are way outside my brief.'

The priest, who didn't return the courtesy of an introduction, seemed unsurprised by the revelation of Trezise's sex life. He'd heard it all under the seal of the confessional no doubt. The silence was awkward.

'I think we can bring this to a close with all parties walking away satisfied,' I said, feeling confident that I was close to brokering a deal that would impress Clutterbuck.

'Miss Capshaw is understandably bitter, but she has no case against my client. She is motivated purely by the ugly desire for revenge. She is, I assure you Mr Trezise, sleeping with you simply to use your expertise to attack Mr Clutterbuck. She can't afford to hire you so she's paying you not in cash but in kind.'

Trezise remained impassive in the face of this unpleasant aperçu. I began to think that he might be aware of Anna Capshaw's ploy, and be indifferent to it. So long as she slept with him, what did he care what her motives were?

'I'm sure,' I continued, 'that it would do your career and your marriage no good if word got out that your business practices included sexual relations with clients.'

I let that hover between us.

'Of course, no word of this will get out so long as Anna Capshaw stays out of my client's life. I don't care how you manage it, Mr Trezise, but she must be reined in. You may have to withdraw your services along with your cock.'

The obscenity was perfectly pitched, and hit Trezise with the force of a slap. Before he could speak the priest said, 'This is a sacristy, Mr Power, not a bar room.'

I turned to this thin, Irish virgin.

'Trezise brings his grubby adultery into every room he enters. If he was sitting in the Pope's lap Anna Capshaw would be there with him.'

This was too much for Trezise. His face turned the colour of an over-ripe plum.

'Blasphemy!' He stood and raised his hand as if to strike me.

The priest stepped between us.

'That's enough!'

The crack of his voice acted upon us with the power of an exorcist's command.

'All I'm saying,' I said quietly, 'is that there's no reason why your wife need ever be told about your indiscretion.'

Trezise laughed.

'You're welcome to tell my wife whatever you like. You'll need a Ouija board and a medium. She's been dead for four years.'

A cathedral ought to be the ideal place in which to undergo a crisis, and here I was with a priest to hand and the resources of this outpost of the Vatican at my disposal, but I felt completely disarmed, and regretted mightily that I had told Trezise much more than he needed to know.

'My relationship with Anna Capshaw is my business. I've never heard of this Clutterbuck person. I certainly had no idea that she'd ever been married at all, let alone to someone with such a ridiculous name.'

Trezise seemed to have had no reason to lie at this point, so to say that I felt bamboozled is to grossly understate the case.

'You *are* a lawyer,' I said.

'I'm an engineer. So if Anna is offering sex in return for advice I could maybe help her build a bridge or pass on the secret of load-bearing walls.'

'Let's not descend into sarcasm,' said the priest. 'Mr Power's misinformation is positively Masonic in its scope, but the fact that he's been hired at all is the really unpleasant part of all this.'

There was a certain smugness in the priest's tone that raised my hackles. My most urgent need was to get out of this stuffy sacristy. I'd take the information to Clutterbuck, and get some sort of explanation from him as to what exactly was going on. I decided to be brazen.

'Why should I believe a word you say? My job is to protect the interests of my client, and his interests are being threatened by his ex-wife. It defies belief that this person with whom you are intimate would neglect to mention her recent, ugly, and impoverishing divorce.'

'Let me spell this out for you,' Trezise said, and sighed with ostentatious patience. 'Miss Capshaw and I have been intimate once, and that was the night you followed us. I met her for the first time at a meeting of the Movement a few weeks ago. She approached me and, you may have noticed — although perhaps you didn't — she's a very attractive woman. She told me that she'd been recently widowed, and naturally I told her the same. We met once or twice after that, for a meal, and we got along very well. She was keen to get involved with the Movement. Both of us knew that our meeting at the hotel was sinful, but we're weak vessels, and although it's no excuse, there is a war on and so we went ahead and spent the night together. I'm sure that Anna has made a good confession, as I've done, and we've agreed to wait now until we're married before we have sexual relations again.'

'So it must surprise and disappoint you to learn that she lied to you, and that she's divorced, not widowed.'

I felt as if I was regaining some ground, and with the memory of Trezise's arm crushing my larynx, I didn't spare him.

'As far as I know Mr Trezise, Anna Capshaw isn't even a Catholic. That, too, must come as something of a surprise.'

Trezise plunged his hands into his pockets and said, 'Frankly, Mr Power, where women are concerned, I'm not surprised by anything.'

The priest gave a little nod of approval, indicating, by this slight gesture, that vulnerable men would always be subject to the predations of rapacious women.

Neither the priest nor Trezise had any intention of preventing me from leaving, so I assured Trezise that I would no longer be tailing him, and slipped into the cathedral proper. The angelic, displaced *Hitlerjugend* were still warbling a hymn of praise. I could hear it faintly even after I'd passed through the front door.

I saw James Fowler immediately. He was on the opposite side of the street; standing, watching. I didn't react and he must have believed that he hadn't been spotted because he moved off quickly, but in a studied way, as if he didn't want to draw attention to himself. I hurried after him, and by the time I'd reached the spot where he'd been standing he'd disappeared. I couldn't join the dots here. Why was Fowler following me? His interest, from whatever motive, was in Clutterbuck. The resolution of this puzzle would have to wait.

I thought Clutterbuck would be relieved to hear that Trezise was an engineer and that Anna Capshaw wasn't attempting to interfere with his engagement to Nigella. Where had Clutterbuck acquired the notion that Trezise was a lawyer? I needed to sit down and marshal the facts of these matters on paper. Maybe then I'd see connections that weren't yet apparent to me.

On the whole the encounter with Trezise had turned out better than it might have. I thought that Clutterbuck could rest easy, and that the outcome reflected well upon me. I'd been unprepared for what Trezise had told me, it's true, and I'd shown my hand too early — a lesson from which I would learn — but on the whole a difficult matter had been brought to a satisfactory close. As I walked from the cathedral I began to think about Gretel Beech. She'd been buried for just over twenty-four hours. It was urgent that I find her killer and allow her the dignity of a decent funeral. The need to find Darlene vaguely asserted itself, too, although I'd be a hypocrite if I declared that it compelled me in quite the same way as poor Gretel's murder.

I walked slowly down Collins Street. The pavement was thick with drones making their way grimly to their soul-destroying, pointless jobs. I was filled with a longing to speak Shakespeare's verse, to be elevated by the majesty of his poetry. I wanted to spread my arms, or my good arm at any rate, and declaim something grand to these drab subjects of a stuttering king. I missed the stage. My skills as a PI were growing, but how marvellous it would be, I thought, if I could combine the ecstatic joy of acting with the satisfying grind of detection.

It was the grind that concerned me now. George Beech and James Fowler. I turned these names over in my mind and may even have spoken them out loud. Pursuing Fowler was the option I favoured. I'm not ashamed to acknowledge that Beech's propensity for thuggery over conversation was at least partly responsible for my decision to go after Fowler. Besides, I had no straightforward way of locating Beech, and I wasn't in the physical condition to match him if I did find his lair. I knew James Fowler was close by, having seen him, and I wasn't afraid of him, although if he had killed Gretel Beech I might have good reason to be. Still, the educated killer was a more attractive option than the drunken, murderous brute.

I lingered outside the Melbourne Club on the off chance that Mr Fowler Snr. might emerge. I would ask him for his son's business address if he did do. The offices of Native Policy for Mandated Territories would surely be in the city — if such a bizarre occupation warranted an office. It sounded more like the kind of job done out of a tent. No one went in and no one came out of the Melbourne Club. I toyed with the idea of knocking on the door and asking to see Mr Fowler but, unshaven and gravel-rashed, I didn't think I'd get a positive reception.

The decision about what to do next was taken out of my hands by James Fowler, who tapped me on the shoulder and asked, 'How was confession?'

'I wasn't at confession. Not that it's any of your business, I'm not a Catholic. You've been following me.' I thought it best to avoid obfuscation.

'Well, Will, I was always told at school that I was more likely to follow than lead, so I guess old Mr Pyers was quite a perceptive fellow after all.'

'So you don't deny it.'

'No.'

He stood grinning, as if he was acknowledging nothing more controversial than that it was an overcast day.

'Why? Why would you want to follow me?'

'I have your best interests at heart, believe me.'

I scoffed theatrically.

'You're being drawn into things,' he said, 'that are unpleasant and dangerous. If I were you I'd move back to your mother's house and leave Clutterbuck to his own devices.'

There was a lot to digest in this brief riposte. How did Fowler know about my mother? What 'things' were dangerous?

'You know a lot about me for a person who met me only yesterday.'

'Thank you,' he said. 'I'll take that as a compliment.'

'You're barking up the wrong tree if you think you'll scuttle Clutterbuck's marriage plans by tailing me. Is that what it's all about?'

'No, Will, that's not what it's *all* about, although I'll be frank and admit that Nigella could do better. Don't you think so?'

James Fowler couldn't have detected my inclinations towards his sister. I wasn't fully aware of them myself during yesterday's afternoon tea. I felt, though, that he was offering a kind of mild imprimatur to me as a suitor, and my feelings towards him shifted accordingly. It was with a jolt that I remembered that he may well have ransacked Clutterbuck's room, and worse, that he may have murdered Gretel Beech.

'I've only known Paul Clutterbuck for a few days,' I said. 'Your sister's attraction to him is understandable, but ...'

'But his to her is less comprehensible? I quite agree, Will. I think you and I both know that Paul Clutterbuck is not a respectable man, and that he thinks he can marry and change that.'

Our conversation was interrupted when a car pulled up at the kerb and a man got out and hurried over to where we were standing. He drew James Fowler away, and the two of them spoke briefly. Fowler came back to me and said that he'd been called to his office. He didn't elaborate, but I found it hard to believe that there'd been a sudden crisis in the area of native policy. Before getting into the car he asked if I'd have dinner with him that night, at the Menzies Hotel. He'd pay, he said, and he'd explain to me then why he'd been following me, and a few other things besides. I agreed, believing that I would learn much that was useful about James Fowler and his family.

I was now at something of a loose end, and I needed time to think. As I passed the Australia Cinema the poster for *Romeo and Juliet* caught my eye. I couldn't quite see Leslie Howard as Romeo, and the idea of Norma Shearer as Juliet was grotesque. Nevertheless, it might fulfil my craving for a bit of the bard, so I bought a ticket and went in just as the morning session was beginning. 'Advance Australia Fair' (which had recently supplanted 'God Save the King) was played and people dutifully stood. It was followed by 'The Star Spangled Banner' and several patrons sat down before it had concluded. After this, an amateurish bit of propaganda thundered at us from the screen. I hoped this wasn't one of Nigella's efforts. Fields of rippling wheat and pastures of grazing sheep flickered behind an insistent, almost hysterical voice, decrying: *Australia. To the Japanese Australia has always meant room to live in. It has long been eyed with malicious envy by Japanese jingoists. In Australia just beyond their reach are many of the strategic minerals of warfare — wealth that would make Japan one of the world's most powerful nations. They believe that once they have Australia and its seven million people to work for them as slaves, their position will be impregnable.*

Here images of serried ranks of Japanese soldiers marching before Hirohito, seated grandly on a horse, reinforced the fact that we were in terrible peril of being over-run. No one in the theatre uttered a sound during the short. The idea of enslavement made whistles and cat calls die in the throats of the usual wags who might have been tempted to make them.

Romeo and Juliet surprised me. I'd expected it to be laughable. Instead it was lavish and not at all silly. Someone had coached Norma Shearer well enough to enable her to speak the verse adequately. Leslie Howard I never could abide, and it was a bit of a stretch to imagine two middle-aged people as teenagers, but I've always been willing to suspend disbelief when occasion demanded.

Looking back on it, I calculated that it was while I was watching Romeo and Juliet that Anna Capshaw was murdered.

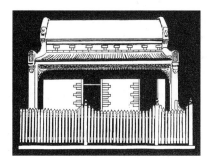

Chapter Eight

SHINING KNIGHTS

I EMERGED FROM THE AUSTRALIA CINEMA into the lunchtime crowd. There was no point remaining in town, so I braved a tram and headed back to Carlton. I arrived at Clutterbuck's house just as he was letting himself in. He was wearing his American army uniform again. I felt sure that there was more to this deception than the acquisition of sex and pantry items.

'Were we running low on cream?' I asked.

He made a small noise of assent and said, 'I wasn't expecting you.' His words were slightly slurred, as if he'd been drinking. 'Still, I'm glad you're here.'

Once inside, Clutterbuck went upstairs to change and told me to help myself to a whisky. I don't usually drink at lunchtime, but Clutterbuck's whisky was first rate and a single malt at any time of the day isn't to be declined.

When he came downstairs he was wearing a thick woollen shirt and baggy, casual trousers. I'd never seen him so dressed down.

'There are some people I want you to meet,' he said, and brooking no opposition propelled me to his car. 'We won't be long and you can tell me how you've been earning your money on the way.'

'Where are we going?'

'Never mind. You'll see. Now, tell.'

The car headed up Sydney Road and Clutterbuck wasn't driving as carefully as he might have. He impatiently blew his horn at a horse and cart, spooking the horse and infuriating the cart's driver.

'I've met with Trezise,' I said.

I thought he might react badly to this, but his response was muted.

'Oh, yes?'

'You have nothing to worry about there. He's not a lawyer, and he thought Anna was a widow. He didn't know you existed.'

'But he does now.'

'Well, yes, but it's not information he can do anything with, and besides, he's not interested in you or your engagement at all. You got the wrong end of the stick with Trezise. He's just a sad, lonely bloke who's eaten up by guilt because he was intimate with someone outside the sacred bonds of marriage. You don't have to worry about him at all.'

Clutterbuck leaned towards his open window and yelled an obscenity at another horse-drawn cart, this one with the name of a grocer printed on its side.

'You should be interned, you Italian bastard!'

I'd never seen Clutterbuck like this.

'You seem a bit rattled. Trezise isn't a problem, believe me.'

'I'm not worried about Trezise. Not at all.'

Having said this he assumed his usual demeanour and even managed a small smile. We drove deep into Brunswick, an area of Melbourne with which I was unfamiliar. We turned right into Albion Street and a few streets along, left. Here there were rows of workers' cottages which might have been pretty in their day but which were now showing the neglect that poverty and indifference promoted. I could see why Clutterbuck had changed his clothes. I felt grimy just looking at these houses. He parked the car — it was the only car in the street — and knocked on the door of a residence with a small, riotously overgrown patch of garden. This was no Victory Garden bursting with healthful vegetables. It was a tangle of thistles, milkweed and dandelions. There could have been splendid rows of produce in the backyard, but I doubted it.

'Who is it?'

The voice, though muffled by the door, was suspicious and uninviting.

'Paul.'

The door opened to reveal a short, misshapen man. The air that escaped was stale and smelled of dripping and unwashed bodies. We walked down a corridor to a small, dark living room. There was only one bedroom, as far as I could tell, and in this living room the tumble of malodorous bedclothes in the corner suggested that it doubled as a second bedroom.

'This is Mr William Power,' Clutterbuck said. 'And Will, this is Mr Ronnie Oakpate.'

I looked at this strange creature closely. He walked with a pronounced limp and his shoulders were so rounded that I suspected an incipient hump beneath his filthy shirt. He was bald with dark hair growing in a half circle above his ears. It didn't end at the nape of his neck but grew abundantly down beyond his collar and crept round his throat to meet a black puff of it emerging from his shirt. His appearance was so simian that it would shake the faith of the most committed opponents of Darwinism. I couldn't tell his age, unused as I was to estimating the lifespan of gorillas. When he spoke he showed a mouthful of yellow teeth and emitted a powerful and penetrating exhalation of halitotic breath.

'What's he want?' he asked.

'It's not what he wants, Ronnie, it's what we want that counts, and Will here can help us.'

'He doesn't look too flash,' said the hunched and hirsute Mr Oakpate. Given that he looked more like he'd climbed down from a tree than a pedestal, this was rather a nerve.

'I fell over,' I said, my indignation obscuring my curiosity about our reason for being there.

A noise from the next room, a kitchen I surmised from the intensity of the odour of things greasy wafting through the door, indicated the presence of another person.

'Mary Rose!' Clutterbuck called. 'Come here and meet Mr Power.'

A woman in her mid-twenties came into the living room. She was dressed severely, almost institutionally, and her lank hair, the colour of fouled straw, had the appearance of having been styled by a blind man in a deep cellar. With the greatest will in the world I could not describe her as pretty and her plainness was exacerbated by a slackness of muscle that caused her to look simple.

'This is Mary Rose Shingle,' Clutterbuck said, 'and ironically, considering her name, she is, I'm afraid, a shingle short.'

Miss Shingle didn't react to this callous assessment of her mental capacity, thereby, I suppose, confirming his diagnosis.

She may have smiled, but it may have been nothing more than a spasm pulling her mouth upward.

'Where's his nibs?' asked Ronnie, and he leaned his hunched body against the doorframe. Before Clutterbuck could answer, there was a knock at the front door and Oakpate detached himself from his support and scuttled down the corridor with the awkward dexterity of a mandrill. He returned with a man whose remarkably small head sat atop a broad, thick torso. The initial impression was that he was fat; he would certainly have been expensive to feed. There was nothing flabby about him however. His first words were, 'Who's this?' and he pointed at me with a stubby, dirty thumb.

'This is Will,' Clutterbuck said. 'He's useful. And Will, this man-mountain is Crocker.'

Handshakes were clearly not among Mr Crocker's repertoire of social niceties so he merely grunted. I returned the compliment.

The room was now crowded. Clutterbuck sat in a filthy armchair, its antimacassar stained beyond hope of cleaning. He didn't lean back. Crocker folded his bulk on to a lounge that had long ago ceased to invite lounging, and Oakpate prodded me into sitting beside him — Crocker that is. Oakpate remained standing. He shooed Miss Shingle into the kitchen and resumed his position leaning in the doorway. This was strange company for Clutterbuck to keep, and it was stranger still that he should bring me here. I presumed his purpose was about to be revealed though it wasn't Clutterbuck who spoke first. It was Oakpate.

'I sacked the last of those bastards today,' he said.

'Good,' said Crocker. 'They're like a fucking cancer.'

'Will might be wondering whom you're talking about,' said Clutterbuck. 'I haven't filled him in properly yet about our organisation.'

At this point I began to feel uneasy. It was the word

'organisation'. I remembered Clutterbuck's dismissive reference to 'Jews and communists'. Was this dingy, little house in Brunswick a fascist cell, a bolt-hole for fifth columnists?

'Well, what's he doing here then?' asked Crocker, and turned his blunt, thuggish gaze upon me.

'He's on our side, aren't you, Will?' Clutterbuck smiled encouragingly at me. Out of the corner of my eye I saw Oakpate put his hand down the front of his trousers and scratch at his crotch.

'Which side are we talking about?' I asked.

'The right side,' said Oakpate, and came into the centre of the room. He stood close to Clutterbuck and his malignant, ugly face became suffused with blood pumped in anger from that organ which in anybody else would have been identified as the heart.

'Why'd you bring a stranger here?' he hissed.

'Will's not a stranger,' Clutterbuck said calmly. 'He's a private detective.'

Both Oakpate and Crocker snapped their heads in my direction and Crocker's fists clenched.

'He's employed by me, and he's good, but even he would be having trouble putting all this together, and neither of you is creating a very nice first impression. What must Will be thinking?' He paused as if he thought I might reveal the answer to his question. Frankly, I was all at sea, horrified and paralysed by the thought that Clutterbuck was an Axis sympathiser, and that I'd been caught in his orbit.

'I can tell from the look on your face, Will, that you've jumped to the wrong conclusion. You think we're the enemy within, don't you. Nothing could be further from the truth. Mr Oakpate and Mr Crocker are captains of industry. They may look like stokers, but they're captains. Mr Oakpate here owns this lovely house, which he shares with the delicious Miss Shingle.'

This ludicrous assessment of his common-law wife made Oakpate smile.

'Mr Oakpate also owns and runs a factory here in Brunswick. I've never been sure what he manufactures but I'm sure it's something terribly dull and metallic. Mr Crocker is the proprietor of a dark, satanic mill as well, and like every other factory owner in this city they're sick to death of unions and of strikes.'

'It's the bloody Catholics in the bloody unions,' said Crocker. 'They're everywhere — and it's up to us to stop them.'

I found my voice.

'Stop them?'

'That's right,' said Oakpate. 'Stop them.' These last words were loaded with menace, as if stopping them meant much more than sacking a few troublesome workers.

'So now we've all met,' said Clutterbuck. 'This isn't going to be a full meeting. I just wanted to bring Will here so that we could get acquainted.'

Crocker was about to say something but Clutterbuck silenced him with a hand motion. There was no further discussion. We said our farewells and returned to the car.

On the way home I didn't feel much wiser about what had just taken place.

'You said something about an organisation back there.'

'Ah, yes. The clubhouse isn't very salubrious I grant you, but we're doing good work, Will.'

'Who's "we" and what's the work?'

Clutterbuck didn't miss the note of annoyance in my voice and he replied in a tone that was carefully modulated to appease me.

'We are a group of like-minded people who believe that the Catholic Church is determined to undermine the war effort by infiltrating the union movement, and our "work" is to stop that from happening.'

It took a moment for this extraordinary declaration to sink in. 'You can't be serious,' I said.

'Like most people, Will, you don't know how influential and destructive a man like Mannix is.'

'Are you a communist?'

'Now it's you who can't be serious. Do I look like a communist? No. Do I live like a communist? I hate communists, Will. The papists and I agree on that, but the Catholics are worse than the communists and they're infiltrating every level of government.'

He must have realised that his voice was betraying him in some way because he took his eyes off the road and looked at me.

'I'm not a fanatic, Will. If you knew the stuff I know, you'd want to be a part of it. It's just politics.'

'Politics can hurt people.'

'That's why it's important that only the right people get hurt.'

This chilling little policy statement transformed Paul Clutterbuck on the spot from harmless dilettante to frightening fanatic, despite his protestations to the contrary.

'I'm not really interested in politics,' I said.

'Interested or not, Will, you're involved. You've been to Oakpate's house, you've met Crocker. You're one of the few people I've introduced to the members of the Order.'

'What are you talking about, Paul? What Order?'

'The Order of the Shining Knights.'

'Is that like the Round Table? Are you serious?'

Clutterbuck wasn't amused.

'It's not some schoolboy secret society, Will. We've been active since 1932 when my father and a few of his friends set it up. It's a serious business, well-funded and well-connected.'

'The headquarters don't inspire confidence.'

'Oakpate's house isn't where we usually meet. I'd like you to join us, Will. We need people like you.'

'I'm not a joiner, Paul.'

'Well, now that you know how important our task is at least you won't be surprised by some of the surveillance work I might get you to do.'

I didn't reply to this, having already determined that I would be doing no further work for Paul Clutterbuck. I knew, though, that it wouldn't do to dismiss the Shining Knights as a benign, amusing hobby group. It was well to remember that no one thought the goosestep was funny any more.

Very little was said for the remainder of the short drive back to Clutterbuck's house. It wasn't until we were walking up the stairs to our bedrooms that Clutterbuck said, 'There are some things that I *will* want you to do, and I think we understand each other well enough now to know that you *will* do them. They're just small things; nothing nasty, I promise.'

He put his hand on my shoulder and gave it a little pat.

'This is Melbourne, Will, not Berlin. I wouldn't want you to break any laws — although I suppose burying poor Gretel was a bit unlawful, wasn't it?'

I knew I'd been out-manoeuvred. What I needed to do now was lie down and formulate a strategy for disentangling myself from the sticky web Clutterbuck was beginning to weave.

'Of course I'll give consideration to any job you offer me,' I said, trying to create the impression that nothing had changed between us. I was relieved when I closed the bedroom door and stretched out on my perfectly made bed.

I hadn't thought I was tired, but watching Norma Shearer wrestle with Shakespeare, and being exposed to the Misters Oakpate and Crocker, to say nothing of the faintly repellent Miss Shingle, had taken enough out of me to ensure that I fell asleep almost as soon as my head hit the pillow. I woke with a start to the slam of the front door downstairs. It was 6.30 p.m. The afternoon had vanished in dreamless sleep. I was to meet James Fowler at 7.30 in the dining room of the Menzies Hotel, where the austerity menu would, I presumed, be unimaginatively if competently prepared. I washed my face and changed my shirt. Shaving was still not possible without aggravating the damaged skin on half my face. I combed my hair and was pleased to note that the darkness of my stubble made me resemble Tyrone Power even more closely than when I was freshly shaved.

By the time I had completed my ablutions it was seven o'clock. I was obliged to take a tram. If I took shanks's pony I would have to half-walk, half-run to make it on time, and I didn't want to arrive drenched in perspiration.

James Fowler was already seated when I got there. He was expensively dressed — much more elegantly than I was — and his hair was oiled and glistening. He looked like he was on a date. I was immediately disconcerted.

The dining room was full. Crisp American officer uniforms were everywhere, and the women were wearing their best evening clothes. The noise was considerable as was the tobacco smoke.

Fowler rose to meet me and shook my hand in a gentlemanly fashion. His hand was soft, but strong, and it made me a little queasy to think that it might recently have been around Gretel's throat, strangling the life out of her.

'I'm glad you came, Will. There's a great deal we need to discuss.'

'Indeed.' I managed to inject both rigid formality and quizzical scepticism into that single word.

'So, Will, you missed the Grand Final by just a few days. Pity. Your mother's house being just across from Princes Park and all.'

'I'm not really interested in football. I'm not sure who played, let alone who won.'

Fowler shook his head in mock disapproval.

'Essendon won, Will. Richmond lost.'

'If you invited me here to discuss football it's going to be a short evening.'

'All right. Let's order and we'll take it from there.'

The menu was limited and I didn't have high hopes for what would come out of the kitchen, despite its pretensions to being both French and *haute*. There were no hors d'oeuvres, of course, in line with the regulations. If I chose carefully I could extract three courses and come in under the mandated five shillings. I chose half a dozen oysters on the shell at two shillings, and sweetbreads Toulouse at two shillings and sixpence. With sixpence to spare I added a Baroness pudding. If Fowler was paying I might as well go the distance. Fowler declared an allergy to oysters and ordered consommé Celestine at sixpence, Tournados béarnaise at four shillings, and apple pie Chantilly at sixpence. When the waiter had retreated Fowler dropped his bombshell.

'You were following a man named John Trezise this morning?'

'I didn't know his first name was John, but yes.'

'He was arrested late this afternoon. It seems like a pretty open-and-shut case. He strangled a woman named Anna Capshaw — here in fact. Upstairs.'

My mind raced to accommodate the fact that James Fowler should be in possession of this knowledge so soon after the event, let alone that he would know the names of both the victim and the perpetrator. Unless, of course, he was involved in the crime in ways which were not yet apparent.

'How do you know this?'

'The police told me.'

'And why would the police run to you with details of a murder? I don't think Trezise or Anna Capshaw were natives in need of your expertise.'

If I sounded brittle, and I'm sure I did, it was because the news of this murder had temporarily disabled my ability to think calmly and logically.

'I'm glad that you at least acknowledge that you know both parties,' Fowler said.

'I've never met Anna Capshaw. I only know her as Clutterbuck's ex-wife and Trezise's mistress.'

'So that's the line Clutterbuck's been running is it? That Anna Capshaw is his ex-wife? He's never been married, Will.'

After my experiences in Queensland I was familiar with this feeling of certainties dropping away, and I didn't like it one little bit.

'You seem to know an awful lot about Clutterbuck. Been looking in his sock drawer have you?'

'Ah, you saw that. That was careless of me.'

'Ransacking his room is a little more than careless. I'd call it wilful.'

He narrowed his eyes.

'I didn't ransack his room. I left no trace.'

'Well, someone did a thorough job of turning his room upside down.'

'Perhaps I'm not the only person interested in Paul Clutterbuck's private life.'

The oysters arrived and I was disappointed to find that they'd been drained of the fluid in which they sat. Fowler declared his consommé to be well flavoured and properly clarified. Between spoonfuls he said, 'I should introduce myself fully. You know the basics already. What you don't know is who I work for — who I really work for.'

I was swallowing the last of the oysters when he said, 'Army Intelligence.'

I thought it best to offer no more than a careful, 'I see.'

'We're interested in Paul Clutterbuck because we believe he's a dangerous person. The fact that he intends to marry my sister complicates matters somewhat, but Nigella's not the sort of person who'll be told who she can and can't marry.'

'Clutterbuck's politics aren't nice, as I've just discovered, but dangerous?'

'You've been acquainted with Clutterbuck for only a few days. We were curious to see whom he would choose to rent his room to.'

'You've been watching him?'

'On and off. He'd rejected half-a-dozen people before you. He obviously saw something in you that he could use.'

'I hope you're not accusing me of being naïve.'

'I try not to make rash judgements about anybody, and my opinion of Clutterbuck hasn't been formed in a hurry. We haven't caught him doing anything too illegal. I don't count his dressing up as an American soldier. We think, however, that something is brewing with him. He belongs to a group that is for all intents and purposes a fascist organisation.'

'The Order of the Shining Knights.'

'Precisely.'

'I met them this afternoon.'

'I know. You were tailed. Let me tell you about them. Have you heard of the White Army?'

I shook my head.

'It was around in the early thirties under a variety of names — the White Army; the New Guard; the League of National Security. They thought Australia needed a sort of secret army to counter insurgents like Catholics and communists. The people in these groups were a mixed bunch: farmers, public servants, just ordinary people. Some of them were sympathetic to European fascism, but most of them were responding to old prejudices and fears. It all came to nothing, of course — sabre rattling more than anything else. However, as always in these situations, a few extremists refused to let go of their paranoia and formed their own little breakaway groups.

'Paul Clutterbuck's father was one of these, and he formed a nasty group called the Order of the Shining Knights. This was way back in 1932. Don't be deceived by the silly name. They were suspected of setting fires in several churches, and of being responsible for a few assaults. Clutterbuck's father died in 1934. A stroke. Nothing suspicious, but his son inherited his hatred of Catholics, and has maintained links with the Order. We don't know much about the people in the group these days, and we haven't had the resources to watch them closely. They're too small and they've been quiet for a long time. We suspected that they just got together to whinge about popery. Naturally, my interest now is both personal and professional. I have a hunch, based purely on Clutterbuck's acceptance of you as a tenant, that they're planning something. He was so obviously waiting for the right person that there must be some significance in his choice.

'Why you? You've been thoroughly checked out by us, of course. I know all about the mess you were involved in up in Queensland, and I know you left there in unhappy circumstances. I also know that you have no affiliations with any political groups. As far as I can tell from the people I've spoken to, despite giving you poor references, I have to say, no one has accused you of anything resembling fascist leanings. Your opinion of yourself might be over-inflated, but your poor opinion of others isn't based on race, colour or creed.'

'Should I take that as a compliment?'

The main courses arrived and I found myself unable to give the sweetbreads the attention they deserved — they were excellent — because Fowler's story was unsettling.

'I admit that my superiors don't share my concerns about the Order of the Shining Knights, and they're reluctant to use man hours to investigate them. It's become more or less my little project, and that's where you come in Will.'

'Wait. Wait a minute. Can we just go back to Anna Capshaw? What's her death got to do with this?'

'Nothing as far as I know. She met Trezise in a room upstairs; they argued, and he killed her. He denies it, of course, but he was the one who alerted the police — said she was dead when he arrived. Looks like a classic *crime passionnel*.'

'But why would the police tell *you* about it?'

'Because of the connection with Clutterbuck. Anna Capshaw was being used by him to trap Trezise into compromising himself. I'm not sure why yet, but clearly it's got something to do with Trezise's position in the Church. Her death will be a blow to Clutterbuck. He won't be happy.'

'Clutterbuck thought Trezise was a lawyer trying to shake him down with the help of his ex-wife.'

'No. There was no ex-wife, remember?'

I couldn't escape a horrible feeling that I'd somehow been responsible for Anna Capshaw's death. I'd given Trezise information that might have inflamed him against Anna. I kept this concern to myself.

'I need someone who has access to the Order of the Shining Knights. It's clear that either Clutterbuck trusts you, which is unlikely, or that he's using you, in which case he might try to find a way of securing your loyalty, so watch out. Either way, you need to work for us. Unpaid, of course. I hate to sound like one of Nigella's propaganda shorts, but it's patriotic work, Will.

You'll be contributing to the war effort in a significant way. Paul Clutterbuck may not be a fifth columnist, but he's a loose cannon and he needs tying down.'

I didn't feel any loyalty to Clutterbuck. My meeting with his unholy trinity of friends had opened my eyes to his dark side, and I realised now that I'd given in too quickly when it had come to the cover up of Gretel's death and the disposal of her body. On the other hand, I knew nothing about James Fowler beyond what he was telling me. How did I even know that he was who he said he was? He acknowledged this point, when I made it, and said that after the meal he'd take me to his office in the Victoria Barracks in St Kilda Road.

'It's not much more than a broom closet,' he said. 'Our unit is understaffed.'

I agreed, in principle, that working for Army Intelligence, unpaid though it was, was an interesting proposition. It made sense to me. James didn't know about Gretel Beech. He'd have said something if he did, and if he knew about my sister-in-law's kidnapping he would have said something about that, too.

It was during dessert that the evening's real bombshell exploded. We were talking generally about how I might be useful when a woman's voice broke free from the surrounding chatter and struck my ears. Recognising it, I turned in disbelief to see Darlene seated a few tables away, her face in profile, her hand resting on the hand of an American officer. He said something to her and she laughed before leaning across the table and kissing him lightly on the lips.

'Is something wrong, Will?' Fowler asked.

Ignoring him, I stood up and walked across to Darlene. When she saw me her face acquired a glaze of determined self-righteousness.

'Will.'

'What the hell is all this?'

The American got to his feet.

'Don't talk to my fiancée like that, buddy.'

My incredulity barely had time to express itself before the American grabbed the front of my shirt and breathed consommé Celestine into my face.

'No one talks to my fiancée like that.'

By now, the whole room was watching. The inevitability of my being hit was so strong that when the blow came I simply surrendered to it. The next thing I remembered was lying on the floor of the Menzies Hotel dining room, my head under the overhanging cloth, close to Darlene's thick ankles. I thought that if I just lay there quietly all would resolve itself into the dream it must surely be, until the point of Darlene's shoe was jabbed meanly into my neck and there was no doubt that I was wide awake.

PART TWO

Chapter Nine

ARMY INTELLIGENCE

MY LOATHING FOR DARLENE was not diminished by the shaming act of her American paramour dragging me from beneath their table in the elegant dining room of the Menzies Hotel. The blame for this hideous humiliation could be laid squarely at her fluid-swollen feet. I was dazed and confused as my throbbing head was pulled into the light. Thankfully, James Fowler appeared out of nowhere and took charge of the situation. He helped me to my feet and assured the American stranger that there would be no further trouble. I was momentarily deprived of the faculty of speech and, with my head still spinning, Fowler directed me firmly towards the exit.

The blow to my head must have been a solid one because the faces and sounds in Collins Street merged into a kaleidoscopic display of colour and noise. As we crossed Princes Bridge I was peripherally aware of people milling about Wirth's Circus tent, and suddenly we were at Victoria Barracks. The monumental bluestone façade of the Barracks loomed in the brownout, like a neat, sharply defined cut-out in the very fabric of space. We entered through an impressive door, after passing muster at the main gate. Fowler apologised again for the unimpressive space he'd been allocated — it was no more than a partitioned corner of a much larger room. He had a desk, a phone, a wooden filing cabinet and a shelf that was held up more by faith than nails.

'Welcome,' he said, 'to Army Intelligence.'

'We're going to lose the war,' I said.

'This is just my section, Will. The big boys have, oh, twice as much space as this.'

He ducked outside and returned with a chair into which I gratefully collapsed.

'Dinner *and* a show,' he said. 'You provide real value for money.'

Given my surroundings, and the fact that the soldier at the gate had let us pass without demur, I had to believe that Fowler was indeed working for Army Intelligence, and that he was now an unlikely suspect in Gretel Beech's murder. I was simultaneously disappointed and relieved — a comfortable paradox I put down to a slight concussion.

'You might want an explanation for that debacle,' I said. 'I'm sorry if you were embarrassed.'

'Embarrassed? Certainly not. Entertained? Definitely.'

I told him as much as I knew about Darlene's scripted kidnapping, and didn't spare him my feelings about my gravid sister-in-law. I also told him about Brian's affair in Maryborough, and the attack upon him on the train.

'Your brother seems to be attracted to unusual women.'

'I'd never have picked Darlene as unusual. Unusual implies

interesting and believe me, the words *interesting* and *Darlene* have never appeared anywhere in the same sentence.'

'Until now,' he laughed.

'For diagnostic purposes only.'

We weren't alone, despite the late hour. There were several people working on the other side of Fowler's partition and the clatter of typewriters and the ringing of phones made a reassuring impression that the war was being fought around the clock. As my head cleared I became confident that James Fowler would be a useful ally, and when he asked me how I'd broken my arm I took the opportunity to give him my version of events in Maryborough. He listened attentively, and nodded sympathetically from time to time. When I'd finished, he said, 'I admire your willingness to admit that you were a bit of a nong.'

I wasn't aware that I'd been doing any such thing, but he spoke without malice so I let it pass.

'When does the cast come off?'

'Monday morning. I can't begin to tell you how much I'm looking forward to that.'

Over the next two hours James Fowler outlined how he wanted to proceed. I came close to revealing that I'd foolishly helped dispose of Gretel Beech's murdered body but couldn't bring myself to do it. I wasn't ready to upset his confidence in me. Besides, I could fix that mess myself. Most pressingly, I had to get home and tell Brian and Mother what I'd seen. James apologised for not being able to provide a driver to get me there quickly. 'I'm low down in the pecking order.'

We arranged to meet the following day in the crypt of the Shrine of Remembrance. I thought this a strange location, but James said it was conveniently close to the Barracks and that he needed to be at his desk for most of the day. We made a time — two o'clock — and he escorted me onto St Kilda Road.

'Stick to this side,' he said. 'The other side is the busiest queer beat in Melbourne. They call it 'the chicken run'. We keep an eye on it but there's never any trouble. Half the Yank army comes here, literally, and many housewives in Camberwell would be very surprised to know what hubby gets up to after dark.' He laughed. 'There's this big dance hall down towards the circus, the Old Green Mill, and on Saturday nights it's packed with Yanks. If they don't get lucky with a woman they'll cross the road, pop into the park with some bloke, and then head back to the dance.'

Fowler's tone was so uncritical of this behaviour that I suspected he thought he was doing me a favour by providing me with information I might find useful. I tried not to be offended. Perhaps he was simply revealing something about himself.

It was quite late so I took the expensive step of catching a taxi to Mother's place. Even so, it was close to midnight when I knocked on the door. To my surprise it was opened almost immediately by Brian.

'We've been waiting for you. We know what happened at the Menzies. She rang.'

Mother sat in her usual place in the living room. She was bearing up, rather self-consciously I thought, under the strain of what must have been a startling piece of news.

'I suppose I should say, "Well done."'

Brian interjected. 'I'm afraid I told Mother about your new job. I didn't think you'd mind, having had this success so quickly.'

I was on the point of revealing that my finding Darlene had been an accident when it struck me that this was a small, irrelevant detail. I'd found Darlene, and if Mother and Brian chose to see this as proof of my investigative skills, so much the better. I hadn't forgotten Brian's crack about finding my arse.

'What did she say?' I asked. My tone was businesslike,

prurience being anathema to a good PI.

'Just that you'd found her and that there'd been an altercation.'

I made a derisive little chortle.

'And did she say who that Yank was?'

'They're coming here tomorrow,' Brian said. 'Both of them.'

'I almost can't believe I'm saying this, Will,' said Mother, 'but it seems you were right to dislike Darlene.'

'She's asked for a divorce.'

'But she's pregnant.'

There was a ghastly pause.

'Yes, well,' said Brian. 'Although she was only on the phone for a couple of minutes she managed to tell me that it's not my child. It's the other bloke's.'

Mother stood up.

'She'd been having an affair with him for months. Right under our noses. Neither Brian nor I noticed. It's inexplicable. Inexplicable.'

I wondered if it was really so very inexplicable, and whether Brian's affair with Sarah Goodenough wasn't in some way a response to his suspicion, or knowledge, about Darlene's infidelity. I'd press him on this point when Mother had retired.

'How she must have hated us,' Mother said, 'to smile and lie so easily.'

Mother looked suddenly old; exhausted perhaps by the realisation that even someone as dull as Darlene couldn't be relied upon to stay true to type.

'She's got a nerve, coming here tomorrow,' I said.

'Yes,' Mother said. 'I admire that, I must say. Anyway, I'm going to bed. Goodnight Brian darling. Goodnight Will.'

When Mother was safely out of earshot I asked Brian why he seemed so calm after this devastating revelation.

'I'm relieved that the police will have to eat their words and admit that they were wrong. I haven't started to think about the other stuff, and I don't want to discuss it now.'

'Do you want me to be at the meeting with Darlene tomorrow?'

Brian's relief at no longer being a suspect had restored some of his natural gracelessness.

'Good God, no. You can't possibly imagine that it'd be helpful to have you in the room. You can't stand Darlene and she loathes you.'

It would have been unfair of me to point out that Darlene's fondness for Brian was, at the very least, under review.

'Did you suspect that Darlene was having an affair?'

Brian's face became tinged with an angry pink.

'No, I didn't, and I said I didn't want to discuss this now. I'll see her tomorrow and sort things out then. It's bedtime.'

I decided to spend the night at Mother's place. I didn't want to walk across the park at that hour, and I wanted to put some distance between myself and Clutterbuck. It was important that I not betray that I felt I'd been duped by him, especially if I was to effectively infiltrate his creepy brotherhood. It was only as I was falling asleep that I wondered if anybody had told Clutterbuck about Anna Capshaw's death. I suspected that it wouldn't be news that would disturb him to any great degree. Nevertheless, I didn't want to be the person who told him. He wasn't a fool, and he'd want to know how I'd discovered the grim fact. It would be better if I feigned ignorance.

I woke late on Saturday morning. Brian and Mother were dressed, fed, tea'd and waiting downstairs for Darlene to arrive. I offered again to be present and Brian again insisted that it was an appalling idea. He was supported in this by our mother, who said that she wouldn't be present either, that she would greet Darlene and withdraw.

'I just want to look into the eyes of the creature who smashed my best china. You should go now, Will. It would only complicate matters if Darlene saw you here, and please shave darling, you look scruffy and really rather frightening.'

'Perhaps I'll grow a beard.'

'Oh, no dear. You don't have the face for it. You'd look like a prisoner of war, or a homeless person.'

'I'll come back later. I want to know what Darlene had to say. I'm sure she's committed some sort of crime by staging a kidnapping.' On the spur of the moment I added, 'Oh yes, Brian … I want to discuss a little proposal with you. It's to do with work.'

This suggestion arrived in my mind unbidden, but as soon as I'd made it I realised it was a good one. Having Brian to assist me now that he was out of teaching would surely make the task of infiltrating Clutterbuck's Shining Knights much less daunting.

As I crossed Princes Park I began to formulate a plan whereby Brian would become Fowler's primary mole. I'd already indicated my indifference to the ideals expressed by the Knights so a sudden enthusiasm might arouse suspicions. I could introduce my brother as a person whose prejudices matched Clutterbuck's — a fellow traveller in the war on Rome. I decided to put this idea to Fowler when I met him later at the Shrine.

Clutterbuck wasn't at home, and as his car wasn't in the garage I assumed he was up in Brunswick with the terrible trinity of Oakpate, Shingle and Crocker — names that conjured some bleak law firm or office of architects. I looked into his bedroom and found it restored to its former, astonishing orderliness. Mrs Castleton must have been busy.

There was a note on my bed from Clutterbuck telling me

that he was driving to Ballarat and that he wouldn't be back until Monday afternoon. Petrol rationing wouldn't affect Clutterbuck. Like anything else he wanted, he'd purchase it on the black market. He didn't mention Anna Capshaw so I surmised that he'd not yet been told of her death, and I doubted that news of it would reach him in Ballarat over the weekend.

Alone in the house, I wandered through its rooms and almost convinced myself that Clutterbuck wasn't such a bad fellow after all. His politics were unsavoury, but his whisky was good and his digs were superb. Had I been too ready to see him through James Fowler's eyes? Did I want to attribute faults to him that would make it easier for me to come between him and Nigella?

I stood in the kitchen and thought about the uncompromising order in the house. I don't know much about modern psychiatry but I thought it might be a symptom of something unhealthy and morbid. Certainly, the alacrity with which Clutterbuck had suggested disposing of Gretel Beech's body was symptomatic of *something*, and his momentarily risen stakes plummeted.

A knock at the front door echoed down the corridor and made me jump. There's something about the unexpected knock in a silent house that is discomposing. I knew it couldn't be anyone looking for me, so whoever it was would have business with Clutterbuck. Having met the type of troll-like people with whom he fraternised, it was with considerable reluctance that I answered the door. Nigella Fowler stood there wearing crisp white gloves and a jaunty hat, accessories which distracted the eye from her rather dull, woollen skirt and jacket. She was an unadventurous, sensible dresser, and she couldn't quite carry off the hat; she wore it nervously as if she thought that perhaps she'd gone too far and that the hat might excite comment and outrage. It would, of course, do neither. Even in these dour, austere times, it would take more than a jaunty hat to make the horses bolt. I found her couture reticence touching, and felt an overwhelming desire to carry her upstairs like an antipodean Rhett Butler and deny Clutterbuck the gift of her virginity. I must have been staring because she raised her hand to her hat and laughed nervously.

'The hat's too much, isn't it,' she said.

'Oh, no, I love the hat. It's not too much. It's too too.'

'I'm not quite sure what that means, but I'm glad you think so. Is Paul in?'

I explained that he'd gone to Ballarat and that he'd be back on Monday. We agreed that it was negligent of him not to inform her of this, and Nigella said that Paul was sometimes careless about telling her things.

'But he does apologise very sweetly when I point this out to him. May I come in?'

With proprietorial nonchalance she went straight to the kitchen and began to make us a cup of tea.

'I should disapprove, but it's a comfort to know that Paul will always have tea, sugar and milk, no matter how tough the rationing gets.'

'We all use the black market in some way,' I replied. 'I don't subscribe to the idea that a soldier dies every time someone eats an illegally acquired chop.'

'Ah, you see, I'm failing. My job is to make you believe precisely that.'

She laughed, and my desire for her threatened to break through containment lines.

'I went to the pictures yesterday,' I said, 'and I saw a terrible propaganda short. I hope it wasn't one of yours.'

I performed it for her there in Clutterbuck's kitchen, and she laughed so much her jaunty hat broke free and slipped to her shoulder. She pulled it off and threw it to me. I placed it on my head and struck a pose, but then remembered my gravel rashed, unshaven face, and felt foolish.

'Don't marry Paul Clutterbuck,' I said suddenly.

'What an extraordinary thing to say. Why on earth not?'

'You don't really know what he's like.'

'And you do, having known him for what? A week?'

I was reduced to stammering an incoherent apology for the impertinence of my remark. Nigella took pity on me, smiled, and said that as her brother and her father had given her similar advice she could hardly pretend that the general antipathy to Clutterbuck was unknown to her.

'I don't need protecting, Will.'

I wanted to ask her if she'd been warned about Clutterbuck's political activities, but an instinct told me that my relationship with her brother needed to be kept hidden. If he'd warned her about Clutterbuck, she was choosing to ignore his advice. If he hadn't, it wasn't my place to jeopardise his operation against the Order of the Shining Knights by providing Nigella with information that she might take straight to Clutterbuck.

With the tea made, we settled in the austere living room.

'So why do you think Paul is an unsuitable match? Apart from his taste in furniture, of course.'

I'd given her the right to ask such a direct question by so overtly challenging Paul's character. But I stalled.

'Well, good furnishings are important,' I said lamely.

'You mean we'll need somewhere comfortable to sit while we're arguing. So what do you think we'll be arguing about?'

I stalled again.

'The state of your underwear drawer probably.'

'You were so adamant a moment ago. No one gets adamant about underwear. What do you think is so bad about Paul Clutterbuck that it would cause you to issue an all points warnings on our second meeting?'

'Third,' I said.

'We weren't formally introduced the first time and you were rather informally dressed.'

Her voice was light, but her tone was steely. She was determined to get an explanation for my outburst.

'My motive was selfish,' I said, and I didn't have to perform embarrassment. I blushed profusely and was overcome by schoolboy awkwardness. This was the unpleasant consequence of telling the truth, or a large part of the truth. 'I find you very attractive, and however dishonourable it sounds, soon after meeting you, Paul went from being my landlord to being my rival. I know that doesn't say much about my character, but people sometimes do behave badly when they're … when they're …'

'In love?'

'I obviously can't seriously declare that. It would be too silly.'

'But terribly flattering for me, Will. No one has ever fallen in love with me at first sight.'

'Does Paul love you?'

She took a moment to reply.

'Now that really is an impertinent question.'

'Is there a pertinent answer?'

'I'm not a romantic person, Will. Does Paul love me? He's never said so, and he can't therefore be accused of lying to me, or misleading me. No, I don't think he loves me. He likes me well enough. The thing is, Will, I love him, and love makes me selfish enough to claim him, whatever his motives in settling for me. I suppose that sounds dreadful, like I have a low opinion of myself. On the contrary, I have a high opinion of myself — high enough to believe that when we're married his philandering will stop — oh yes, I know about all that — and I don't mean that the love of a good woman will turn dross into gold. It won't be love that makes Paul faithful; it'll be money. I have it; he needs it.'

'You're willing to buy his love?' I couldn't keep the shock out of my voice.

'No, Will, I'm not buying his love. I'm buying the means to express and enjoy mine.'

Her words made me feel a sickening surge of despair, and I thought that if I didn't leave immediately I would retch, or burst into unstoppable, humiliating tears. I made a hurried apology, and bundled into it an expression of the hope that she wouldn't repeat anything I'd said to Clutterbuck, and left the house.

My feelings about the encounter with Nigella were mixed. My desire for her was undiminished, although she was tougher and more calculating than I'd supposed. On the surface it seemed that Clutterbuck could need protection from Nigella, rather than the reverse. I was glad that I'd declared myself, and as I walked down Royal Parade, with no destination in mind, I thought that I'd acquitted myself rather well. I hadn't revealed any of the information given to me by James Fowler, and I felt confident that I needn't be shy about reaffirming my feelings at subsequent meetings with Nigella. She might rebuff me, but she would be neither shocked nor offended. Indeed, given her own approach to these matters, she would understand, perhaps even admire my determination to succeed with her. I couldn't buy her love; but I could perhaps overwhelm her with mine. The idea of giving free rein to my feelings actually made me whistle, even if it was, inexplicably, bars from *There'll Always Be An England*.

With several hours in hand before I was to meet James Fowler, I decided to attempt to track down George Beech. The light of day made this seem a little less frightening. I remembered that Mr Wilks, the drawing master, had offered me work at the National Gallery Art School, and with no better plan to hand, I headed towards the National Gallery in Swanston Street. If Mr Wilks was there he might be able to shed some light on the

Beech marriage, even though he'd claimed to know nothing of substance about either Gretel or George. Careful questioning might reveal something that he didn't know he knew — a piece of conversation, an off-hand remark — something. Experience had taught me that the truth can sometimes lurk behind the most inconsequential comment or gesture.

The entrance to the drawing school was in LaTrobe Street in an annexe to the gallery that clung to its northern side like a ghastly afterthought. After I passed through its doors I found myself in a strange otherworld peopled by plaster casts — some life size, some larger than life and some on a more modest scale. Scattered among these copies of the world's masterpieces were fragments of arms, feet and hands and one or two weird and frightening sculptures of flayed bodies, their muscles and veins exposed. This long shed allowed no natural light, but was lit by overhead bulbs that made the space seem bleak and cold.

There were three people scratching at boards but the place was so quiet the sound of charcoal on paper was absurdly amplified. I approached a young woman who was producing a serviceable charcoal copy of the Venus de Milo and asked her if Mr Wilks was anywhere to be found. She pointed towards a door at the end of the room and said that he was in there, conducting a life-drawing class.

'And why are you out here?' I asked.

'This is my first year. You don't get to do life drawing until your second year. I don't mind. I like statues. They don't talk back.'

'Neither do life models, I assure you.'

She looked me up and down and asked in an offensively dubious tone, 'Have you worked as a life model?'

'Yes,' I replied, 'but mostly I'm an actor.'

'I guess they need all types,' she said dismissively and returned to her drawing.

'When will Mr Wilks be free?'

She shrugged.

'About ten minutes I should think.'

She drew back from her drawing, lined up her charcoal stick with the plaster cast, and pretentiously made a small correction before she put her charcoal down and wiped her hands on her filthy smock. She was young and rather lovely but I could see in her demeanour that art was making her hard and superior. I wouldn't like to be dissected and delineated by her sharp, stabbing little pencil.

The other students were a young man, labouring over an elaborately realised acanthus leaf, and a woman who must have been in her fifties, erasing highlights into a dull representation of a sandaled foot. I walked among the chaotically displayed casts and marvelled at their power to intimidate and excite, despite lacking the sheen and white blood of marble. This was as close as I was going to get to the Belvedere Apollo and it seemed like an adequate substitute for the real thing.

The sudden intrusion of voices into the relative silence of the cast room indicated that the life class had finished, and half-a-dozen young men emerged followed by a thin, red-faced and red-bearded man who looked half asleep and whose features exhibited the ravages of alcohol — clearly they were getting their models from among Melbourne's most desperate classes.

I went into the room and found Mr Wilks carefully examining a partially completed drawing. He looked up and said, 'Oh, you've come for some work. Excellent. That last chap stank.'

I hastily corrected him on this point — not the smelliness of the sitter, but my looking for work. I told him that I was actually a private inquiry agent and that my client was interested in the whereabouts of George and Gretel Beech. I hoped this half-truth might jolt his memory. He hadn't known, he said, that

Gretel was married to George.

'So you managed to find this George chap at some stage, did you?'

'Oh, yes, and it was the right George. He was able to confirm this by producing his penis.'

'I got the impression when he was modelling for me that he wasn't a shy man. He managed to put his member front and centre, as it were, in every pose he struck. My ladies were quite distracted by it. Only Nigella Fowler drew it as she saw it. The others reduced it to more classical proportions. Would you like a cup of tea, Mr Power?'

There was a long table in the tearoom of the drawing school, with one young man seated at the far end eating a sandwich out of a brown paper bag, and smoking.

'This used to be quite busy,' Mr Wilks said. 'The war has badly affected our numbers.' The attendance problems of the art school were of no interest to me and I started to think I'd made a mistake in allowing myself to be trapped in a pointless conversation. Mr Wilks, obviously skilled in watching the subtle movement of muscle under flesh, observed, quite correctly, that I seemed agitated.

'I was rather hoping that you could help me, that's all.'

'I'll be frank with you, Mr Power. When you modelled for my class you told me a blatant lie about Gretel owing you money. It wasn't the debt that gave you away; it was the ridiculous size of the debt. Now you tell me that you're some sort of spy.'

'A private inquiry agent, not a spy. I'm simply a private detective.'

To me, the sound of these words was thrilling. They didn't have the same effect on Mr Wilks.

'I don't like private detectives,' he said. 'They poke about in other people's business and bring misery to them. You're just the grubby tool of jealous husbands and vindictive wives, and vice versa.'

'You seem to speaking from personal experience.'

'Oh, I am, Mr Power, I surely am.'

'Let me assure you that my client is not concerned about sexual morality. He would be the first to acknowledge that his own morals are, shall we say, flexible.'

I suddenly found myself on an explanatory course that might take me into turbid waters. Having started, I couldn't stop.

'My client's interest in the Beechs stems from his concern that Gretel Beech, with whom he was having an affair — that should allay your fears about his reasons for employing me — that Gretel Beech has gone missing.'

I knew this was a risky disclosure. Mr Wilks was now the only other person to know that Gretel's whereabouts were unknown, and that this fact was sufficiently suspicious to justify the employment of a private detective.

'By gone missing I presume you mean your client suspects foul play?'

I nodded.

'Why hasn't he gone to the police?'

'There are sensitive issues here and he wants discreet inquiries made first. I'm not really privy to his motives. I imagine he's reluctant to have the police blundering about in his private affairs until he's certain there's a good reason to expose himself in this way.'

I was pleased with this neat improvisation. Mr Wilks was satisfied with it as well.

'And you think George Beech — her husband you say — might have something to do with her disappearance.'

'It's possible. He's a violent man.'

'He did that to your face, did he?'

'He took me by surprise, and he threatened to do worse. He's a man with something to hide.'

'A secretiveness that doesn't extend to his penis.'

Mr Wilks' willingness to make a small joke indicated that the facts of this case had softened his attitude to my new profession.

'All right, Mr Power. I'm reluctant to do this but I can find Gretel Beech's address for you. She's on our books as a regular model and her details are filed away.'

'But you said you didn't know where she lived.'

'I wasn't about to give her address to a stranger, and anyway, I don't actually know it. I'll have to look it up.'

This was a tremendous breakthrough. There was, however, a price to pay for the information.

'I'll get you the address, Mr Power, on the condition that you do something for me. Quid pro quo. I assume Gretel is going to miss her next session with my ladies, and finding a replacement for such an amateur group is difficult. So, next Thursday? Same time?'

I agreed, thinking that between now and Thursday any number of things could happen to prevent me keeping the appointment. The important matter was to get the address. Mr Wilks duly went off and returned with the address of a boarding house in St Kilda written neatly on a scrap of paper. It was only outside the gallery, in the shadow of Frémiet's Joan of Arc bronze, that it occurred to me that Nigella Fowler would be in the drawing class again. I couldn't possibly keep the appointment. After what I'd told her, the imbalance of my being naked while she looked on, clothed, was too much to contemplate.

With some time to spare I wandered slowly through the city. It was much quieter than on a weekday but there were still people window shopping — mostly couples, and mostly Americans with local girlfriends or companions. The windows seemed dismal to me, victims of the notion that it was in poor taste and unpatriotic to flaunt luxury. I noticed that there were frequent, low-level displays of unpleasantries whenever a shabby Australian soldier passed a dapper ally. The tension was palpable, and I thought how this made a mockery of the catchy little tune that was current and which insisted that we were all in clover because the Aussies and the Yanks were here.

As I crossed Princes Bridge, and passed Wirth's Circus, I thought how tawdry circuses looked in daylight. The big top was diminished to grubby canvas and guy ropes by the illusion-shattering blast of the sun. Hobbled camels grazed desultorily, and a shackled elephant swayed with boredom. I kept to the left hand side and walked along the path that James Fowler had called the 'chicken run.' I wondered how many pints of semen had been ejaculated the previous evening onto the ground I traversed, and I made a mental note to pause before walking barefoot through any park again.

I mounted the steps of the Shrine and passed into the Sanctuary — a place that had made me a bit weepy on the two or three occasions I'd visited it in the past. The centre was surmounted by a monumental cap, shaped to evoke the great temple at Helicarnassus; but to me it was reminiscent of the inside of a camera's snout. There were a few people in the Sanctuary, maintaining the silence the space demanded. At the back I turned right and walked down a short flight of steps, then turned right again where a longer flight felt like the approach to a pharaoh's tomb.

The crypt was dimly lit and smaller than I'd remembered it. Regimental colours hung beneath the ceiling and the air smelt of wet sandstone. I was alone. I could hear the echo of footsteps above, and muffled, subdued voices as people moved around the Shrine. For no rational reason I experienced a kind of panic. The damp, dark, flag-bedraped crypt suddenly became less a place of reflection and more of a trap into which I'd walked. I began to sweat and feel dizzy; the claustrophobia to which I was prone came creeping from my subconscious into the wide open spaces of my susceptible mind.

'Will?'

James Fowler's voice was low.

I turned, expecting to see a gun pointed at me. Instead he was standing with his hands on his hips. Even in the poor light, my pale, glistening, panicked face caused him to ask if I was feeling ill.

'Hay fever,' I lied. 'Could we go outside do you think?'

'That seems a little illogical, Will, but if you insist.'

I followed Fowler up onto the exterior balcony of the Shrine. From here the centre of Melbourne lay before us, and my eyes skipped over the ugly factories on the Yarra River's bank to collide with the lumpish, failed grandeur of Flinders Street Station, and then onto the true splendour of St Paul's Cathedral.

'All these things will I give thee,' Fowler said, and swept his hand over the vista, 'if thou wilt fall down and worship me.'

'That sounds like something you'd hear on the chicken run.'

'Do you mean me, personally, or is that a more general "you"?'

'I'm sorry,' I said hastily, 'it was just a poor joke.'

'Have you thought any further about what we were discussing last night?'

Without hesitation I told James Fowler that I would do whatever Army Intelligence asked me to do.

'I'm glad you're on board,' he said. 'I'm sure Clutterbuck thinks that he can rely on you to help him, advertently or inadvertently, in whatever he's got planned. He's slippery enough to arrange things so that you're never told quite what it is you're being used for.'

I resented, slightly, the implication that I mightn't be bright enough to know when I was or wasn't being exploited. Nevertheless, I agreed that it would be satisfying to know that while Clutterbuck thought he was keeping an eye on me, it was actually me who was keeping an official eye on him.

Fowler was anxious to point out that he didn't expect, indeed didn't advise, that my role in infiltrating the Order of the Shining Knights would be a very active one. All that was required was that I attend a few of their meetings and pass on the gist of their discussions to him.

'They won't tell you anything of real significance probably, but you might be able to tip us off about something.'

'Both Oakpate and Crocker have been sacking people from their factories. I know that,' I reported.

'Nasty but not illegal. But we have had some vague intelligence about an attack of some sort which may be planned. We don't know where or when, or even if, really. That's what I need you to keep your ears open for.'

As Fowler was outlining the job he wanted me to do, I waited for an opportunity to raise the issue of bringing Brian in on all this. The more he spoke, the more certain I became that the less he knew about my plans for Brian the better. Army Intelligence was all very well, but there was something to be said for Power Intelligence. It always pays to have something up your sleeve.

James Fowler and I parted on excellent terms. I was tempted to mention my conversation with Nigella. I didn't, because such an intimacy was at odds with the professionally distant relationship I wanted to maintain with him, at least until the whole Paul Clutterbuck issue had been resolved.

'I have to get back to my cubby-hole,' he said. 'Be careful, Will. Don't take any risks or you'll give yourself away.'

We shook hands.

'I'm an actor James. I can play the wide-eyed naïf. I won't be giving anything away.'

⌀

It was very late in the afternoon when I returned to Mother's house. The football season had finished so the hoi polloi wasn't milling about in Princes Park. There was a baseball game in progress, watched by a handful of locals and quite a number of grunts from Camp Pell. I assumed that Darlene and the father of her unborn foal would have left. They hadn't. The living room door was closed but I could hear Darlene's flat, penetrating voice through the wood. I found Mother in the kitchen and she told me that they'd been talking for hours, the three of them. They hadn't even stopped for a cup of tea. Voices had been raised, but generally it had been a civilised affair. I said that I thought it was extraordinary that Darlene could be so deaf, dumb and blind to decency that she would bring her adulterous gigolo to the very house that had welcomed her as my brother's wife.

'He's not a gigolo, Will, and you've certainly never been guilty of welcoming Darlene.'

'How can you defend her?'

'Oh, for heaven's sake, I'm not defending her, but I have no patience for that tone of yours. It's most unpleasant and unhelpful.'

It's remarkable how one's childhood can be summoned by a single, sharp reprimand. Conversation was now impossible. I'd grown out of the sullen silence with which I used to meet correction, obviously, but I didn't feel I had anything to apologise for so I simply made myself a cup of tea. I put the teapot on the table without offering to pour Mother a fresh cup. I hoped she'd appreciate this gesture as a pointed riposte to her short-tempered reaction to my perfectly reasonable question.

'I'm going upstairs to write to Fulton,' she said. Before leaving the kitchen she added, 'When you speak to Brian try to keep the awful note of glee you sometimes get, out of your voice.'

I ran my hand over the stubble on my face in lieu of a rejoinder.

'You really are frighteningly like your father sometimes, Will.'

With that, she went upstairs, and I was left to ponder whether this observation was a compliment or an insult.

The door to the living room opened — I could see it from the kitchen — and the American came down the corridor towards me.

'I'm after some water for Darlene,' he said.

I hadn't really had the chance to examine him closely the night before. I noticed he was a captain, though without his uniform he would have been Darlene's equal in colourlessness. If I were casting him in a play I'd put him somewhere down the back, his only use to 'swell a progress.'

'You're the guy I slugged last night. Darlene's brother-in-law. I guess I should apologise for that.'

He put out his hand. I ignored it.

'OK,' he said and withdrew it. 'Darlene warned me that you were an asshole.'

'Darlene has specialist knowledge in that area, and I see she's exercised it in her choice of lover.'

'You talk like a homo.'

'You Americans have never really got the hang of English have you.'

'Water,' he said, and nodded in the direction of the tap. He found a glass and filled it.

'Darlene's usually more comfortable with a trough,' I said.

'You're a funny guy. You could get hurt you're so funny.'

He returned to the living room and only a few minutes later he re-emerged, this time with his arm through Darlene's. I was standing in the kitchen doorway and watched as she pulled gloves over her trotters and pointlessly attempted to improve the way her hat sat before going into the street. It was pleasing to note that her pregnancy was wreaking havoc on her appearance. She wasn't glowing; merely swelling and sloughing. She saw me and curled her lip. She said nothing, words as usual failing her.

In the living room Brian was standing by the bay window, staring at them as they walked down Garton Street.

'How could she this fair mountain leave to feed and batten on this moor?' I said.

'She's a cunt, Will.' His tone was dramatically inexpressive, as if he was repeating a bland truism. He wasn't upset; exhausted perhaps and showing none of the agitation I'd expected.

'I won't have you using that kind of language in my house, Brian,' Mother said. She'd come in silently behind me. On any other occasion Brian would have stammered an immediate apology — I'd never heard him utter so powerful an obscenity before — but he must have been numbed by his lengthy negotiation with Darlene, because he paid no heed to Mother's injunction.

'I'll give it some thought, Mother, but for the moment "cunt" is all the English language has to offer to describe her.'

He spoke slowly and deliberately. He'd entered emotional territory he'd never been in before and he was taking careful steps.

'Sit down,' he said to both of us. 'I'll give you the short version and I don't want to answer any questions. Darlene has been seeing Captain Spangler Brisket — yes, that's his real name — for six months. They met at one of the Comfort Fund do's that Darlene attended. Darlene and I hadn't been intimate for a while — I suppose we were going through a bad patch, like any marriage. She and Spangler — that name — hit it off and she became pregnant. As soon as she discovered this she had sex with me, just to cover herself until she decided what to do. Spangler wasn't going to be in Melbourne forever, although he'd managed to stick around for longer than most of them. He's got a cousin on Macarthur's staff who pulled a few strings.

'Darlene freely admits that the kidnapping stunt was appalling, but she only decided to do it after she found out about my affair with Sarah Goodenough in Maryborough. Sarah did ring her, just as the police said, and told her everything, and with stunning hypocrisy she took offence, said I was my mother's son, whatever that means, and that she wanted to punish us all.'

He paused, and I know both Mother and I were tempted to fill the pause with questions. With disciplined reticence neither of us did so. Brian could see us straining at the leash but went on:

'Darlene's been unhappy here for a long time. She said that she never felt comfortable; that Mother always made her feel clumsy, and treated her in the off-hand way she might treat a servant. Will, of course, she detested.'

I thought that 'of course' was a bit much, and I could see from the aggrieved look on Mother's face that Brian's words had come as something of a shock.

'She wants a divorce and she intends to marry this Spangler Brisket and move to the United States with him. She wants nothing from me except the divorce. Anyway, given her pregnancy it would be ludicrous for her to make any demands. Spangler, by the way, is happy to replace the crockery Darlene smashed. He didn't entirely approve of her kidnapping scheme.'

Mother finally interrupted.

'The crockery is irreplaceable, as Darlene very well knows. It was a wedding present from your father's family.'

'At any rate, he's going to replace it. Now I'm tired of talking. I'm going upstairs to lie down and think about things.'

'Of course, darling, you were in there with Darlene and this Spangler person for hours. You must be exhausted. We'll sort it all out later.'

'It's sorted out, Mother. I'm giving Darlene her divorce and she's going to America. Simple.'

Brian left the room. I hung fire, not wishing to attract any further criticism for misheard tone.

'Well, that's that,' Mother said. 'I hope Mrs Spangler Brisket will wear her name with all the pride it calls for.'

'And I'm sure Spangler Junior will be the child they richly deserve.'

'Let's have a whisky, Will, and you can tell me about this private detective business. When Brian told me I must confess I thought the strain had made him silly.'

There was nothing to be gained by telling Mother all the details of my recent investigations. I sketched a rough picture and left her with the impression, I think, that in a very short time I'd become as fine a detective as I was an actor. Never one to lavish praise and approval on her children, she acknowledged that finding Darlene had been a coup, and she congratulated me on doing so.

'I'm doing a bit of work now for Army Intelligence. It's hush-hush, so you mustn't tell anybody, and that includes Fulton. I'm telling you because …' When I came to 'because' I realised I didn't know why I was telling Mother this sensitive material. I floundered and she filled the gap.

'You're telling me because you want to let me know that you're doing something useful. That's nice, Will, but you know you don't have to impress me. I always thought your acting was a fine profession to follow. I'm glad, though, that you're having some success with your detecting. I want my boys to be happy. You don't have to compete with Fulton or Brian.'

I'd always found these blessedly infrequent assurances that Mother distributed her affections equally, embarrassing, and I moved to head off further maudlin and deeply unconvincing observations.

'As I said earlier, Mother, there's an opportunity that I need to discuss with Brian, and I'm afraid it can't wait. I'm sure he's very tired but I'm also sure this will take his mind off his troubles.'

I went upstairs to Brian's room — until recently Brian and Darlene's room — and found him lying on the bed, his hands behind his head, staring at the ceiling.

'I'm not here to talk about Darlene,' I said hurriedly. 'I've got a job I think you might be interested in doing.'

By the end of my account of all that James Fowler had told me about Secret Armies and Shining Knights, Brian's interest had been aroused. The idea of playing the part of a rabid, angry, volatile, anti-Catholic, anti-government, anti-just-about-anything agitator was appealing to him. With his professional and personal life in ruins, a risky, potentially violent adventure was just the tonic he needed. He didn't even mind that there was no salary attached. The sudden, seismic shift from plodding teacher with wretchedly dull wife to Army Intelligence mole so energised him that he leapt from the bed and began stuffing Darlene's clothes into a suitcase.

'I'll give these to the Red Cross. She'll be ropeable, but bugger it, Captain Spangler can fork out for a new wardrobe.'

'The Red Cross? I always said her wardrobe consisted of stuff you'd only wear in an emergency.'

Brian began to say something, probably a reflex defence of

his wife's taste, but caught himself in time and laughed instead.

'When do I start?'

'Right now. I'll take you to Clutterbuck's. He won't be there until Monday, but I think you'll find his house quite instructive.'

Chapter Ten

VERY POOR DECISIONS

UNTIL THE ARRIVAL OF THE AMERICANS, Melbourne slipped into a coma each Sunday. Influence was brought to bear, however, when thousands of troops wandered the city's streets, bored and dismayed by the absence of entertainment. A bored and dismayed doughboy is liable to make his own fun, so the city fathers, with the greatest reluctance, and with the noisy disapproval of church mice from various denominations, decided that perhaps the veil of the Temple would not be rent in twain after all if movie houses were permitted to operate.

This is why the centre of the city was quite busy when I passed through it on Sunday morning on my way to the Beech residence in St Kilda. I was slightly hung over, having had more of Clutterbuck's whisky than I'd intended. This was Brian's fault. He'd been impressed by the house, and even more impressed by the quality and quantity of Clutterbuck's single malts. My reticence about drinking it had faded with every nip, until we'd disposed of most of a bottle. Brian said it might be a good introduction for Clutterbuck to Brian Power, anarchist.

'Anarchy,' I said, 'is the last thing Clutterbuck is after. He's a controller. His idea of anarchy is a poorly folded sock.'

'Anyway, Will, I'll take responsibility for the whisky. I'll say I was toasting the death of all Vatican vultures, and got carried away. I'll stress how much you tut-tutted and tried to stop me.'

At first I thought this was a bad idea, but then it occurred to me that it would be very useful if Clutterbuck thought that there was tension between my brother and me. I explained this to Brian and he agreed, saying that licensed and unbridled attacks on my character and personality would be endlessly entertaining for him.

'All in a good cause, of course,' he said. 'Having a go at you in front of this Clutterbuck will be a kind of patriotism.'

I counselled him not to go too far, that any rivalry between us needed to reflect the banality of real life, not the excess of a Sheridan Restoration comedy.

The morning was grey, exacerbating the disappointment of the late Spring bud burst. I didn't know my way around St Kilda at all. Although it was a suburb only a few miles from where I'd grown up in Princes Hill, it might as well have been on the other side of the continent. It faced the sea, which made it seem alien to me. My internal geography was calibrated to dry land, and it seemed to me that Melbourne resolutely faced away from the turbulence of the ocean in favour of the sluggish predictability of the Yarra River. St Kilda was, as well, terribly déclassé, and in my memory it smelled unpleasantly of brine and salt-rotted timber.

Finding the boarding house where Beech lived turned out

to be surprisingly easy. The first person I asked — the female driver of a horse-drawn bread delivery cart — pointed me in the direction of a street that ran off the Esplanade. It was close to Luna Park, and as I approached it I was reminded of the occasion I had visited this fun fair with my father. I must have been ten years old, and this was supposed to have been a treat. Perhaps it was my birthday. I hope the visit wasn't a substitute for a present, because I recall finding the experience hideous and upsetting. I've always found fairgrounds and sideshows and circuses rather sinister, and the great, gaping mouth at the entrance to Luna Park didn't seem to me then, and doesn't seem to me now, to be an invitation to fun and games. Its sheer size makes it grotesque, and the unavoidable conclusion that children passing beneath its teeth are being swallowed whole was disconcerting to a sensitive ten-year-old.

My father was deaf to my protestations, and I was harried onto the Scenic Railway without really being aware that it was neither scenic nor a railway, but a rollercoaster of terrifying antiquity. The howls of delighted hysteria from the other passengers convinced me at this early age that the general public are, sadly, never at their best. I didn't enjoy that day; I endured it. My sense of my father being so vague, I can't know for certain whether my discomfort was seen by him as being evidence of a job well done. He certainly made no attempt to shield me from every ghastly excess Luna Park had to offer.

As I turned into George Beech's street the Scenic Railway clattered its way to the top of a rise, and screams and laughter flew over the rooftops as it hurtled into a dip. I knew I could never live within earshot of Luna Park, but it was obviously not a concern that troubled Beech. The house where he boarded was only two doors away from the Esplanade. It was a two-storeyed building which would once have been a single home, although even in its heyday it would never have been considered grand. It was both bland and ugly, with stained and flaking stucco walls, and window frames that were peeling and splitting with rot and neglect. I didn't have to walk through the front door to know that the conversion into flats would have been cheap and nasty. This wasn't a house that would attract a better class of tenant. This was a house that actually preferred the George Beech's of this world, and it shared his odours of drink, smokes and sweat.

I discovered which was Beech's room when I peered through a grimy window. George Beech was sprawled on a mattress on the floor, dressed only in his underwear, with one arm covering his eyes against the light. He was deeply asleep, his chest rising and falling in the steady, slow rhythm of the comatose. I surmised from what I knew of the man that this was an alcohol-induced sleep, so I had no qualms about going into the house and trying the door to his flat. It was unlocked and opened soundlessly.

The air in the room was stale and, among all the other foetid odours, I detected the sweet taint of perfume, probably arising from Gretel's clothes which were still strewn about. George Beech showed no sign of having heard me come in; he continued to sleep and breathe deeply. Beech grunted and I turned to look at him. His hands were enormous; great plates of flesh with powerful fingers that would have closed easily around his wife's throat. I could picture the sinews moving beneath the skin of his arms as he applied and adjusted pressure to Gretel's neck. It was clear from the state of the room that George was determinedly slovenly. Clothing, shoes, bits of paper, books and newspapers lay where they'd fallen. I had no idea what I was looking for, and anyway, finding anything significant would be unlikely, and given that I had to move gingerly, impossible.

There was a desk beside the mattress on which George lay;

the legs on its right side just a few inches from his head. It was risky to approach it, but as it was the most promising object in the room, I had no choice. Its top was strewn with cosmetics and other detritus of domestic life, and its drawers were stuffed with socks and undergarments. In the second drawer I pushed these aside and revealed a neat pile of papers. They were of a design which was familiar to me because every citizen was required to carry them. My own was in the wallet in my back pocket. They were ID papers, the kind Manpower officials checked on their regular raids. I suddenly recalled that one of the men who'd been at the Petrushka with George had had inky fingers. George Beech and his friends were in the business of counterfeiting ID papers. No wonder he'd been so quick to accuse me of being a copper. I picked up a bundle and riffled through them. They were utterly convincing to my eye. If George was the artist, or one of them, his thick fingers were nimble.

I was considering this when those very fingers closed around my ankle. I looked down into George's open, if bleary eyes, and the expression on his face wasn't a welcoming one. He was sluggish but his grip was tight, so tight that it felt as if he might crush my bones. The greater danger, though, was that he might yank my foot out from under me and tip me onto the ground where I would stand as much chance as a small animal in the jaws of a crocodile. I had the slight advantage of being awake and sober, so I groped on the desk top for a weapon. I found a paperweight that was simply a heavy lump of rock with crystals protruding from it, and, almost instinctively, I hurled it down at George Beech's head. It caught him above the right eye and bounced onto the mattress.

His grip relaxed immediately and his eyes juddered from side to side before they seemed to roll upwards so that only the whites were showing. Then his eyelids closed, slowly, as if the mechanism needed oiling, and he lay still, a bloom of blood spreading around his head. All this had taken place soundlessly, although I quickly became aware of my own rapid breathing, and the muted squeals of excited girls on the Scenic Railway. Beech's great paw lay palm upward at my foot. I nudged it, hoping to make it twitch. His chest was no longer rising and falling and his face was already assuming the pallor of the dead. I'd never killed anyone before, and I was shocked at how easily a life could be extinguished. George Beech had looked as if it would take a blunderbuss to bring him down, and all it had required was a paperweight.

I stepped away from his body and tried to gather my thoughts. His death had been an accident, but the police wouldn't believe this, so involving them was out of the question. The man was a criminal — definitely a counterfeiter, and in a time of war that made him a traitor, too — and probably a murderer. It wasn't as if the country had suffered an irreparable loss. My reaction may seem cold, but you can't work in Army Intelligence *and* be sentimental about life and death. I slunk out of the room and fortunately met no one in the corridor. Beech's body would be found soon enough, and there wasn't a thing in the world to connect him to me. There were threads, it's true — I'd asked Mr Wilks for Beech's address; Beech's friends had seen me at the Petrushka; the police would want to find Beech's wife — but I couldn't see how any of these threads could be pulled together. The police would have no reason to speak to Mr Wilks; Beech's friends had no way of identifying me, and Gretel wasn't about to speak from beyond the grave.

With Beech dead, of course, I would now be unable to deliver him as Gretel's murderer. As I walked along the Esplanade I began to consider the awful possibility that Gretel would have to remain where she was. Two things then struck me forcibly at once. The first was that if I was unable to produce Gretel's killer, Clutterbuck had only to open his mouth to put me in a very delicate position indeed; the second, and more immediately pressing, was that I'd left my fingerprints all over the paperweight that had clobbered Beech. To be implicated in the murder of both husband and wife was quite beyond the pale. I had no option. I had to go back to Beech's room and wipe that piece of stone clean, along with the doorknob.

I retraced my steps and stood nervously outside his door for a moment. I couldn't linger in case one of the other tenants appeared, but I was reluctant to re-enter Beech's room. The knowledge that there was a corpse in there filled me with superstitious dread. Coming upon the dead suddenly is very different from knowing about a body in advance. I girded my loins and went in.

George Beech was not where I'd left him. He wasn't, in fact, in the room at all, and if there's one thing more disconcerting than the expected presence of a corpse, it's the unexpected absence of one. I was so befuddled that it took me a moment to register the sound of running water somewhere in the house. I opened the door and located its source — a kitchen at the end of the corridor. It only took a few steps to see George Beech, bent over a sink, splashing water on his face. The relief was so profound that I felt like throwing my arms around him, but I knew that would have led to my own death, so I withdrew without betraying my presence. At least I could now alert James Fowler to the counterfeiting operation — information that was certain to impress him and inspire confidence in my abilities — and if I shared my suspicions about Beech's role in Gretel's demise, perhaps this line could be vigorously pursued during interrogation, to the point where he might confess. This seemed beautifully neat to me. Army interrogators would surely be ruthless in extracting information from a traitor like Beech. Falsifying ID's must constitute a kind of treason.

When I returned to Clutterbuck's house I allowed myself one more whisky from his depleted supply to celebrate the serendipitous confluence of events that had provided me with a successful parallel career to my acting, as well as a solution to the seemingly intractable problem of the illegal disposal of Gretel Beech's body. With the murderer nabbed it wouldn't be too difficult to explain the circumstances under which this had been essential, and given the outcome of my strategy, how could the courts argue with my method? Occasionally, in my past, after a particularly gratifying performance, I would permit myself the indulgence of private self-congratulation. As I sat in one of Clutterbuck's uncomfortable chairs I permitted such congratulations to flow through me. It was a delightful sensation and I savoured it. I'm not a vain man. I had no wish to share it, or bruit my achievements abroad. This was personal; a well-earned luxury.

I telephoned the number James Fowler had given me. He was at his desk, and I simply told him that I had information that I'd uncovered in the course of an investigation, unrelated to the operation involving the Order of the Shining Knights, but which he would nevertheless find interesting. He stopped me and said that if this was connected in any way to national security it shouldn't be discussed over the phone — he'd call on me as soon as he could get away. I was to stay put. I impressed upon him that there was some urgency, that the person about whom we were speaking might begin to destroy the evidence of his activities. He said he'd be at Clutterbuck's as quickly as he could.

Fowler was as good as his word, and within three-quarters of an hour he'd arrived and I'd begun telling him all that I knew about George Beech. But I lost my nerve when it came to telling him the whole truth about Gretel. I couldn't, understandably, bring myself to say, 'I helped dispose of the body.' It spoiled all the rest. I told him only that I was certain, more than certain, that Gretel had been murdered and that her husband had done it. He wanted to know, quite reasonably, how it was that I was so sure of this. Where was Gretel's body? All I could do was ask Fowler to trust me; that locating the whereabouts of the victim was a part of my ongoing investigation. What I needed from him was an assurance that Beech would be confronted with the accusation of murder, and that he would be leaned on heavily. Fowler said that murder didn't fall under his team's terms of reference, but that he was sure it could be raised among the questions asked of Beech.

'And yes,' he said, 'considerable pressure can be brought to bear.'

Fowler made a phone call and left, saying that George Beech would be picked up in a very short time and that he'd keep me informed of all developments.

'Oh, by the way,' he said on leaving. 'Well done. I knew I'd chosen the right man. We may have to find you a permanent job.'

I slept soundly and woke with the pleasant expectation that the cast on my arm was to be removed that morning. I walked to the surgery of Doctor Spitler, a man who'd tended all our family's ills from the time we'd arrived in Princes Hill. I had no memory of him ever being young, and when I looked down on his age-spotted skull as he cut away the cast, I couldn't imagine how he might have looked as a young, vigorous man. I don't know whether he was incurious, or discreet, but he made no inquiries as to how I'd come to break my arm, or how I'd managed to graze my face. I volunteered that I'd fallen over on both counts, although the accident with the arm had happened seven weeks previously.

Doctor Spitler's nicotine-stained fingers wielded the shears skilfully, and in a few minutes my arm was released from the wretched plaster. I didn't recognise the pallid, mottled limb as my own. Doctor Spitler assured me that with daily exercises it would rapidly return to normal.

'Try to avoid falling over,' he said.

I thanked him for his, as always, impeccable medical advice.

'How's your mother?' he asked. 'She's a remarkable woman. She almost died having you. Did you know that? I trust you've made it all worthwhile.'

The world is packed to the gunwales with impertinent people.

I returned to Clutterbuck's house at midday and was surprised to find him drinking whisky with Brian, who was either acting as if he was inebriated, or was in fact inebriated. Clutterbuck, as usual, showed no effects of the alcohol.

'I've confessed,' Brian said. 'I've told Paul here that we got into his whisky.'

'You mean that *you* got into his whisky, Brian.'

'Oh, and I s'pose that you didn't have any.'

'I had some, yes, but not as much as you did.'

Brian sneered.

'Anyway, we agreed to take it out of your wages.'

He burst into laughter and Clutterbuck joined him. Even though I knew Brian was acting as we'd decided he should act, I still flushed pink.

'Oh, come on, Will,' Clutterbuck said. 'Brian's just kidding.

I don't mind if you hop into my whisky. You know that. Here, have one yourself.'

'No thank you. It's a little early in the day.'

Brian pulled a face to indicate that my refusal was entirely consistent with his opinion of me as a wowser.

'I'm sorry I wasn't here to formally introduce my younger brother,' I said.

Brian snorted.

'It wasn't necessary, Lady Bracknell. Paul and I got along fine without you.'

I saw one of Clutterbuck's eyebrows rise a fraction — enough to tell me that he accepted the tension between Brian and me as genuine. I hoped Brian wouldn't ruin it by taking too many liberties.

'What are you doing here?' I asked him.

'I came to see you, and Paul here answered the door. I need a bit of cash, Will. Just to tide me over.'

'Brian told me he's just lost his job,' Clutterbuck said.

'Wasn't the right fucking religion,' Brian said. 'Excuse my French.'

He'd got the tone just right; a good mixture of disappointment and resentment.

'What line of work were you in?' Clutterbuck asked.

'Just a clerk in an office. Nothing flash. The boss is a king Catholic and he gave my job to another left-footer. Arsehole. Those bastards stick together.'

'Indeed they do,' Clutterbuck said. If he'd risen to the bait, this was the only proof of it. He was not a man who made any unconsidered remarks or movements, and he immediately changed the subject, as if the issue of the great Catholic threat was of no interest to him. I could see that the care he took to camouflage his prejudice was evidence enough that he was already considering how he might turn Brian's bitterness to his advantage.

I had to admit that Brian was a naturally talented actor — with some training he could possibly achieve something on the stage.

We were rescued from the threat of Brian going too far in his performance by his need to go to the toilet and the simultaneous arrival of Nigella. There was no awkwardness between us. She acknowledged me gracefully, and informed Clutterbuck that she was taking him out to lunch so he could tell her all about his trip to Ballarat, and perhaps explain why he'd neglected to let her know he was going. This last was delivered rather icily. Clutterbuck wasn't enthusiastic, but he acquiesced and they left before Brian returned. We were left to ourselves and Brian's tipsiness was replaced by sober smugness.

'Do admit,' he said, 'I carried that off very well.'

I agreed that he'd set himself up quite nicely, and was lavish in my praise of his performance. After all, he'd had a couple of nasty shocks recently and it cost me nothing to put a little salve on his bruised ego. I was happy to do it. I've never been stingy in my praise of others — when it was warranted.

'What were you talking about before I arrived?'

'I was telling Paul what a prig you can be.'

'No, really Brian, what were you talking about?'

'No, really Will, I was telling him what a prig you can be.'

I cautioned him again about over-exaggeration, and he said that nothing he'd told Clutterbuck had been a surprise. 'I see your plaster's off. That must be a relief. Your face is looking better, too. Soon you'll be your old self Will.'

Brian's chirpiness was strangely at odds with the dramatic turn his life had taken.

'This isn't a game, Brian. This is a dangerous thing that we're doing. Paul Clutterbuck may not be a violent man, but I can't guarantee that his friends are as civilised.'

'I'll meet them soon enough. Paul's eager for new recruits. He's already hinted that he might be able to find work for me. He said he's got a friend who's laid off some workers. I'm in, Will. Paul Clutterbuck can't wait to sign me up. I don't think he's as bright as he seems. Money makes people look smarter than they are.'

'Brian, I know he's not as wealthy as all this makes him seem either. It's inherited and squandered.'

As I said this I experienced a spasm of anger that Nigella was prepared to prop him up. I was anxious to get her alone again to demonstrate the compelling truth of my fervour. In a day or so I'd be able to shave again without damaging my face. I'd get a haircut and restore the shimmer of Hollywood that surrounded me. I believed I could then tempt Nigella Fowler into my now fully liberated arms.

Brian stood up and announced that he had to go home to weed the vegetable garden.

'Come round for dinner,' he said. 'Mother's got some halfway decent beef and she's making a Scotch broth.'

I thought about it, and even though I knew that the essential element of barley would be replaced by inedible, but available, oatmeal, I accepted the offer.

'Is there anything Mother needs to bulk out this broth?'

'It's only soup, Will. It's no big deal.'

'Good food makes life bearable, Brian. What else is she putting in this broth?'

'I'm not a cook and as far as I'm concerned if it's edible that's all that matters.'

I ignored his culinary philistinism.

'Do you have herbs?' I asked.

'Yes,' he said, with undisguised annoyance. 'Darlene planted plenty. She was sending them off to the Australian Fighting Forces Herb Auxiliary. She used to say that her marjoram might just be making some poor bastard's food palatable up in New Guinea.'

'A paragon of patriotism. Shame about her loyalties closer to home.'

Brian would have bridled at this as recently as the day before. Now he accepted it without comment.

'I'll tell Mother to expect you,' he said.

Brian had barely left Clutterbuck's house, clutching a note scribbled to Mother showing her how best to use carrots in the broth (shredded so finely that they dissolve and provide background sweetness), when the phone rang. I didn't recognise the voice until it introduced itself as Oakpate. It was impossible, I know, but I almost believed I could smell his foul breath travelling along the wire and emerging from the mouthpiece at my end. He had a message for Clutterbuck. He said it was imperative that the Knights meet with him that evening and it was even more imperative that the meeting be held at Clutterbuck's house. I assured him I would pass this on.

'Tell him we're all coming. He knows where to contact me if there's a problem.'

I assumed that Clutterbuck would be back from lunch soon — Nigella had work to do, after all.

I lay on my bed, flexing my hand, gently exercising the weakened muscles in my newly repaired arm. I heard Clutterbuck return and went downstairs to give him Oakpate's message. Stopping outside the living room door, I heard two voices, both male. Clutterbuck's voice was measured and calm, the other voice was raised so that words were audible.

'It wasn't my fault. It should've gone off.'

I leant down to the keyhole, like a maid in a farce, to hear Clutterbuck's response.

'If we can't manage to incinerate a fucking country church, what chance have we got with St Patrick's,' he said.

Ballarat, I thought, or a church near Ballarat. Fowler was right. The Shining Knights were on the move.

I went back upstairs and ostentatiously slammed my bedroom door before descending again, this time in the throes of a manufactured coughing fit. I wanted to give Clutterbuck and his companion plenty of time to arrange their features into an approximation of bland sociability.

The living room door was open now, and a thickly bespectacled man in his late forties, with full jowls and hair the colour and dull sheen of axle grease, was walking towards the front door. No introductions were made. When I entered the living room Clutterbuck showed no sign of discomposure, or that he'd only moments before been speaking about blowing up St Patrick's Cathedral. He was his normal self, but I now saw that there was something about him that was unsettling and a little frightening. It had always been there, I realised, but I'd missed it. This was an unusual and uncharacteristic lapse in perceptiveness. I gave him Oakpate's message. He nodded and said that while he appreciated that I wasn't enthusiastic about the Knights, perhaps I'd tell Brian that he'd be welcome to join that evening's meeting.

'You're welcome, too, of course, but your scepticism won't go down too well, so I'd advise you to stay upstairs if you're going to be home.'

'Will Nigella be at this meeting?'

He laughed.

'Nigella and I don't discuss politics. Like sex, we're going to wait until after we're married.'

'I see. Well I hope you'll excuse me if I don't come.'

'That suits me fine. I want you to be doing something for me then anyway.'

I inwardly rebelled at being spoken to like an employee, although in truth that was precisely how Clutterbuck saw me.

'I want to know what Trezise is up to. I haven't heard from Anna, and Trezise's movements are of interest to the Knights.'

So he hadn't been told. It surprised me that Trezise hadn't mentioned Clutterbuck during what would undoubtedly have been a gruelling interview with the police. I'd given him Clutterbuck's name, unadvisedly — although I'd been cured of feeling guilty about this by recent revelations concerning his character. Perhaps Trezise didn't remember the name. It was far more likely, though, that the police were certain that they'd got their man, and any story he told about Anna Capshaw's ex-husband would be compromised by the fact that the police would be aware, with very little checking, that Anna Capshaw didn't have an ex-husband.

I couldn't tell Clutterbuck that the woman he'd sent to seduce Trezise was lying in the morgue without exposing my connection to James Fowler, and I had no intention of doing that. I agreed, therefore, to spend the evening tracking the incarcerated Trezise down. I thought I would go to the pictures instead, or the theatre, maybe. A lightweight bit of nonsense called *Robert's Wife* was playing at Her Majesty's. But I knew it would depress me to see second rate actors garnering applause for undemanding rubbish — and getting paid handsomely for it — so I scotched the theatre idea.

'How was lunch?' I asked.

'Lunch was fine. Nigella was a bit peeved that I hadn't told her about going to Ballarat, but she came round as she always does. I'm having dinner with her and her father this evening. I'm becoming quite one of the family.'

A little wave of self-satisfaction passed across his face, and I experienced a similar emotion when I considered that in all likelihood, in a very short time, Clutterbuck and his cronies would be locked up. Nigella would surely be grateful that I'd played some part in saving her from marriage to a fascist bully. I was anxious to get away from Clutterbuck as soon as I could. The less we saw of each other the better. My attitude towards him was hardening into a kind of contempt and the more time I spent with him, the more likely he would be to spot this.

'I'll start on Trezise now,' I said. 'He'll be at St Patrick's I imagine. I'll tag him for the rest of the day.'

'Nice building, St Patrick's. All that money.'

If he was hoping for an argument, I didn't oblige. I had no desire to get into a discussion which would provide him with a platform for the expression of his ugly philosophy — if his beliefs could be dignified by that term.

'I'll tell Brian about the meeting. He's more inclined to your way of thinking than I am.'

With that, I left and headed towards Mother's house.

I'd decided to telephone James Fowler from there, tell him what I'd overheard and tell him, too, about the gathering of the Knights that evening. I'd leave him with the impression that it would be me, and not Brian, who attended. This didn't seem too deceiving. I didn't think I was weaving a tangled web.

I didn't go out again after settling into Mother's house, but I helped in a desultory sort of way to weed the vegetable garden.

It gave me an opportunity to talk to Brian about that night's meeting. I stressed that Clutterbuck's cronies — certainly the ones that I'd met — were awful people, and that some of them, no doubt, had the fascist taste for violence, although I'd seen no evidence of this in Clutterbuck. Brian thought that the idea of blowing up St Patrick's Cathedral was laughable.

'It sounds to me like they're a bunch of Don Quixotes, more dotty than dangerous.'

The Scotch broth was excellent and afterwards Mother produced some first class brandy that had escaped use in Darlene's Comfort Fund fruitcakes. At nine-thirty Brian said he was going for a walk around the park while Mother and I chatted about Fulton and what he might be up to in Darwin. This was a topic that she could both happily and unhappily speculate upon for hours at a time, and in so doing she was not as likely to stray into one of her incidental analyses of my character. She went to bed finally, and felt less concerned I think about the danger Fulton was in for having spoken about it at uninterrupted length.

I intended to wait up until Brian returned from Clutterbuck's meeting, but when he still hadn't shown up at 2.00 a.m., I surrendered to sleep.

When I woke at seven, Brian had still not returned. I wasn't concerned, but I knew Mother would be, and as she'd retired last night in an almost euphorically exhausted state, induced by her unimpeded monologue about Fulton, it seemed a shame to wake her with worrying news. Her Fulton monologues didn't bother me at all, but her claim that her affection for her children was evenly distributed was patently untrue. I couldn't imagine her falling into a blissful sleep with my name on her lips.

I left her a note explaining that Brian and I had decided to go to the Melbourne Baths for an early morning swim. As this was something Brian did from time to time, she would be unsuspicious and remain pleasantly combobulated. I hurried across the park to Clutterbuck's house and found Brian asleep in my bed. The air was positively vaporous with whisky fumes. He'd obviously made a night of it. I shook him awake and the groans that issued from him were painful to hear. We went downstairs and I made him a cup of Clutterbuck's purloined coffee with cream. I told Brian that he should appreciate the fact that the entire American military establishment was now being used to cure his hangover. Before he could reply, Clutterbuck joined us, and, as usual, he showed no ill-effects from the previous night's drinking. I watched him closely, looking for any sign that Brian in his drunkenness had given us away. Clutterbuck seemed inordinately pleased with himself and, from the manner in which he put his arm around Brian's shoulder, clearly he thought he'd found in my brother a fellow fanatic. God knows what vile rubbish they'd spent the evening discussing.

'Your brother,' Clutterbuck said to me, 'is a good man.'

'By good, I presume you mean that his unsavoury views mesh with yours.'

'Get fucked, Will,' Brian said, with a completely convincing edge of detestation in his voice.

He pushed past me into the living room. Clutterbuck followed him and I stayed where I was. I'd find out soon enough from Brian what had transpired the night before. For now, he and Clutterbuck could continue to strengthen the bond between them under more sober conditions. I went up to my room and very carefully shaved. I took an unpatriotically deep bath, luxuriating in being able to put both arms under water. Perhaps it was the warmth of the water, or the freedom from that wretched plaster cast, or the pleasing knowledge that the Shining Knights had been infiltrated, but I felt for the first time in a very long time indeed, that God was in his Heaven and all was right with the world. By this hour the following morning God had changed his address, and chaos had been unleashed in my world.

Chapter Eleven

PIECES OF BRISKET

I DIDN'T SEE BRIAN for the remainder of that Tuesday. He and Clutterbuck went off somewhere together — probably, I thought, to that dank little Camelot up in Brunswick where they could hatch some vile plan in an appropriately vile atmosphere. Clutterbuck hadn't asked for any details about Trezise's movements, which surprised me, and the only way to account for it was the probability that something big was afoot.

Brian's absence meant that I didn't yet know what anti-Catholic outrages had been planned. When I was in possession of pertinent information I'd have to pass it on, of course, to James Fowler. Would I then tell him about Brian's unsanctioned role? I thought not. Having found in the past that the truth is more of an impediment than a lubricant to good relations, I opted for avoiding James Fowler altogether.

I spent the day wandering about the city, checking the theatres and despairing that the people of Melbourne were turning out in large numbers to hear Gladys Moncrieff sing, or queuing to see barely dressed showgirls stand stock still at the Tivoli (the rule being that any movement would transform an artistic tableau into something of interest to the police). I noticed in that day's *Age* that a production of *Othello* was being mounted by a group called the Art Theatre Players, but it had the air of amateur theatricals about it, and there are few things more dispiriting than Shakespeare's lines flattened, mangled and stuttered in characterless suburban vowels. Whenever my thoughts turned to such matters I felt a profound longing to get back on stage to reveal the exquisite beauty of properly read verse.

I returned to Mother's house at six o'clock and she told me that a man I assumed to be James Fowler had telephoned for me. I needed to catch up with Brian, who was having a bath, before talking to Fowler. As there was little chance of Mother hearing, or intruding upon, our conversation while he was in the bathroom, I sat on a chair over which his clothes were draped, and listened as he told me the Order of the Shining Knights' extraordinary plans.

'There seem to be only about eight of them,' he said. 'Last night that Oakpate bloke got hot under the collar about some other bloke's incompetent arson attempt near Ballarat. The arsonist then started yelling about second-rate equipment, and Clutterbuck had to come between them. Talk about a bunch of misfits. I'm surprised someone like Clutterbuck has anything to do with them.'

'I showed you his underwear drawer. He's a different kind of misfit — but he's a misfit, all right.'

I didn't want to give Brian the impression that I lacked confidence in him, but I needed to know if he'd been indiscreet under the influence of what had been rather a lot of alcohol. When I asked him he accepted the question without rancour, although he shifted uncomfortably in his shallow, tepid bath.

'I told Clutterbuck about Darlene and Captain Spangler Brisket, and I added for good measure that I thought Brisket was a Catholic. I think that was a good lie to tell. It certainly gave him the impression that I had good personal as well as professional reasons for hating popery.'

'So you didn't let anything slip?'

'Of course not. He trusts my hatred. No one held back at the meeting. They spoke openly in front of me about attacking St Patrick's, and today, Will, at Oakpate's house, Clutterbuck and a bloke called Crocker decided that what they'd do instead of blowing anything up was assassinate Archbishop Mannix.'

He delivered this plum with the enthusiasm of a little boy who knew he was pleasing an elder whose good opinion he craved. I couldn't wait to pass it on to James Fowler.

'Assassination is a more manageable abomination. How and when?'

'They haven't worked that out yet. They think he's the most dangerous man in Australia. They really do. Mannix is the face of everything they despise.'

I told Brian that I thought he'd done a good job and that I had to inform Fowler immediately.

Although it was close to six-thirty, Fowler answered the phone. Did he have a home to go to? I told him what I'd learned — withholding, of course, Brian's role in the collecting of information. He was disappointed that the details were vague, but I assured him that Archbishop Mannix's life was now officially in danger. Would he be told? Fowler thought not; at any rate, not yet. There was no point agitating the Catholic hierarchy until something more definite was known.

'The last thing we need,' he said, 'is priests thundering from pulpits about persecution.'

I returned to Clutterbuck's house just as he was cutting slices from a nut of corned beef. He offered me some and I took it, not having eaten. It was quite good, although Mrs Castleton — for it was she who had made it — had been too generous with the cloves and this is a flavour of which I've never been particularly fond. The meat itself was excellent, of a quality that was unobtainable except from the black market. We put the beef between buttered slices of good bread — Clutterbuck wouldn't stoop to using dripping — and washed it down with Ballarat Bitter — another commodity that was getting harder and harder to buy legally.

Nigella arrived soon afterwards and I went up to my room to read *Timon of Athens*, a play I'd long dreamt of producing. I had no desire to sit and watch Nigella and Clutterbuck bill and coo, knowing that for every coo there was a corresponding bill of a very different kind. I fell asleep in my clothes and didn't wake until the clanging of the telephone downstairs demanded to be picked up. It was 7.00 a.m., and the horrifying Wednesday was about to get underway.

I answered the telephone. It was Brian, and the fear and panic in his voice tumbled into my ear in an incoherent demand that I get over to Mother's house immediately.

'What's happened?' I asked, my own voice now taut with the contagion of alarm.

'Just get here,' he cried, and hung up.

I was already dressed, so I left Clutterbuck's at once and ran almost the full distance to Garton Street.

Mother was on the porch, wrapped in her nightgown and with an expression on her face that I'd never seen before. She was speechless, her eyes wide, but dulled by shock. I don't think she saw me, and didn't respond when I asked her if she was all right. I went into the house and found Brian pressed against the wall of the corridor leading to the kitchen. It was a strange and disconcerting attitude to strike, and it filled me with a kind of terror. I tried to speak but had to swallow first.

'What? What's happened here?'

Brian stared through me, and with a jolt was suddenly aware of my presence. He pulled himself together and led me into the kitchen. At first I saw nothing amiss. Then I saw them — four severed fingers and a thumb, lying on the bench.

'They were in the cutlery drawer,' Brian said. 'Mother found them.'

I walked over to the bench and looked down at them. They'd been severed cleanly. I noticed that the nails were well manicured.

'They're not Darlene's, are they?' Brian asked.

'Not unless she had hairy knuckles.'

Even in this bizarre situation I couldn't stop myself from suggesting that this didn't necessarily rule her out.

'Have you checked anywhere else in the house?'

Brian looked even more stricken; I don't think the possibility that other parts of this person might be scattered around had occurred to him. I pulled open the drawer under the cutlery drawer, expecting to find something grisly, but it contained nothing out of the ordinary.

It was Brian who found the next body part. In a saucepan on the stove top someone's right foot sat as if waiting for water and a *mire poix* to make a stock. A rapid search of cupboards turned up a left hand, and in the refrigerator, bloodied, unidentifiable viscera wrapped in yesterday's copy of the *Truth* newspaper.

Neither Brian nor I were capable of making any sense of this. We had no idea whose body this was. All we could surmise was that sometime in the night, someone had come into Mother's house and planted the butchered remains of an adult male. In a fog of revulsion and dread we left the kitchen to look in all the downstairs rooms. Brian went into the living room and I, having caught sight of something in the umbrella stand near the front door, approached this receptacle. Rammed among the brollies, and poised in a ghastly parody of them, was an entire left leg — from the hip bone down — the remainder of a right leg, and two, handless arms. I touched nothing, of course, and through my disbelief and dreamlike state of disconnection, I noticed principally that the cuts were clean, precise and surgical. Whoever had done this hadn't attacked the corpse in a frenzy. There was skill and deliberation in this dismemberment. The deliberation extended, I was certain, to the choice of Mother's house in which to distribute the carcass.

I was on the point of joining Brian when the front door flew open and detectives Strachan and Radcliff burst in, followed by three uniformed policemen. The umbrella stand immediately commanded their attention.

'Jesus Christ,' Strachan said, and one of the uniformed officers visibly blanched and hurriedly went outside, presumably to be ill. My eyes darted to the living room door, and this didn't escape the notice of Messrs Strachan and Radcliff. They pushed it open and there, in the middle of the room, stood Brian, a look of uncomprehending surprise on his face — a look that was mirrored on the startled face of Captain Spangler Brisket, whose severed head Brian held by his side.

'It fell out of the cupboard,' he said, as if this explained everything. This was entirely the wrong moment for Mother to push her way to the front, but she was a mistress of the wrong moment. She uttered a peculiar little cry and collapsed into a nearby chair. The remaining policemen were at Brian's side in a moment, and Radcliff took Brisket's head by the hair and lowered it to the floor, where it lay like a discarded stage prop. Strangely, nothing was said. We simply left the living room in a group, a policeman was stationed outside its door, I took Mother upstairs, and Brian was taken away.

I sat with Mother in silence. For the moment, words couldn't convey the enormity of what had happened downstairs. The house had been turned into an abattoir. Detective Strachan intruded upon our dumb contemplation by telling us that we were to remain where we were, and that a contingent of coppers would go over the house and try to locate all of Spangler Brisket's body parts.

'Like humpty dumpty,' I said. Strachan looked at me with distaste, as if this harmless remark were the most vulgar thing he'd ever heard. 'You've arrested Brian,' I added flatly.

'We've taken him in for questioning. He hasn't been arrested.'

'Do you really think he'd do this in his own house?'

Strachan sighed wearily and gave a surprising answer.

'No. For the moment though, he's our best bet. Unless you'd like to put your hand up.'

I looked at him with an unmistakable expression of utter contempt for his deductive abilities.

'Your arrival was very convenient,' I said.

'We were tipped off by an anonymous American serviceman who said we'd find the body of a Captain Spangler Brisket at this address. He also said that this Brisket had been having an affair with your brother's wife. Turns out Brian had threatened

Brisket's life just the other day.'

'That could only have come from Darlene.'

Strachan gave a noncommittal shrug.

'We're keeping an open mind. We do seem to be spending a lot of time at this house.'

Mother suddenly found her voice.

'Brian couldn't …'

'If you want my opinion, Mrs Power, I agree with you. This is the work of a deranged and violent person and your son just doesn't strike me that way. You'd have to agree, though, that we found him in something of a compromising position.'

'So ridiculously compromising,' I said, 'as to be almost a proof of his innocence.'

Strachan produced an insultingly pitying expression and wondered aloud if I mightn't like to keep quiet.

'An American army officer has been murdered and violated. The Americans aren't going to be too happy about that, and they're going to want a culprit, and they're going to want him now. They dealt with Leonski with ruthless speed, knowing full well what a disaster that was for relations with the Australians. They appeased the locals and they're going to demand a bit of *quid pro quo* on this one. I guarantee it.'

'They wouldn't sacrifice an innocent man,' I said.

'Leonski's going to hang in a few weeks time. It doesn't bother them that the man is insane. He's been killing Australian women and *that's* what matters. He has to die and the legal niceties of his mental state are ignored. Now, Brian had motive and opportunity, and issued a threat. They might be tempted to run with that. Tensions are pretty high between the Yanks and our soldiers. They're going to want to douse this before it really catches fire.'

Strachan made mollifying mutterings to the effect that he'd

try to ensure that the investigation stayed out of American hands as much as possible, and he reassured Mother that this time they'd be working to prove that Brian was innocent. I said nothing, believing it to be unwise to remind Strachan of his recent errors of judgement. I wanted to ask him if John Trezise had confessed to Anna Capshaw's murder, but I restrained myself, realising just in time that it would be foolish to establish a link between Trezise and me.

Mother and I sat in her small study for three hours while police downstairs put Spangler Brisket's body back together again, piece by bloody piece. Eventually detective Strachan told us that they'd found all of him.

'His torso was in the vegetable garden.'

We were told that it wouldn't be possible for us to remain in the house that night. It was a crime scene and we would have to vacate until it had been thoroughly investigated.

'That's fine,' Mother said. She'd reclaimed her verve. 'I can stay with Will, at least for tonight. I'm sure he'll find room.'

'There's plenty of room,' I said without thinking. I'd never expected Mother and Paul Clutterbuck would ever meet, and there was something perilous about this.

As we walked across the park — I was lugging a suitcase that Mother insisted contained only the bare essentials for a one night stay, but the weight of which suggested that the bare essentials included several bricks — I gave Mother a brief account of how things stood with Paul Clutterbuck. I left out any details that were pertinent to Army Intelligence's interest in him. I did hint that his politics weren't quite as liberal as her own and that politics wouldn't be a fruitful conversation starter.

When Mother finally met Clutterbuck, shortly after our arrival, he couldn't have been more charming. I took her bag up to my room — Clutterbuck said that there was a cot bed somewhere that I could set up in an empty spare room — and the two of them repaired to the living room where they began chatting as if they were picking up the threads of a conversation only recently abandoned. When I joined them I found Clutterbuck's brow knitted in empathetic distress as Mother related the horrible events of the morning.

'And poor Brian,' she was saying, 'the first time he was falsely accused was bad enough, but now this. You've met Brian, haven't you?'

'Yes. He's been here to see Will a couple of times. He certainly didn't strike me as the murderous type.'

Mother spoke rapidly, and as was always the case with her, the more she spoke, the calmer she became. Clutterbuck reassured her that there was really nothing to worry about with regard to Brian's being in custody. With the detectives on his side this time, he'd probably be released as soon as he'd been questioned . Mother was relieved to hear him say so, more relieved than when I'd said the very same thing — several times — barely an hour previously.

'You're more than welcome to stay here, Mrs Power, for as long as you need to. It will be no inconvenience at all. I imagine you're reluctant to go back to your house after, well, after that body was strewn about there.'

Mother thanked him, but said that she wasn't afraid of the dead and that there'd be stains to get out.

'Would Marlene have any reason to do something like this?'

'Darlene,' Mother said.

I expressed the view that it was unlikely that psychopathy was among her vast catalogue of personality defects, a moody pregnancy notwithstanding.

'She's quite capable of boring someone to death, and I wouldn't have been in the least surprised if Spangler had woken up next to her one morning and opted for suicide, but in the current situation the dismemberment rules that out.'

Under normal circumstances, such a remark would have prompted a sharp response from Mother, and I detected the automatic beginning of one, but she checked herself, realising, I suppose, that the days of leaping to Darlene's defence were over.

'I imagine Darlene is in a state of shock,' she said. 'She no doubt believes that Brian had something to do with Captain Brisket's death. I'm sure she'll realise how absurd this is.'

'Is there anybody else who'd want to put Brian in this terrible position?' Clutterbuck asked, and the obvious, disingenuous nature of the question — which Mother missed — indicated that Brian had told him about his affair with Sarah Goodenough in Maryborough. Without embarrassment or reticence, Mother sketched the facts of Brian's grim little adultery and its consequences. It was possible, she said, that Sarah Goodenough had an agent in Melbourne who was charged with harassing Brian, but it beggared belief that such a person would be licensed to kill and butcher an essentially innocent man — a man whose only crime was to fall in love with Darlene.

'And that,' Mother said firmly, 'is not a crime.'

'Just a gross error of taste,' I said.

'So the only person who has done anything even remotely similar in the way of setting Brian up, is Darlene,' Clutterbuck said gently. 'I wonder if this is a double blind. What if this Spangler Brisket was deliberately chosen to be nothing more than a convenient victim. What if there's a third man, the real father of Darlene's baby and the real object of her attention.'

'Darlene bakes fruitcakes,' I said. 'Reading the recipe is as close as she's ever come to literature. She wouldn't have the nous to execute such a slippery plot.'

'She mightn't,' he said, 'but what about her partner?'

'Look like the innocent flower, but be the serpent under't,' I said.

I could tell from the rigidity of Mother's posture that Clutterbuck's hypothesis had run through her like an electric charge. She'd just that morning opened the cutlery drawer and found four severed fingers and a thumb. This was bound to affect her sense of what was or wasn't outlandish, and what Clutterbuck had said wasn't outlandish at all — not to me, and not to Mother either.

'Oh, my goodness,' was all she said.

By the time Mother was settled in Clutterbuck's house it was past midday. She'd contacted her solicitor, Peter Gilbert, so she knew that Brian's interests were protected. She was surprisingly sanguine about his removal for questioning, as if the shock of the first time around couldn't be repeated. It was also remarkable how rapidly she seemed to have assimilated the awful desecration of her house. She'd never been superstitious though, and had always insisted that the dead were just that — dead. The idea that they could annoy the living was primitive nonsense. She thought about religion in much the same way.

'Churches,' I remember her saying when I was quite young, 'are places where people with no common sense gather to express their stupidity. It makes them feel better to know that there are lots of other people as silly as they are.'

Clutterbuck suggested that we join him and Nigella for lunch at a café in Collins Street, and he took the extravagant step of driving us there.

'You have to eat,' he said, 'and it might take your mind off things.'

His Studebaker, unencumbered by the ugly charcoal burner attached to the back of so many vehicles, drew attention to itself by virtue of its sparkling duco, polished to a high sheen that made any car near it seem grubby and shabby. He parked out the front of the café and hurried round to open Mother's door, as if she were a dowager empress. I'm afraid she's prone to taking enormous delight in such old-world etiquette, and Clutterbuck's manners were impeccable. A polite fanatic always says 'excuse me' before pulling the trigger.

When Nigella arrived she did so with her brother in tow. Clutterbuck made a good show of being pleased to see him, and James took a well-acted moment to recall that he'd met me at afternoon tea the week before. They were, of course, enthralled by Mother's version of the morning's discoveries. James Fowler listened with the air of a man hearing decent gossip, and Nigella uttered small gasps at appropriate junctures. I could tell that behind Fowler's bland response a great deal of agitation was lurking.

When Mother told them about Clutterbuck's theory, they both nodded and said that it was so clever it must be true. I was glad that I hadn't told James about Brian's being my eyes and ears among the Shining Knights. If he'd known this he might have leapt to an unfortunate conclusion about Brisket's murder, and regretted trusting me with this sensitive task. He did catch my eye at one point, and I detected the slightest narrowing of the lids, indicating I think, no more than that he was pleased with the ease with which he and Clutterbuck were speaking. Clutterbuck was never guilty of an unguarded action, and his complete absence of suspicion as to James Fowler's real position reassured me that Brian and I had been successful in establishing a usefully ambiguous relationship with him and his unsavoury Knights.

The meal was filthy, even for these straitened times. No one commented on this — the lamentable state of Melbourne's kitchens now being an accepted part of daily life. The conversation became more general, with Clutterbuck asking Fowler if the natives under his jurisdiction were becoming restless, and Nigella complimenting Mother on her dress. My eyes strayed around the dim café and settled on a startling poster affixed to the wall opposite me. A top-hatted, big-toothed, short-sighted, Japanese gentleman sat in a rickshaw being pulled by an obviously decent, Australian man in striped shirt, suit and sensible hat. Behind them rose Flinders Street Station, its face marred by Japanese lettering above the clocks, and the Rising Sun fluttering from the dome. A tram trundled evocatively to one side. 'A united, fighting mad Australia can never be enslaved!' screamed the tag. 'Beaufort bombers are the key to victory!'

'Did someone in your department come up with that?' I asked Nigella.

She turned to look at it and couldn't contain a charming chuckle.

'It's good, isn't it,' she said, 'in a hideous kind of way.'

The poster seemed to give Mother something of a fright, and she closed her hand over Nigella's arm and asked, 'You don't really think they'll come to Melbourne, do you?'

'I'd like to say no, Mrs Power, but we've spent most of the war underestimating them, to our cost. Anything is possible.'

This wasn't a comforting answer, but I could see that Mother appreciated Nigella's frankness. I knew that she'd embrace her as a daughter-in-law without hesitation. Nigella's intelligence was self-evident, and she lacked Darlene's bovine complacency. My marrying Nigella was hardly a foregone conclusion, of course, and even though I knew that Clutterbuck's exposure as a member of a vicious circle of misfits would be accomplished soon enough, Nigella's insistently proprietorial attitude to him was discouraging. She touched him again and again, and drank from his water glass. No one watching would have doubted that intimacy of some kind existed between them.

'Oh, Will,' Nigella said suddenly, 'I've got a small acting job for you, if you're interested.'

'Well, yes, of course,' I said unthinkingly. There are some things I'm not prepared to do, especially if they stray too far from the notion that acting is an art.

'We're filming one of our information shorts tomorrow afternoon, and we're looking for someone to play the sort of male lead. It's really quite straightforward and the pay is good.'

Nigella briefly outlined what passed for the plot of this short film. When all was said and done I was to play an air force chap who gets on to a tram and is very pleased to be confronted by a female trammie. I had no dialogue, but Nigella said that she thought she had enough influence to get the narration job for me.

'Jack Davey doesn't have to do them all,' she said, referring to the ubiquity of Davey's voice on propaganda reels.

I was actually pleased to accept the job, not only because I quite liked the idea of hearing my voice intoning jolly, morale-boosting pap from the cinema screen — or, if more narration came my way, dire warnings of impending invasion — but because the work would almost certainly bring me closer to Nigella.

'So what do I need to do?'

'I'll give you the script after lunch, and we'll meet tomorrow at Henry Buck's in Swanston Street. They've agreed to fit out our man with an air force uniform. It's much more photogenic than the army uniform, don't you think?'

'Indeed. Do you want me there early?'

'No, we're not filming until after lunch, which is convenient for me. I've got my drawing class at ten.'

When she said this my stomach lurched and my heart sank. Was tomorrow Thursday already? I'd promised Mr Wilks that I'd pose for him, and when I'd made that promise Thursday had seemed an age away. I couldn't let him down, having no desire to antagonise anyone even remotely connected with Gretel Beech. Even though I have an actor's indifference to personal modesty, the prospect of standing exposed and examined before the object of my as yet unreciprocated affection was not one I could face with anything approaching equanimity. I wouldn't have minded if we were already lovers — the gaze of the matrons who were her drawing class mates was of no consequence to me — but as things stood I felt at a considerable disadvantage. The element of surprise was all on her side.

A solution presented itself when I heard Clutterbuck comfort Mother with an unfounded reassurance that he was certain that Brian would be released from custody before nightfall. Brian. Brian could take my place in Mr Wilks's class. I'd have to explain to him that you couldn't expect to work for Army Intelligence and not be required to do some odd things. Look at Mata Hari and what she'd been willing to do. At least he wasn't being asked to sleep with any of the matrons. I thought that he'd take some persuading and possibly a hefty amount of cash. If he refused I'd be in a bind, so I'd have to proceed on the principle that whatever his state of mind after his interrogation, refusal was not an option. My determination had to secure his acquiescence.

After lunch we all walked to Nigella's office, which was little more than a flimsy, temporary structure in the grounds behind Parliament House. It seemed peculiar to me that neither James nor Nigella, both of whom were doing what I thought was important work, had decent space in which to do that work. I suppose all the ritzy offices were the demesne of pompous, career public servants who didn't do anything, but who had come to expect that they'd have elegant rooms in which not to do it. I fell back on our way up to Nigella's office and managed to say a few words to James Fowler.

'I hope you don't think all this business with my brother compromises my intelligence work.'

'Not at all. Your mother and Clutterbuck seem to get along very well.'

'Mother doesn't share his views,' I hastened to assure him. 'She only met him this morning and he's gone out of his way to charm her socks off.'

'That's good, Will. It might be a way of showing you some loyalty, of letting you know that he trusts you.'

This was a reasonable supposition for Fowler to make, but I knew it was wide of the mark. If Clutterbuck was showing loyalty to anyone, it was to Brian.

✒

Back at Clutterbuck's, Mother composed her daily letter to Fulton.

'You'll have plenty to write about today,' I said.

'Oh no. When I write to Fulton I'm like a one woman propaganda ministry. I won't have him worrying about us. He can be cross with me for keeping things from him later.'

We had the house to ourselves. Clutterbuck had dropped us at the door and continued elsewhere, up to Oakpate's house in Brunswick probably, where their plan to assassinate Archbishop Mannix was taking shape.

Mother retired for an afternoon nap and I lay on my bed and

read the script Nigella had given me. She'd warned me that it was set in concrete, that it had been approved and that not a word would now be changed. I read: *Women tram conductors have replaced trammies, and are the citizens glad of it! Smart and trim, they're a credit to their city which expects to heavily increase its tram traffic immediately! Tram travelling now has ooomph!*

At this point the script called for a shot of an air force man waiting at a tram stop. He boards. *He's up in the air about it. They don't say mind the curves any more, but you'd better just the same!*

Drivel; pure, unmitigated drivel, which I was to deliver with all the faux cheeriness I could muster. Still, I'd bring what I could to the part of the air force officer, putting in a bit of business — perhaps even suggesting something of the doomed airman as counterpoint to the vulgar narration.

Nigella had slipped in another job for me, and a note: 'We need you to record this at the same time as the other one. It won't take any time at all, and you'll be paid separately for it, of course.'

This propaganda gem featured women painting army vehicles, and as they smilingly daubed the chassis I was to intone: *Their knowledge of camouflage — a woman's secret weapon — is useful in this sort of work. It's grease instead of hand lotion, lubricant instead of lipstick, for these ladies of little leisure.*

It wasn't exactly 'Once more unto the breech', and I knew that whatever dignity I could impart to it would be undercut by the ludicrous, rollicking music that invariably accompanied these shorts. The only satisfaction to be derived from the job was financial, and I'd use the money to pay Brian to take his clothes off for Mr Wilks' ladies.

Brian was set free late that Wednesday afternoon. He came, as arranged, to Clutterbuck's house accompanied by Mother's solicitor, Peter Gilbert. Brian didn't look haggard or drawn. He said that the police had been quite pleasant, that they genuinely believed that Spangler Brisket had been carved up elsewhere and delivered piecemeal to Garton Street — a cursory examination of the body had convinced the police pathologist that it had done most of its bleeding at a different location. He told us that there'd been an American military policeman present during the interview, and while he'd seemed more hostile than Strachan or Radcliff, he'd accepted their general assessment of the situation. It was their belief that the manner of Captain Brisket's death pointed to someone with a long held antipathy towards him — a rage against him that had built and built over an extended period of time. This meant that whoever killed him, also knew something about his private life. Brisket's friends and associates at Camp Murphy — the American army camp set up at Melbourne Cricket Ground — were also being investigated.

Brian's position, as the offended husband of the woman Brisket had taken up with, naturally provided a ready-made suspect. I was waiting for Mother to postulate Clutterbuck's theory about Darlene's possible involvement, but she was silent on this point, I think because she believed that despite all that Darlene had done, and despite Brian's recent, obscene description of her, he wasn't yet ready to hear her characterised as a cold-blooded killer, or killer's accomplice. I certainly wasn't going to provoke him by mentioning the theory, not when I had to convince him to model the next morning.

Peter Gilbert told Mother that the police had finished at Garton Street and that she could return there at her convenience. He was willing, even eager, I suspected, to stay the night. Mother thanked him and to my surprise said that yes, it would be lovely if he stayed the night. I looked at Brian to try to gauge from his expression whether Peter Gilbert was a regular overnight visitor. He studiously avoided my eye, which I took to mean that this was a piece of information he'd deliberately held out on giving me.

Peter Gilbert went upstairs to help Mother pack, and forgetting for the moment that I needed Brian on side, I asked him, a bit peevishly, why he thought it wasn't worth mentioning that Mother had taken a lover.

'I wasn't sure you'd approve,' he said.

'I'm not a prude, Brian.'

'No, but you can be a bit priggish, and besides, it's Mother's business, and if she wanted you to know before now she'd have told you herself. It wasn't my place to gossip about her private life.'

'The fact that our mother is conducting an affair isn't gossip Brian. It's news. There is a difference.'

Brian shrugged. 'Anyway, now you know.'

Further consideration of my mother's private life would have to wait. There were more urgent matters to be addressed. I told Brian that when Mother and Gilbert came down with the luggage he should say that he wanted to stay and talk to me. He agreed, thinking, no doubt, that we'd be discussing the Order of the Shining Knights and what our next move would be. After Peter Gilbert had helped Mother into his car, and after I assured her that I'd thank Clutterbuck profusely for his hospitality, he drove her home to Garton Street, and the stains which she'd set about removing immediately. At the front gate of Clutterbuck's house I told Brian that I had a straightforward but demanding job for him.

'You'll never have been asked to do anything like this before. It's not dangerous; it's Army Intelligence at its most obtuse, but it's terribly, terribly important. Are you up for it?'

'Of course. If it's not dangerous, how hard could it be?'

I told him exactly what he'd be required to do. He baulked, and wanted to know what posing naked for a posse of old ladies had to do with Army Intelligence, and why I couldn't do it if it was so bloody hush hush and important. I was able to tell him, with pleasing truthfulness, that I had in fact already done it. And that the only reason I wasn't doing it again was on account of Paul Clutterbuck's fiancée being among the art students — the only one under the age of fifty. I hadn't known her at the time, but now that I'd met her, she might think it odd if I turned up again in her class.

'I don't know whether she's involved in the Knights or not,' I lied, 'but I don't want her expressing any suspicions about me to Clutterbuck.'

Maintaining my policy of holding small bits of information back, I told Brian that her name was Nigella, but didn't tell him that she was the sister of my contact in Army Intelligence, the man he knew of only as Jim.

'Mother met Nigella at lunch today,' I said. 'I'm sure she'll confirm that she's Clutterbuck's fiancée. I want you to take careful note of who else is in that drawing class. I'm sure it's a front for something.'

'What if this Nigella woman twigs that I'm your brother?'

'Why would she? We don't look that much alike and you'll use a false name.'

'And speak, maybe, with a slight foreign accent.'

Brian's *Boy's Own* sense of adventure bubbled over and it was evident that I wouldn't have to tempt him with payment.

'I could be Ziggy Swiebodsinski, a Polish-Jewish émigré,

living in Carlton. I can do that accent perfectly.'

It was true. Brian could do a vowel perfect Polish accent. His closest friend growing up had been the son of one of the Jewish families who'd moved to Carlton in the twenties.

'All right,' I said. 'That's a good idea. Even if Nigella thinks she sees a family resemblance the accent will throw her off.'

'So what am I looking for?'

'I'm not sure, but pay particular attention to the woman who owns the house you'll be going to. Her name is Lady Bailey. I'm pretty sure she's a fifth columnist of some sort.'

Brian swallowed this nonsense hungrily, so that by the time we'd finished talking he couldn't wait to get to the house in East Melbourne, introduce himself as my replacement, and tear his clothes off. I almost felt guilty about gulling him so effectively. Almost.

Like the changing of the guard, Brian had barely left when Clutterbuck arrived home. He was excited about something but said it was the sort of thing that would appeal more to Brian than to me, so it was a pity Brian was in custody. When I said that he'd been released Clutterbuck seemed taken aback for a moment, then said that he wanted to contact him urgently.

'I've got something that'll take his mind off his troubles. A bit of fun.'

'Is it anything to do with the Knights?'

'You're more than welcome to join us, Will, you know that.'

I waved his invitation away, but changed my mind when I realised that whatever Clutterbuck's plans with the Knights were, they would involve lawlessness of some kind, and if Brian was to be a part of it, he might be at risk either of injury or arrest, or disabling drunkenness. Any or all of these possibilities threatened his ability to stand in for me the next day. He'd need a chaperone, and if this meant tagging along at whatever vulgar entertainment had been planned, then so be it.

'All right,' I said. 'I'm curious enough to find out what your idea of a good night out is to join you.'

He lifted his eyes and widened them in exaggerated surprise.

'We're honoured,' he said facetiously. 'Perhaps you'll enjoy it so much you'll want to fight the good fight after all.'

'I think you know, Paul, that your idea of the good fight and my idea of the good fight are not quite the same thing.'

With the infuriating condescension of the blindly committed he said, 'One day, Will, you'll come to understand who the real enemy is.'

I was about to say something about despising his methods but I had to preserve the illusion that I didn't know about them.

'We're meeting here at nine o'clock. Just a few of us, and we're just going to take it from there.'

That colourless expression wasn't being used to indicate an evening of backgammon. I was nervous about what I might be getting into, but was confident that the evening's entertainment wasn't to be the assassination of Archbishop Mannix. I knew that that was as yet only a vague plan, or rather a vague notion that might never go beyond the bravado given expression in a dark, run-down house in Brunswick. I imagined that the night's excitement would amount to daubing slogans on a church or presbytery wall. I could tolerate being witness to that, so long as I wasn't asked to take part in the vandalism. Brian, on the other hand, would be quite willing to enter into it with gusto, partly because he knew it would strengthen his ties to the Knights and to Clutterbuck, and partly because the whole Army Intelligence exercise had uncovered in him a real pleasure in transgression.

When I rang Brian to tell him that the Knights were to be engaged in what for them passed as a social event, he was eager to join in. He was less enthusiastic about my coming along, as if my mere presence would put a dampener on his fun. I pointed out that the presence of someone they didn't fully trust might act as a brake on their actions and prevent anyone from going too far. They wouldn't want a witness to anything seriously illegal or criminal. It would also give us both some idea about the kind of people we were dealing with. I suspected it would confirm my belief that the Order of the Shining Knights was all ugly, adolescent, secret-society talk, and no action. I believed that they'd do something minor and silly, and probably unpleasant, and then talk about it for weeks afterwards as if it had threatened the fabric of society.

At nine o'clock, in Clutterbuck's living room, six men, including me, were fortifying themselves with whisky. Ronnie Oakpate limped back and forth and, as always, resembled an angry, deformed pongid; Crocker spoke to Clutterbuck, and Crocker's small head bobbed forward and backwards on his absurdly broad shoulders; Brian was talking to a man I'd never seen before — a man who bore an uncanny resemblance to Herr Goebbels. He was wiry and rat-like, and smoothed his hair continually in response to an obsessive vanity which must have told him that it had shifted in some unflattering way between swipes. He had the air of a man who'd spent his childhood torturing small animals. Clutterbuck was resplendent in his American serviceman's uniform. He looked even more fiercely well-groomed than he usually did, and I caught the waft of an expensive cologne. I idly wondered whether Oakpate might be encouraged to splash some on himself, or maybe gargle with it.

Nobody spoke to me, reinforcing their sense of me as an outsider. If they seriously resented my presence, though, they were disciplining their expression of it, being content to ignore me.

Both Brian and I were still in the dark about the nature of the night's program. I approached Brian and the poor-man's Goebbels and tried to insinuate myself into their conversation. In keeping with the role Brian was playing he reluctantly and dismissively introduced me to his cadaverous new chum, whose name was MacGregor, and who spoke, unexpectedly, with a Scottish burr.

I was rescued from the awkwardness of making small talk by Clutterbuck's announcement that it was time to be on our way. I couldn't miss the shiver of excitement that passed through Clutterbuck's three acolytes, and I suddenly began to feel that I'd made a terrible mistake in deciding to be involved in this. The charge in the air was too electric to have been generated by an impending bout of graffiti writing. Something of a very different order was in the wind.

We filed out into Bayles Street, now dark under a cloud-covered sky. Clutterbuck had a partly masked torch which we followed like overgrown moths. No instructions were given but it was understood that we were to proceed in silence — up Bayles Street towards Royal Parade, along which an occasional car travelled. When we reached it we turned left, and crossed Degraves Street. A pool of nausea in the pit of my stomach began to bubble and plop as I realised we were headed towards St. Carthage's Catholic church.

Unusually for a church, it was built right up to the pavement, with no forecourt. Its front door, closed and locked, was just a few feet from the traffic. We stopped, and Clutterbuck switched off his torch. He reached into his pocket and withdrew a small, glass bottle which he passed to MacGregor. He knelt before MacGregor and threw his head back. MacGregor pulled the stopper from the bottle and slowly poured its dark contents onto Clutterbuck's face, so that it ran in rivulets from his forehead down onto his cheeks and into the collar of his uniform. He kept pouring until Clutterbuck's features were all but obscured. The torch was shone briefly onto Clutterbuck's face and I couldn't disguise my sharp intake of breath at the sight of so much blood. MacGregor nodded with satisfaction. Clutterbuck stood, and in the dim light I saw his perfect teeth revealed in what could only have been a smile. I was sure that Brian was as alarmed as I was about what was going to happen next. Clutterbuck's bloodied face wasn't for our benefit.

A narrow walkway separated the church from the double-storeyed terrace on its left. Clutterbuck pushed open the terrace's iron gate and knocked urgently on the door. When it wasn't immediately opened he hammered again. This time I heard the click of the locked being disengaged and it opened. There was the faintest of lights from deep in the house, sufficient to palely illuminate the gory face that confronted the priest who'd answered the knock.

'Please, Father,' said Clutterbuck in an American accent, 'I've been cut up real bad.'

He fell forward against the door jam, almost into the priest's arms. It looked, from where I was standing, as if the priest was trying to hold Clutterbuck up. In one deft movement, Clutterbuck was behind him, his forearm pressed into his throat, gagging any sound.

'That thing pressing in your back isn't my cock, Father, it's a gun, so don't get excited. Now you just do what I tell you or bits of your spine will end up on the other side of Royal Parade. Have you got a key to the church on you?'

The priest must have nodded because Clutterbuck shoved him towards us. As they came closer I could see that the priest was a young man, perhaps in his late twenties, and his eyes were wide with uncomprehending fear. There was nothing of the stoic martyr about him — he was just a young bloke scared out of his wits. Oakpate, Crocker and MacGregor were careful to keep their faces turned away. Neither Brian nor I thought to do the same until it was too late. Even though it was dark, the priest could probably have made out our features. Clutterbuck propelled him swiftly towards the door of the church, and in a matter of seconds it had been opened and we were all inside, with the heavy door closed behind us. Clutterbuck pushed the young priest roughly up the aisle, his cassock making a flapping noise that was strangely amplified by the space. We followed dumbly.

On either side of the small interior were five tall windows of clear glass which gathered all the available light and dispersed it thinly through the church. This light died when it reached the wooden ceiling so that I couldn't tell how high it rose above us. The only other light was the red, flickering candle of the sanctuary lamp hanging above the altar, before which Clutterbuck had unceremoniously dumped the priest. Clutterbuck must have struck him because he lay quite still. Oakpate, Crocker and MacGregor each came forward and delivered a brutal kick to the priest's body. Without waiting to be prompted, Brian did the same, although I'm certain his kick didn't land forcefully. Each of the others had been accompanied by a sickening thud. There was no noise from Brian's blow. No one commented on this — they were obviously too wrapped up in the exhilaration of their violence to notice.

Clutterbuck stood back from the prone form at the foot of the altar. I thought he was preparing to land his own kick. Until this evening I'd have thought that he'd be disdainful of committing violence himself. That sort of savagery was best left to underlings.

'This meeting of the Order of the Shining Knights is now in session,' he said, 'and we have here a very special guest — a man in a dress.'

He leaned down and rolled the priest onto his back. The priest groaned and instinctively rolled onto his side and drew his knees up to his chest. Clutterbuck repeated his action, placed his foot on the priest's chest and told him that if he moved again, he'd put a bullet through his left eye, the specificity of the threat making it somehow more potent.

'Blindfold him,' said Crocker from the shadows. Clutterbuck grabbed the hem of the priest's cassock and tore from it a strip of cloth with which he bound his eyes. He then lifted another part of the cassock and using it as a rag, wiped his face clean. Now Crocker, Oakpate and MacGregor came forward and stood around the priest, who so far hadn't uttered a sound, apart from moans and whimpers. Oakpate giggled and said, 'Should I piss on him?'

'I wouldn't piss on him if he was on fire,' Clutterbuck said. 'How about you, Brian?'

'Waste of piss.'

The hollow acoustic in the church disguised the lack of conviction in Brian's voice.

A sudden burst of brilliant moonlight feebly illuminated the two narrow, stained-glass windows in the wall behind the altar. I looked up at the subtle change in intensity of the light. The window on the left was a representation of St Carthage — whoever he was — and the one on the right was of St Therese, of whom I'd vaguely heard. I was concentrating on the windows because the spectacle of Clutterbuck and his cronies standing over the injured body of the young priest was becoming unbearable. I wanted to flee but I couldn't leave Brian alone in a situation like this. I also wanted the priest to say something, to protest at this outrage, but he remained dumbly terrified, unless of course one of those kicks had so wounded him that speech was impossible.

'What'll we do with him?' MacGregor asked.

In response, Clutterbuck held out his hand to Oakpate who produced from his coat a flask. Clutterbuck took it and emptied its contents onto the priest's garments.

'Auto da fé,' he said. 'Welcome to the Order, Brian. If you'll do the honours.'

He gave Brian a box of matches and no further instructions were necessary. It was clear that Brian was expected to put a match to whatever inflammable liquid had been splashed over the cassock. The priest knew now what was imminent, and he made an attempt to stand. He was pummelled back to the ground and a handkerchief was unnecessarily stuffed into his mouth.

I was paralysed with horror. There wasn't sufficient light to see the expression on Brian's face clearly. It's a big leap from schoolteacher to priest burner, and he must have been in turmoil. Would carrying out this atrocity — and it was something from which he'd never recover — serve the greater good of preventing the assassination of Archbishop Mannix? If he refused he would have no further access to the Order of the Shining Knights. If he struck a match he would be their creature forever — we would all be witnesses. Was this the case with each of the others? Had each of them committed a grave crime under watchful eyes?

I had slipped into a kind of anaesthetised reverie, retreating from the reality before me. I was brought out of it by the scrape of a match along the striking board and the flare of bright fire at its tip. Brian's face was lit for a moment with the brilliance of a klieg lamp and he was staring down at the priest fiercely, as if he was blaming the young man for putting him in this impossible position. He then dropped the match onto the wet cassock and I cried out, expecting the 'woomph' of exploding gasoline. There was no 'woomph.'

The cassock became decorated with flickering tongues of blue fire, and there was the smell of burning cotton. The priest began ripping the cassock from his body and nobody stopped him. By the time he'd thrown it to the floor the flames had burnt themselves out. Clutterbuck had made a poor choice of combustible liquid. The priest now stood, blindfolded still, and with the handkerchief still in his mouth, shivering, despite his black woollen trousers and white shirt. Clutterbuck removed the gag, and maintaining his American accent, said, 'You make a crappy martyr, buddy.'

MacGregor stepped forward and punched the priest first in the groin and then in the side of the head. He fell unconscious to the ground.

'Time to leave,' Clutterbuck said. 'Our work here is done.'

Clutterbuck had gone upstairs to change. Oakpate and Crocker had gone home, citing early starts the next morning. MacGregor sat with Brian and me, his face flushed either with whisky or with the almost post-coital heat of lust satisfied.

'Serves him right,' he said. 'A good punch in the balls isn't going to matter to someone like him, is it?'

Clutterbuck returned, his face washed and his hair neatly combed. He was wearing a bathrobe over his pyjamas. Once I might have thought this elegant. Now I thought he looked like a pale, pale imitation of Noël Coward.

'Shall I explain?' he asked me.

'Attempted murder doesn't really require much in the way of explanation.'

'You have a tendency to exaggerate, Will. No one was in any danger of dying tonight.'

I spluttered my disbelief.

'Only because your fuel wasn't good enough.'

Clutterbuck laughed.

'The fuel was perfect.' He paused to let that sink in. 'I'm not a murderer, Will.'

'You're not seriously going to rationalise what happened tonight.'

'Oh, for heaven's sake. The priest was roughed up a bit, that's all. He can offer it up to the suffering souls in Purgatory, so a good time was had by all. He'll have a few bruises and a story to tell, and by the time he's finished telling it he'll be the hero who wrestled some Yankee anti-Christ and won.'

'So it was all just a bit of fun, was it? Scaring someone witless and beating him up is your idea of a good night's entertainment.'

'It's a bit like high melodrama, Will. It's not everyone's cup of tea, but it isn't without a point.'

'And the point is?'

Clutterbuck settled into a chair and swung one knee over the other.

'The point is that Brian proved himself a worthy member of the Order tonight. We needed to know where his loyalties lay, and as he was prepared, without argument, to drop a lighted match onto what he thought was a highly inflammable priest, I think his loyalty's been well proven. From the priest's point of view, and maybe even from Brian's, I suppose you could argue that it was attempted murder. Neither of them knew that the liquid was pure alcohol or that it would burn itself out without doing too much damage. More of a flambé than anything else. I was careful not to get it on the priest's skin, although I don't deny I was tempted. We had you there for security, Will. My fellow Knights argued that because I'd introduced you to them you might at some stage decide to talk to the wrong people about us. We thought you'd be less likely to do this if it meant implicating your brother in something which an unsympathetic policeman might construe as violence with menaces, or worse, and as you were present and did nothing, I don't think young Father Arsehole, or whatever he's called, will be offering you absolution if it ever came to a prosecution.'

'You already knew I wouldn't say anything.'

'It's always good to make assurance doubly sure, and now that both you and Brian are nicely woven into the fabric of our little group we can all rest peacefully.'

Brian, who'd been grinning in an effective rendition of a well-stroked and well-pleased village idiot, suddenly dropped his carefully managed persona and asked with real concern, 'What do you mean, Will? How does Paul know that you'll say nothing?'

Fortunately, neither MacGregor nor Clutterbuck noticed the shift in his demeanour.

'Nothing,' I said. 'Just that I'd already told Paul that I wasn't interested in what his group did, and that I certainly wasn't interested in reporting their activities to the police.'

Clutterbuck could have chosen this moment to tell Brian about Gretel Beech, but he settled for saying, 'Will and I have an understanding. And now I think we should discuss how and when Brian and Will are going to kill Archbishop Daniel Mannix.'

Chapter Twelve

THE UNEXPECTED VISITOR

IT WAS MACGREGOR'S VOICE that intruded upon the silent world into which I'd fallen. I think the shock of Clutterbuck's casual confidence that we'd do as instructed had the physical effect of briefly cutting off my air, and I must have blacked out. MacGregor was on his feet and patting Brian's shoulder, when a few seconds ago he'd been sitting exhibiting the odd, rodent-like twitch that jumped around his mouth and making regular infinitesimal adjustments to his hair.

'All the honour will be yours,' MacGregor was saying.

'Well then, I don't want to share it with Will.'

He managed to sound both surly and proud of the honour being accorded him. It was a remarkable performance, and one which even I would have had difficulty carrying off. The more Brian said, the more certain I was that he'd make a very fine actor indeed.

'You can do the deed, Brian, but we'll need Will there to support you and to help you get away safely,' Clutterbuck said. 'You won't have to get your hands dirty, Will.'

'You know, Paul, you have a very strange moral sense. Just because I don't have to pull the trigger doesn't mean I'm not implicated.'

'Now you're getting into philosophy. We'll be here all night if we go down that path.'

In an effort to elicit more information, I decided to play along.

'And while we're busy assassinating the most famous cleric in Australia, where will the brave members of your Order be?'

'Now you're sounding snippy. We will, of course, be in church that day, praying hard for your success — the same church where Mannix will go to his eternal reward.'

'You want Brian to kill Mannix in St Patrick's Cathedral?'

'Can you think of a more appropriate place?'

'He stood up and sonorously declaimed, 'Will no one rid me of this meddlesome priest?'

MacGregor laughed sycophantically.

'It's been an exciting night,' said Clutterbuck. 'I think we should all go to bed now and think about Sunday's assassination.'

'Sunday?'

'No time like the present, Will. Nine o'clock mass. The main attraction. Mannix will be there, the choir will be yodelling away. It will be beautiful. He's a very tall man and he'll fall very picturesquely at the altar, all those expensive robes flowing around him. Very Thomas à Becket.'

'I'm going home,' said Brian. MacGregor said the same and they both got up to leave.

'I'd drive you to your respective homes,' Clutterbuck said, 'but I don't want to. Too tired.'

'I'll walk with you,' I said to Brian. 'I think Mother would appreciate having us both in the house tonight.'

'That's a good idea,' said Clutterbuck. 'You have much to discuss.'

As I passed him on my way out he put his hand on my forearm and said, 'Don't imagine you can stop this from happening, Will. If you did manage to get Brian to change his mind, I'm afraid I'd have to call on you to deal with Mannix, and the body of a young woman currently resting peacefully in the Carlton Cemetery might make an awkward reappearance if you refused.'

I didn't disabuse Clutterbuck of his belief that he had me over a barrel by telling him that Gretel's killer was already in custody, and his confession was inevitable. I manufactured fearful resignation and simply said that Brian was sufficiently deranged to render him unreachable, and that Clutterbuck could have every confidence in his insane willingness to murder an innocent man.

'If you knew anything at all about the extent of Catholic espionage in this country you couldn't possibly accept that Mannix is anything other than a criminal and a traitor. He is the worst of men; a boil that has to be lanced.'

His grip on my arm tightened as he spoke, and his face reddened. I caught a glimpse then of the man he truly was, and I knew without a doubt that no amount of money would protect Nigella from the rages he'd express in private. I must have felt an overwhelming need for a small victory over him because I suddenly told him that Anna Capshaw was dead and that John Trezise had been arrested for her murder. He relaxed his grip on my arm, and said, 'You were saving that up, were you, for just the right moment?'

'No time like the present, Paul.'

I could tell that the news had shocked him. His face became blank, in readiness, I think, for an upsurge of emotion. Whether

Anna Capshaw was his ex-wife or not, clearly he was attached to her in some profound way. I couldn't allow myself to feel any sympathy for him. If I stayed to watch him fill up with grief, it would blunt the edge of my detestation of him and of all that he stood for. I coldly left him to wrestle with his feelings alone.

✑

Brian was waiting for me in Bayles Street. MacGregor had scuttled off to whatever rat's nest he called home.

'These are bad, bad people, Will.'

'You did very well in there, Brian. You almost convinced me that you were crazy enough to assassinate someone.'

'I was shitting myself, Will, absolutely shitting myself.'

As we walked I assured him that neither he nor Archbishop Mannix would be in any danger on Sunday, that the cathedral would be crawling with Army Intelligence personnel, and that the Order of the Shining Knights would be rounded up and charged with enough offences to put them away for a very long time.

'That priest saw our faces you know,' he said.

'Yes I know, but I don't see how it matters unless he sees us again, and I'll be staying well away from St Carthage's, I can tell you.'

'Listen Will, I didn't actually put the boot into him, not like the others.'

'I know that. There wasn't a thud.'

We were silent for a minute or so. With time to reflect on the attack on the young priest, one moment among all the frightful moments reared up and demanded to be spoken of.

'I have to ask you this, Brian. What made you drop that match onto the priest's clothes?'

He stopped and had to make an obvious effort to control his temper.

'Do you really think, Will, that I'd be prepared to set someone on fire just to protect my cover and prove my loyalty to a group of lunatics? Do you really think I'm capable of that?'

'Well,' I said reasonably, 'You did drop the match, Brian, and you did know that his clothes were wet with some highly inflammable liquid. It could have been petrol.'

'You're not a very good PI are you. I knew it wasn't petrol. There was no smell, so I also guessed what it was, and any schoolboy will tell you that pure alcohol burns at a much lower heat than petrol. I also noticed that Clutterbuck was very careful to keep it off the bloke's face and any exposed skin. I knew he was testing me, and I knew that he wouldn't want a full scale murder investigation on his doorstep when he had much bigger plans.'

He paused for breath.

'You know, Will, one thing about you, you never disappoint when it comes to disappointing.'

'All right, Brian. You're wound up, and no wonder, but I had to ask the question.'

'That's what's so disappointing. You didn't have to ask the question. You shouldn't have asked the question.'

He was wrong, of course. It's a PI's job to ask questions, but I attempted to mollify him by apologising and pointing out that this was not the time to be arguing. We were in the middle of the most dreadful and dangerous situation of our lives, and we couldn't afford to allow personal antipathies, many of them spawned in childhood, to interfere with our thinking. It was also essential that Brian not pull out of his commitment to model for Mr Wilks the next morning. Fortunately, as he explained when he'd calmed down, his experience in St Carthage's had made him immovably determined to bring fifth columnists and their ilk to justice. If Lady Bailey was a Nazi spy, and Brian intended to find out whether she was (a statement that troubled me somewhat), he would unflinchingly condemn her to a traitor's fate. I was troubled because all I wanted him to do was strike a few attitudes, not wrestle a patriotic, elderly and titled lady to the ground, especially if he was naked at the time.

I didn't try to dissuade him from taking any inappropriate action because his current moodiness precluded his accepting such advice calmly. I supposed that there wasn't much he could really do in the nude, although his admittedly clever handling of tonight's crisis made me wary of underestimating him. He was capable of great courage, or maybe foolhardiness, with or without clothes. I'd have to trust that Lady Bailey's positively über-banality would immediately convince him that I had, once again, made a mistake — a mistake he'd be more than happy to uncritically accept.

Mother was still awake when we reached Garton Street. She was on her hands and knees in the living room scrubbing at the spot where Spangler Brisket's severed head had inconsiderately dripped blood.

'This is the last of it,' she said, 'and the most stubborn. There was surprisingly little blood anywhere else, given how widely distributed he was. The umbrella stand was unpleasant, of course.'

She chatted to Brian about how very charming Paul Clutterbuck was, and she was pleased that I'd neglected to tell Brian about Clutterbuck's theory regarding Darlene because it meant that she was now able to produce it with an unspoken 'Ta da!', like the surprise lurking on the last page of a whodunit. When Brian failed to express any excitement, she enlisted my support by saying that I fully endorsed the Clutterbuck version.

'I know Darlene better than anyone — recent surprises

notwithstanding — and I can't see her taking time off from her Herbs for Victory commitments to have affairs with two men and oversee the killing of one of them.'

Where Brian saw a mermaid, I saw a dugong. Our widely differing views of Darlene meant that further speculation was a waste of time and I announced that as I had a film to shoot the next morning I would go up to bed. On the way up I ran into Peter Gilbert on his way down. I'd forgotten that he was going to spend the night. My natural inclination was to resent his presence. It wasn't anything personal, unless you consider that the deliberately clandestine nature of his affair with my mother strays into the realm of the personal.

'I'm glad that business in Maryborough sorted itself out for you,' he said. 'I was ready to go up there if necessary.'

I dismissed this as inconsequential small talk.

'How long have you been having an affair with my mother?'

'Four years.' He thought for a moment.

'Let me expand on that. When I say four years, I really mean twenty years. I was only having an affair for the four years that coincided with your father being alive. After his death, for the next sixteen years, we were involved in what is rightly called a relationship. We were, of course, discreet. Even so, it is astonishing that you never noticed — or perhaps not so astonishing after all.'

He said all this with the clipped confidence of the practised solicitor, as if he was laying before me the irrefutable evidence in an open and shut case. How I might feel about such a revelation was of no interest to him. In fact, I felt nothing in particular, except perhaps the slightly distressing realisation for a man my age, that my mother was a stranger. Not wishing to hear any more from him, I said, 'Good night', and went to my old room where I re-read Nigella's dreadful script. I allowed myself to contemplate Peter Gilbert's assertion that he and my mother had begun an adulterous liaison when I was barely twelve years old, and had continued it even through what ought to have been a period of decent mourning for a dead husband, in Mother's case, and close friend in Gilbert's. I fell asleep musing on the inconstancy of human emotion.

Thursday morning was grey and wet — one of those slate-coloured Melbourne days that make you feel like your spirit is being tamped down by a celestial thumb. At breakfast, which was just a cup of tea, Brian asked if there was any heating in Lady Bailey's drawing room. I lied and said that, of course, there was; when, in truth, I had no idea. I'd been so surprised to find myself naked that the air temperature hadn't registered. I do know that there'd been no alarming shrinkage in response to a sudden chill so it was safe to presume that the room was heated.

'When I'm there, Will, what exactly should I be on the lookout for?'

'Nothing in particular. She's not going to give herself away by suddenly leaping to her feet and giving a Nazi salute. All I want you to do is see if you can find out the names of any of the other women. You might overhear one talking to another. This is low level surveillance, Brian. Even if you come away with nothing, it's all right.'

I hoped that Brian would heed my words and not do anything embarrassing. If he could obtain a few pointless names at least he'd feel that he'd done something worthwhile.

'How long have you known about Mother and Peter Gilbert?' I asked.

'I don't know. Years.'

'Years!'

'It was pretty obvious, Will. They spent a lot of time together after Dad died.'

'They spent a lot of time together before he died as well. Did you know about that?'

'No, but it doesn't surprise me. Dad was hardly ever home if you remember, and when he was he wasn't exactly a barrel of laughs.'

I didn't press Brian any further, conscious as I was that the conversation would inevitably decline into an accusation that my ignorance of Mother's private life had more to do with my supposed self-absorption than with her and Gilbert's subterfuge. With the greatest reluctance I had to inwardly acknowledge that there might be a grain of truth in this. It wasn't, however, something that warranted being spoken out loud.

Both Brian and I left the house before Mother and her geriatric paramour came down from their lustful couch. My intention was to return to Clutterbuck's house and take a deep, hot bath — a luxury that would be denied me after Clutterbuck's apprehension. Brian headed off for Lady Bailey's house in East Melbourne, convinced that he was embarking on a task of national importance, when in fact the only legacy of his morning's work would be a few incompetent charcoal sketches of his slightly out-of-condition body.

Clutterbuck was having toast and coffee with the odious Mr Ronnie Oakpate. Of all the grotesques in the Order of the Shining Knights, Oakpate seemed to be the one for whom Clutterbuck had the most time. They were an odd pair; the dapper, handsome Clutterbuck—carefully shaved, perfumed and manicured—and the dwarfish, pug-ugly and frighteningly hirsute Oakpate. Their relationship had the exotic and creepy feel of an unnatural attachment between two different and hostile species. Watching them talk was like watching a chimpanzee vigorously mount an altar boy.

I said a polite good morning, although it was clear to all of us that there could be no normal social intercourse after last night's extravagant festival of violence and humiliation, and went upstairs and drew a bath, adding a good slurp of an aromatic oil to the water. I wanted to look and smell my best for my meeting with Nigella. I closed my eyes and breathed in the sweet-scented steam. I rationalised my slight unease about not having contacted James Fowler by thinking that it would be better to hold off until I had more details. I was also nervous about his reaction to the attack on the young priest. Perhaps he'd think that I ought to have been able to prevent it. No. With his experience he'd know that going along with it was essential in consolidating my position with the Order. He still wasn't aware that it was Brian's position that had been consolidated. The deeper my brother and I had become embroiled with the Order of the Shining Knights the more impossible it became to tell Fowler the truth. I'd have to do it though, before Sunday, and in the calm and enervating warmth of the bath Saturday seemed soon enough.

Oakpate and Clutterbuck were in the hallway when I came downstairs. They both stared at me silently as I walked towards them, and in a strange drawing together they contrived to block my path so that I was obliged to ask if I might pass. They drew apart and provided a space sufficient to allow me to squeeze between them so that one breathed in my face and the other down my neck in a menacing way. Naturally my back was turned to Oakpate, not wishing to suffer the swampy exudation from his lungs. Clutterbuck's breath was inoffensive and smelled only of coffee. He watched unblinkingly as I eased past, our eyes at the same level and only inches apart. This forced, physical contact between Oakpate, Clutterbuck and me felt contaminating in some profound and disturbing way. It was as if each of them had marked me with his scent in an aggressive display of ownership. If I'd had time, and a more extensive wardrobe, I'd have changed my clothes.

Out in Bayles Street I began walking towards Royal Parade, but stopped and changed direction when I realised I would pass quite near St Carthage's. Running into a battered priest was not something I wanted to do.

I arrived at Henry Buck's, gentlemen's clothier, well ahead of Nigella. They were expecting me and had laid out an air force uniform in readiness. The shop assistant, a gruff, ungentlemanly type who breathed so raspingly that I thought he must have inhaled mustard gas for breakfast, said that madam had given him my measurements the day before. I was on the point of protesting how this could be so, but remembered that Nigella was well placed to know them.

The uniform fitted perfectly and confirmed what I'd always known — that blue suits me, not that the colour would be apparent on black and white film. In the half hour or so that I was in Henry Buck's, there were only two other customers, and both of these were women. When I commented on this the shop assistant said rather forlornly that the bottom had fallen out of men's tailoring, and that they only managed to return a small profit, mostly on the sale of ties and handkerchiefs, neither of which required coupons, and regulation kit accessories for all the services, including the Yanks. I regretted asking the question because I wasn't interested in the least degree in Henry Buck's sales figures. I'd only inquired to be polite, and the unnecessarily detailed reply breached the social contract which was understood by most to demand a brief, polite answer to a brief, polite question. He was just beginning to rail against a rival company called Davies Coop which had secured the contract to make service uniforms, when Nigella and a young woman who'd been designated her driver for the day, entered and rescued me. Nigella whistled and said that I looked the part. Her driver, rather a surly lump, twisted her mouth in a way that made her ugly, but conveyed no other readable response.

We were to film this epic of the tramways in St Kilda Road, and on the drive there I asked Nigella if she'd enjoyed her drawing class that morning. She laughed and said it had been a memorable one.

'We had this model who was a young Jewish man from Poland who spoke in the most extraordinary accent. He was in the mould of Tyrone Power actually. Quite good looking, but he rather disgraced himself by getting an erection. I had a three quarter view of him at the time and it just popped into the picture. I suppose the poor man was mortified but he didn't break his pose and Mr Wilks thought that was very professional of him. None of us was brave enough to draw what we were looking at, so we all made small adjustments. At the end of the session the young man stepped down, still stark naked, but more relaxed if you know what I mean, and shook us each by the hand and introduced himself and asked us our names. Quite bizarre, but also rather naïve and touching. Mr Wilks was cross about it. Apparently there is to be no contact between artist and model. He said he wouldn't be employing that fellow again, which raised a howl of protest from the group. We thought he was lovely.'

It was a pleasure to see Nigella so animated, and I wondered how I could ever have thought her plain. It was less of a pleasure to learn what a dog's breakfast Brian had made of a relatively simple task. I accept that standing nude in a roomful of women falls short of hiding in plain sight, but he managed to make it more memorable than was strictly necessary. It was so like Brian to do everything wrong and have everyone love him for it.

'Now, Will,' Nigella said, a note of seriousness entering her voice. 'There's no live sound on this film and we're going to do it all as quickly as possible. The director is a man named Gregory Howden and I'm afraid he thinks he's Howard Hawks. He's competent but he thinks he's an artist. I'm sure you know the type.'

A small smile escaped her reins, and for a moment I thought she was referring to me. This was of course absurd, and merely the oversensitivity one feels when one is in the sure grip of a strong, unreciprocated attachment.

'He spent time in Hollywood in the early twenties and worked in a minor capacity on a couple of Wally Reid pictures, before morphine did Wally in.'

'Ah, poor old Wally Reid.'

'Anyway, Howden treats every short as if he was shooting *Gone With the Wind*, so don't be surprised by the megaphone or the constant stream of barked instructions.' She lowered her voice. 'I'm afraid he wears jodhpurs and riding boots.'

My initial contact with Mr Gregory Howden wasn't all it might have been. He was standing by a camera, with a few assistants taking light readings and making jottings in notebooks. When Nigella introduced me, he pointed the tip of a riding crop at my face.

'What are those ugly marks on this man's face?'

'They're the remains of a nasty gravel rash and they're barely visible now,' I said, perhaps haughtily. 'A little pancake will make them invisible.'

He turned to Nigella.

'In the whole of Melbourne you couldn't find one unscarred actor?'

Nigella folded her arms, stared him down and said with

magnificent finality, 'No. Directors on the other hand are surprisingly plentiful.'

Mr Howden looked from Nigella to me and said, 'Ah, I see. In Hollywood I was used to the casting couch working the other way round.'

Nigella didn't seem to be offended, and I took this as a sign that she wasn't appalled by the idea that someone thought she might be sleeping with me. Mr Howden didn't know it, but his grubby, snide remark served to raise my spirits.

'No close-ups then,' he said. 'We'll shoot you from the less unsightly side and stay in wide shot. I want you over there by the tram stop and when I say 'Action' I want you to look up and down the street as if waiting for a tram.'

'Am I perplexed, worried about it being late? Should I look at my watch?'

'Just look up and down the street. Can you do that Mr Barrymore?'

He was deliberately overplaying his exasperation to unnerve me. Passers-by were stopping to gawk, and Howden's assistants had to keep them moving so that an unrealistic clot of them didn't form at the edges of the shot. I stood at the tram stop and Howden raised his megaphone and shouted, 'Action!'

I did as requested — came forward and looked up and down the street. I took my cap off and ran my fingers through my hair as I did so.

'Cut! I don't recall asking you to get undressed!'

There was a smattering of laughter from his assistants.

'Go again! Action!'

I stepped forward again, and just to do something with my hands, I placed them casually on my hips.

'Cut!' Howden screamed through the megaphone. 'You're an air force officer. Not a chorus girl! Go again!'

My fury was mounting, but for Nigella's sake I submitted to this little Napoleon's commands until after the sixth, unnecessary take, he called, 'Print it! It's lousy but it'll have to do.'

Apart from recording the narration this was all I was required to do. Apparently the rest of the short had been filmed that morning at a shunting yard, with another actor playing the air force officer who gets on the tram. So all that insulting nonsense about not being able to shoot a close-up had been nothing more than a bad joke. No wonder Howden wanted me to keep the cap on. All he needed was an establishing shot of someone in a uniform, seen from a distance. It would be edited together with the material shot in close-up and no one would guess that the man at the tram stop and the man who gets on the tram weren't the same person.

In the car on the way back to Henry Buck's to return the uniform we agreed that Mr Gregory Howden was a kind of monster.

'I thought you did a great job,' she said.

'So you *really* believed that I *really* wanted that tram to come, did you?'

We both laughed, and I leaned across and kissed her quickly and gently on the mouth. Her driver saw nothing. I sat back in the corner of the car and watched for her reaction.

'You really mustn't do that again, Will. You really mustn't,' she said quietly.

'And you really mustn't marry Paul Clutterbuck. You really mustn't.'

Her eyes darted to the back of her driver's head, alarmed that she might have heard this exchange, but the noise of the engine made this unlikely.

'Paul wants us to get married this Sunday afternoon. A civil ceremony. It's all arranged. All I have to do is say yes.'

I had to take my hat off to Clutterbuck — an assassination in the morning and a wedding in the afternoon. Most people would consider this an unworkably crowded schedule. I was confident that neither event would take place. All I said was, 'I see', and avoided anything more consequential.

I recorded the badly written narrations, as agreed, and made no comment about how awful they were. I sat obediently in the booth of a studio that had once belonged to Efftee Film Productions, and which was now an arm of the government's film services, and read the words as if they were poetry. I did each of them in a single take, and was pleased to acknowledge to myself that this was the easiest money I'd ever earned. Afterwards I thought about telephoning James Fowler, but as I was in the city and as the news I had for him was significant, and not suitable for an insecure telephone line, I decided to walk across Princes Bridge and see him in his office. This turned out to be a complicated process. I was canny enough to ask at the gate for the offices of Native Policy for Mandated Territories and was told that this was a military establishment and that whatever I was looking for sounded like the public service. I explained that the fact that the Victoria Barracks was associated with the military hadn't escaped me but that if this dullard to whom I was speaking would just check he'd find that I was in the right place after all.

'The person to whom I wish to speak is a Mr James Fowler.'

With a graceless sneer the soldier made a phone call from the gatehouse and returned with the information that James Fowler was unavailable and that he'd be out of town for several days. Was there anybody else I wanted to speak to? I had no other names and I had no idea how much anybody else in James' department knew. He'd stressed that this whole investigation was at his behest, and I understood that he hadn't gained official approval to undertake it — hence his reliance on my skills. The top brass certainly wouldn't sanction the use of non-military personnel, although my quick success in uncovering George Beech's forgery ring would provide James with a bulwark against their wrath if they were to ever find out.

I couldn't just leave matters unresolved like this. James must have a subordinate who worked closely with him.

'Perhaps I should speak to someone,' I said. 'Does Mr Fowler have a secretary?'

'And a butler probably,' said the soldier, clearly dismissing the whole public service as an extravagant waste of money. I gave this sour comic my name and he phoned Fowler's office again. He passed the handset to me, and a man's voice said, 'I believe you have a message for James Fowler.'

It was important that the message be sufficiently ambiguous to convey meaning only to James or to someone who'd been taken into his confidence.

'I understand Mr Fowler is out of town at the moment, but it's imperative that he keep an appointment at St Patrick's Cathedral at nine on Sunday morning.'

'I see,' was the reply, and it was immediately followed by the click of disconnection.

James' absence posed several serious problems. The thought that Archbishop Mannix's life might now be in my hands frankly made me feel ill. I had no opinion of the man one way or another, but I knew he was a powerful and influential force in Melbourne and that his assassination would divide the city and possibly provoke riots in retribution. Certainly, a murdered religious leader would have a less than beneficial effect on morale generally. It also struck me as rather shocking that he might be gunned down in front of the Vienna Boys' Choir.

I walked all the way from Victoria Barracks to Mother's house in Princes Hill. I was so preoccupied with the dilemma of James

Fowler's sudden posting elsewhere — no doubt to deal with something of grave importance — that the hour that it took me passed rapidly. I was considering a range of strategies Brian and I might employ to both thwart and apprehend any of Clutterbuck's cronies who came to the cathedral on Sunday — and Clutterbuck himself, of course. They must all have thought they'd been terribly clever in manoeuvring Brian into being the assassin. We, however, were several steps ahead of them, which should have given us an advantage, but Brian and I hadn't taken into account the possibility that there would be no military people in the cathedral — and that was now a real possibility unless I found a way to speak to James Fowler before Sunday morning.

I couldn't help but contemplate, as I walked, the dark power of passion that had brought me to this point. All around me was evidence of the havoc it wreaked. John Trezise's passion for Anna Capshaw; George Beech's for Gretel; Sarah Goodenough's for Brian, and Darlene's, perhaps, for someone as yet unknown. Death shadowed each of these attachments, and what must have begun in excitement and pleasure, illicit or not, had soon declined into upheaval and loss. That one person's love for another could be so destructive that it smashed his or her moral compass, that it could be so all-consuming that it devoured common decency and rectitude, was incomprehensible to me, and it was mirrored, I thought, in Clutterbuck's distorted and single-minded hatred of a religion practised by half the population. When Trezise and Beech strangled the life out of the women they supposedly loved, were they proving that excessive love and excessive loathing were essentially the same thing, that the consequences for both the loved and the loathed were similarly dire?

The house at Garton Street was crowded. Peter Gilbert, Mother, Brian and detectives Strachan and Radcliff sat in confabulation. There was no hostility in the air. Indeed, everyone was drinking tea — not from Mother's best china, but this time she wasn't making a point. Her best china had been smashed by Darlene, an action that had made any subsequent atrocity entirely feasible.

The Clutterbuck scenario had been put to the police, but they hadn't found it as compelling as we had. Brian told me, after they'd gone, that Darlene's distress over Spangler's murder had been so extreme that she'd lost the baby. She was under sedation and had made no contact of any kind with anyone. The only constant in her behaviour was her maddened belief that Brian had killed the man she loved, and she expressed this even under the restraint of strong sedatives.

'I think they've fallen,' I said, 'as we all did, for her crust of stupidity and missed the cunning underneath.'

'If the rozzers are right about Darlene it means that there's someone out there who really hated Captain Brisket.'

'Given where he ended up, Brian, it seems more likely that there's someone out there who really hates you.'

'That's not a good feeling. Not that I have to tell you that.'

I would have asked what he meant by that last remark but Peter Gilbert put his head round the door and said that a Nigella Fowler was downstairs and wanted to see me.

'Nigella,' Brian said. 'Clutterbuck's fiancée?'

'Yes, Brian, and I don't think it's a good idea for her to see you here. I believe, by the way, that you gave the ladies their money's worth.'

'You've spoken to her already?'

'Now isn't the time to explain. As soon as she's gone I'll tell you everything. I promise.'

'This gets more interesting by the minute. Two weeks ago I

was telling little boys not to pick their noses. Now I'm up to my neck in murder and mayhem, and you know what Will? I love it.'

✺

'I tried for you at Paul's house,' Nigella said when she saw me, 'but he said I'd find you here, and here you are.'

I immediately spoke about the matter that was on my mind.

'Have you made a decision about Clutterbuck?'

'As I haven't yet given him my answer I'm hardly likely to tell you first, Will. Besides, I haven't come here to discuss that. I'm here because my brother asked me to deliver a message *I* don't understand, but which he said you would, and I'm to relay your reply to a friend of his in his department.'

It struck me as a bit risky entrusting someone so close to Clutterbuck with a message that would concern him, however it was coded.

'How intriguing,' I said, feigning surprise that James Fowler would wish to pass on a message to me.

'James said to tell you that he'd be out of town until early next week, but that if you could confirm that appointment you were to let me know. I didn't know that you and James were, well, what are you and James? Does this message mean anything to you?'

I had to think quickly here.

'I discovered recently that the Vienna Boys' Choir sang in St Patrick's Cathedral. I mentioned it to James — I don't know when — and he asked me to find out when he could hear them. That's all. Nothing mysterious after all.'

'I see. James has never expressed his interest in choral music to me. It must be a private passion.'

'You almost make it sound sordid.'

'And is it?'

'What an extraordinary question!'

'We live in extraordinary times.'

Because extricating myself from the implications of Nigella's innuendo might reveal too much about James' work, I chose to play along to some extent and said only, 'That we do.' I'd clarify the situation with Nigella later. For now it was critical that I give her my vital information.

'Tell James' friend to tell James that the performance is at St Patrick's this Sunday morning during nine o'clock mass. It'd be a shame if he missed it, but if he's away, well, maybe someone else in his office might be interested.'

'You think there's been a sudden outbreak of enthusiasm for boys' choirs in the department of Native Policy for Mandated Territories?'

I didn't want the conversation to go any further, so asked Nigella to just pass on the message exactly as I'd given it. She stood up to go and I offered to walk with her across the park, but she said that she wasn't going back to Clutterbuck's house and that she preferred to walk alone.

All in all, my reaction to this brief meeting was mixed. I was relieved that James, or someone from Army Intelligence, would now know where and when to intervene, and I was impotently livid at Nigella's perverse reading of my relationship with her brother.

'What's wrong with people,' I said out loud.

'That's her all right,' said Brian as he came into the room. 'I saw her leave from upstairs. I wouldn't have thought she was Clutterbuck's type. She's a bit, I don't know, unglamorous.'

'Clutterbuck has a great deal of time for her money.'

'She's a good artist.'

'And did she draw just exactly what was in front of her?'

'I couldn't help it. None of the horses bolted, so no harm

was done, and I managed to get the name of every person in the room.'

He reached into his pocket and handed me the piece of paper he withdrew. 'Mission accomplished.'

If I was going to tell Brian that I'd sent him on a wild goose chase, now would've been the time. I hung fire because he would have become sulky and churlish, and I needed him to be cooperative and alert when I filled in some, but not all, of the gaps in his knowledge.

'Thank you,' I said. 'Now we should stop talking about the drawing class. There are some images that should never enter a person's head, and a fully tumescent brother is one of them.'

He performed a caricature of concentration.

'It's funny, Will, I'm trying to see you like that, and I'm getting nothing. Hang on … nope, nothing at all.'

'That might be because you have no imagination, Brian.'

'So you agree that the idea of you with a decent erection would require a pretty good imagination.'

'Brian,' I said indulgently, 'we don't have time for these silly word games. There are some things that you need to know. I suggest that we go for a walk so that we won't be interrupted, and I think you should then go to Clutterbuck's and find out what they're planning in more detail. I'm sure he's expecting you. At some stage they're going to have to give you a weapon and show you how to use it.'

Brian looked genuinely perturbed, a look I preferred to the smug expression that lingered when he thought he'd won a verbal joust.

'Well, they're not going to get you to kill Mannix by pointing the bone at him, are they. I think they're looking for more immediate results.'

'I hate guns.'

'Don't worry. You won't have to fire one. Army Intelligence knows all about it.'

As we walked around Princes Park I told Brian about James Fowler and his cover in the Native Policy for Mandated Territories department. He couldn't fit Nigella neatly into the picture until I said that she had no idea, and neither did their father, that James was something more than a civil servant. The relationship with Clutterbuck was unfortunate, and I'm afraid I betrayed a little of what Nigella had told me about her reasons for marrying him.

'Do you think there's more to it than that? Do you think James Fowler is in the awful position of having to investigate his own sister? I can't believe she knows nothing about Clutterbuck's politics. If she told you that, Will, she could be lying. What if she's the brains behind the whole thing?'

When Brian began to postulate this absurd theory I redirected him by telling him about Anna Capshaw and the first day I'd followed her and John Trezise, whose name I thought at the time was Cunningham.

'I swallowed Clutterbuck's story about his divorce. Now it seems so obviously unlikely that I can't believe I accepted it. In my defence, one doesn't expect a well-dressed, well-spoken man to be a type of criminal. When Clutterbuck told me they'd be in the bookshop at two o'clock I should have twigged that the only way he could have known that was if Anna Capshaw had arranged the time with him.'

Brian's jaw dropped when I told him that Trezise was now in custody for the murder of Anna Capshaw.

'It's funny how things work out, isn't it? Clutterbuck wanted to get at Trezise because of his connection to the Catholic Social Studies Movement. I'm sure now that what he intended to do, with Anna Capshaw's help, was expose Trezise's sexual peccadilloes and shame him out of the Church. Trezise did his work for him. Fanatics of any stripe are unbalanced in some way, so we shouldn't be surprised that Trezise snapped when he found out the truth about Anna.'

There was a lot for Brian to take in and when I'd finished the Trezise story, I mentioned, just in passing, that I'd also uncovered a ring of forgers while working on something else, and that the leader of that ring was now being interrogated by Army Intelligence. He pressed for more detail.

'No one can accuse you of sitting on your arse since getting back from Maryborough,' he said, and I noted with pleasure the unmistakeable tone of respect in his voice.

'Yes, well, some things have fallen into my lap, I admit, but I've always believed that you make your own luck mostly. You need to be ready to grasp opportunities when they present themselves.'

By the time I'd filled Brian in on most of the details — there was no reason to discuss either Gretel Beech or my interest in Nigella Fowler — we were on the Royal Parade side of Princes Park, and from there it was a short distance to Bayles Street. Brian said that he wasn't looking forward to handling a gun, and that he hoped Clutterbuck was alone.

'That MacGregor bloke is seriously creepy. He'd slip a knife up under your ribs as soon as look at you.'

'We're at a very dangerous stage, Brian. Luckily, Clutterbuck has absolute faith in you as the patsy who'll do his dirty work for him.'

'They'd get rid of me afterwards, wouldn't they?'

'Yes, Brian, I think they would, but there isn't going to be that sort of afterwards. Clutterbuck is in for a big surprise.'

I left Brian and went back to Garton Street. I was going to spend as little time as possible at Clutterbuck's house before

Sunday. Except to take a decent bath and to change my clothes there was no reason to hang about there.

A few times in my life I have experienced a strange and foreboding stillness that presages a violent storm. Thursday night and the Friday following felt like that. It wasn't just the depressing and frightening news from Europe and New Guinea, or the government's announcement that Christmas was more or less cancelled. A ban had been placed on any Christmasy words in advertising, including the word 'Christmas' itself. Words like 'festive season' and 'yuletide' were forbidden, and pictures of Santa Claus were taboo. No tinsel, no holly, no window displays. The prime minister's voice, so desperately in need of elocution, exhorted people from their radios to observe Christmas 1942 'soberly, confidently, realistically', and to exchange savings stamps instead of gifts. They were getting in early — this was still only late September — but I suppose they wanted people to get used to the idea.

When Brian came home late Thursday night he said that the plans were unchanged and that MacGregor was going to show him how to fire a pistol next morning. He'd done a good job, he'd thought, of further convincing Clutterbuck that he, Brian, was the ideal assassin.

Peter Gilbert had departed, for a few days at least. Mother didn't mention him, or discuss her relationship with him, despite having ample opportunity to do so, and I certainly wasn't going to raise the matter with her.

Friday passed slowly. There was no word from the police; Brian learned how to load, point and discharge a hand gun; Clutterbuck was silent; James Fowler was absent, and Nigella made no contact. Somewhere in the bowels of the police building John Trezise was cooling his heels, and so too was George Beech. I spent the day learning speeches from *Timon of Athens*, and blocking out in my head the opening few scenes. Once all this hideous business was over I'd begin the process of gathering together another company and *Timon* would be our inaugural production. The hours slipped by in a pleasant fantasy of as yet unrealised performances.

Mother, Brian and I had dinner together — another vegetable curry made from produce in the garden.

'Nothing on your plates has been touched by Captain Brisket's torso,' Mother said. 'It was quite obvious where it had fallen in the garden, and I picked vegetables well outside the crushed area.'

Nevertheless, we ate slowly and cautiously after that, as if caution alone would prevent ingesting a leaf or a floret that might have touched the mutilated torso. We all went to bed early and I fell deeply asleep very quickly. I hadn't realised how exhausted the last few days had made me.

I awoke to a shrieking noise that at first seemed a part of the soundscape of my dream, but continued at a pitch that made me sit bolt upright. A woman was screaming so insanely downstairs that I think the hair on my head actually stood up. I rushed into the hall and collided with Brian who was struggling into a pair of pyjama bottoms. The screaming continued, followed by the crashing of furniture. I'd never heard sounds like these before. They were inhuman, wild, terrifying. It wasn't Mother because she appeared at the top of the stairs, her nightgown visible in the dark. Her voice quavered when she asked, 'Who is it?'

Brian said, 'It's Darlene,' and began to descend the stairs. I followed, and told Mother to stay where she was.

Light seeped from beneath the living room door. The

screaming intensified and as we came closer we could hear the ripping and tearing of fabric, along with the smashing of china and glass. Brian threw the door open, and there was Darlene, rampaging among the torn and shredded furniture, the air full of floating feathers and horsehair. She'd just plunged the knife into the padding of a beautiful chair when she became aware of Brian's presence. She stopped for a moment, looked at him with mad eyes, and resumed screaming, but at an even higher pitch than previously. It was completely unnerving. If I'd believed in possession I'd have thought I was now a witness to it.

'Stop it!' Brian called, 'Stop it!'

His voice was loud but it made no impression on Darlene. He stepped towards her and there followed a confused flurry of movement. Darlene was suddenly standing near him. She screamed the word 'Murderer!', made what appeared to be a small movement with her hand, and then fell silent. It was as if a plug had been pulled. Brian leant forward slightly and said, 'She's punched me.' His eyes were focussed on her face; she was looking at his stomach, and when he turned towards me, incredulous that Darlene had had the gall to punch him, I saw what Brian hadn't yet seen — the handle of the knife protruding from his abdomen, just above the waistline of his pyjama bottoms. He looked down then, and it was apparent that he couldn't comprehend that Darlene had driven the knife into his exposed belly. He touched the handle gingerly before dropping to his knees. I hurried to him and prevented him from falling forward. I placed him on his side and called for Mother to telephone for an ambulance.

Darlene sat, distracted now, in one of the damaged chairs. She whimpered, and took no further interest in what was happening around her. I drew Brian's fingers away from where they'd curled around the knife's handle. His eyelids closed and he became unconscious just as Mother entered the room and knelt with me beside Brian. She held his hand and wept soundlessly as we waited for the ambulance. Darlene didn't move. Even as Brian was carried out on a stretcher she stayed quite still; present but absent. Mother accompanied Brian to hospital and I was left to deal with this strange creature—the husk of Darlene who'd emptied herself in a storm of screaming and who may well have killed Brian in the mistaken belief that he'd killed her Captain Spangler Brisket. The police were right and Clutterbuck was wrong. There was clearly no third party to whom Darlene was attached.

Darlene sat in this catatonic state for two hours and I sat opposite her, watching her and watching the room as it settled down around her into a chaotic tumble of ruin. She barely moved and eventually fell asleep sitting up, her head lolling forward onto her chest. She didn't wake when the front door opened and Mother came in.

'He's all right,' she said, 'Brian's all right. The blade missed vital organs and it didn't go in very far. He's sore, but he's not in any danger.'

She looked across at Darlene.

'Brian doesn't want her charged with anything.'

'So what do we do with her?'

'What time is it now? Seven o'clock? In a little while I'll call Dr Spitler and he'll know what to do.'

She went upstairs and returned with a blanket that she tucked around Darlene's body.

'Don't you want to slap her, Mother? Look at what she's done.'

'No, Will, I don't want to slap her. Her life is never going to work out for her after this. I think she's lost her way now. It's the end of happiness for her. You go up to bed. I'll watch her.'

'I'll make us a cup of tea.'

'Brian's going to be all right, and that's all that matters, Will.'

That wasn't all that mattered, of course. Who, for example, was now going to shoot Archbishop Mannix?

Chapter Thirteen

MURDER IN THE CATHEDRAL

NOT LONG AFTER DARLENE HAD BEEN TAKEN from
Mother's house into medical care, I crossed the park to tell
Clutterbuck that he'd have to change his plans for Sunday. Brian
wouldn't be able to crawl from his hospital bed to do his bidding.
Clutterbuck took the news well. I'd never seen him rant or rail
and he wasn't about to start now. Indeed, he pretended concern
for Brian's welfare, and said that he'd visit him in hospital.

'It's a shame, but it really only means a slight change of plan.'

'Oh?'

'Brian was always my first choice, but you'll do just as well,
Will.'

I'd been expecting that he'd say this, so it didn't come as a
shock. What did surprise me was the sudden surge of heart-
pounding hatred that I felt for him. It so overwhelmed me that I

was unable to speak.

'You *will* do it.'

I found my voice.

'I will not do it.'

'Yes you will, and afterwards we'll help you disappear and you'll never have to have anything to do with any of us ever again.'

'And what makes you think that I'm prepared to spend the rest of my life hiding from the authorities?'

'You don't have a choice; that's the thing.'

'Ah. Gretel Beech.'

He gave a non-committal shrug.

'If that's the ace up your sleeve, Paul, it's worthless.'

I thought it best not to mention Army Intelligence at this point — I didn't want to run the risk of Clutterbuck changing his plans. I wasn't, however, going to accept the role of assassin, even though I knew it would never come to that. I'd allow Clutterbuck to push me sufficiently hard to give him a guarantee that I'd be there in the cathedral on Sunday, but he'd have to get one of his goons to hold the gun. I didn't care for being the centre of attention in a situation where anything might go awry.

'The police have George Beech and he'll confess to Gretel's murder.'

Things began to go awry much sooner than I'd expected. Clutterbuck said, 'George Beech didn't kill Gretel, Will. I did.'

'That's impossible.'

My mind raced back to the night of Gretel's death. We'd watched her sing and we'd come home so that she could rest and take a bath before her next performance. Clutterbuck and I had had a drink downstairs and then decided to return to the speakeasy before Gretel. As we were leaving, Paul had called up to Gretel to tell her that we were going out. She'd replied that she was due to go on at 12.30, and that she'd meet us there. Paul was never out of my sight for more than a few minutes after that, and yet Gretel was dead when we came back home.'

'You mean, I presume, that you had Gretel killed.'

'No, Will, I don't. I mean that I put my hands around that lovely throat, and wrung it. And I can't believe that you still don't know how I did it, or rather I can believe it because you're not a very good detective, although to give you your due, you did much better than I thought you'd do.'

'All right, Paul, I'll bite. If you really did kill Gretel, how did you do it, and why?'

'I confess I had a little help, Will, but not with the deed, just with the misdirection. When the three of us came home here, Gretel and I went upstairs. I was only gone for a few moments. Long enough to kill poor Gretel. It was quick, and so completely surprising for her that she really didn't have a chance to be frightened or distressed. I wasn't the only person upstairs with her at the time — Anna Capshaw was waiting there. She ran the bath, and it was her voice you heard. You assumed, quite reasonably, that it was Gretel's; the tap was running at the time, so any differences in their voices would have been hard to pick. She also put your tie around Gretel's neck. And why? It was for your benefit, Will. Well, it was to make sure that you'd be useful to us. I couldn't believe my luck when you agreed to help me bury her. I thought I was going to have to work much harder on you, really scare you with the implications of that tie of yours. Your experiences up in Maryborough must have made you very jumpy about the police.'

'And how was I going to be useful to you?'

'Our work is important, Will, and everyone in the Order is essential. What we needed was a person who'd carry out our most ambitious plan, but who we could then afford to lose. As soon as I met you I knew you were our man — the perfect mix of gullibility and misplaced self-assurance.'

I tried to interrupt him, but he stopped me.

'Let me finish, Will. I'll lay everything out before you. Everything.'

'What more could there possibly be?'

He smiled.

'Let's start with Trezise. I'm afraid he didn't kill Anna Capshaw in a fit of jealousy or rage. I killed Anna and, believe me, it broke my heart. It was possibly the most difficult thing I've ever had to do, although I don't expect your sympathy. I don't think you know the first thing about sacrifice. You see, Will, we weren't really sure what we were going to do to strike at the fucking Catholics. Trezise was a target, but the more I thought about him, the more I realised we needed to go after a much bigger fish, so I settled for setting him up for Anna's murder. I think I loved her, Will, I really do, but she wasn't going to stand quietly aside for Nigella. She just couldn't see the bigger picture, and in the end I couldn't trust her to keep quiet about Gretel.

'Trezise'll never prove his innocence. I made sure there was plenty of evidence linking him to the crime, so that gives me pleasure. Even if they don't hang him, he'll spend the rest of his life in prison wondering how his Catholic god could have deserted him. Things were going along swimmingly until your brother turned up, and it was transparently clear that the two of you were up to something. I thought you'd been through my drawers, so I did a more thorough job of it to confuse you. That was a painful thing to do, I can tell you.

'I wasn't convinced by Brian, Will. He's almost as bad an actor as you are. I think you'd got it into your head that you could break up the Knights and establish yourself as some sort of brilliant investigator. It's the kind of thing that'd appeal to your vanity. The thing about vanity, Will, is that you spend too much time staring at yourself in the mirror and not enough time looking over your shoulder.'

He paused, just to let that jibe sink in.

'Brian is a bit different from you, though. He's smarter and therefore more dangerous. I humbly admit that my attempt to get rid of him was a bit of a miscalculation. When he told me about his wife and her American lover, I thought I'd been handed a gift-wrapped opportunity. Spangler was easy to find and even easier to kill. MacGregor did the butchery, out the back of Ronnie Oakpate's factory. It was amazing to watch, Will. Very skilful. When you take a man apart like that, he's remarkably easy to transport — a few burlap sacks is all you need. I planted him around your mother's house, and I *am* sorry if she found it distressing. I like your mother. I'd hoped that the coppers would arrest Brian as a matter of course and take him out of circulation. It had been such a successful strategy with Trezise. What I hadn't counted on was their immediate and accurate assessment that if Brian was the killer he'd be unlikely to foul his own nest in that way. I got carried away with the drama of it all. It was about that time that we decided to execute Mannix. I can't think why we hadn't thought of it earlier. He's the public and ugly face of Catholicism in this country after all. Strike at the head and the body's bound to falter. It was Crocker who suggested that Brian be given the task of shooting Mannix.'

'But if you knew that he wasn't really one of you, how were you going to get him to pull the trigger?'

'We were going to give him a choice — he shoots Mannix, or we shoot you. I was counting on him making the right choice. Now I have to count on you making the right choice.'

I knew what was coming.

'You shoot Mannix, Will, or we shoot your mother.'

It was said very simply, very matter-of-factly, as if he was trying to minimise giving offence. He looked at his watch.

'She should be having a not very nice cup of tea with Mary Rose Shingle right about now. I'm not sure that they'll find very much to talk about, Miss Shingle being a couple of coupons short of a pullover.'

'You don't need me to shoot Mannix.'

'Well, I suppose it's partly personal now, although the reasons I stated earlier still hold. I confess it will give me a great deal of pleasure to watch you do something that goes against your nature and that you're going to find difficult to live with afterwards. I do like actions that lead to a lifetime of punishment. They play in my head like favourite tunes. Ten years from now I'll think of John Trezise languishing in jail, and it will give my day a lift.'

'I've never fired a gun in my life,' I said.

MacGregor and Crocker, who must have been listening at the door, took this as their cue to enter. MacGregor was holding a large hand gun, a Colt 45.

'Mr MacGregor will be pleased to instruct you. He's a man of many talents, our Mr MacGregor. You'll be staying here with us today and tonight, Will, and I'm sorry but you'll be confined to barracks. At least you'll get in one more bath.'

MacGregor showed me how to fire the Colt, but we didn't fire off any live ammunition.

'It's too noisy,' he said. He warned me that there'd be considerable recoil and that I should tense the muscles in my arms in anticipation of it.

'You'll be in the front pew, so you can hardly miss, but I think you should try to get two or three shots off. He's a big target. Aim for the centre of the back. Don't try for a head shot. You'll miss.'

I had plenty of time that afternoon and evening to think about what Clutterbuck had said. For all his murderousness and duplicity, his view of the world was essentially a simple one, and the field of his vision was narrow — so narrow that James Fowler had gone undetected by him. This wasn't really surprising; he'd gone undetected by his sister as well.

It had been decided that Mannix would be shot at the moment in the Mass when he consecrated the host. He would have his back to the congregation, most of whom would have their heads bowed in prayer. I was to stand in the pew and fire, then drop the gun and leave by a side entrance. A car would be waiting and I would be taken to Oakpate's house in Brunswick where I'd have the opportunity to see that Mother was alive and well, and then I'd be driven to Ballarat, where a safe house had been organised. It all sounded neat, and I knew it was all bullshit.

At some point in the afternoon I heard Nigella's voice. Almost immediately Crocker let himself into my bedroom, presumably to prevent me going downstairs and causing some sort of scene. Crocker said that Nigella and Clutterbuck were going to the pictures. He left me alone when he was sure they'd departed. Nigella would be giving Clutterbuck the answer to his proposal for a quick, post-assassination wedding. It was too bizarre to comprehend.

I insisted that I be allowed to speak by telephone to Mother. This, I was told, was impossible. I was assured that she was quite comfortable and being treated with the utmost respect.

The afternoon darkened into evening, and Sunday morning arrived with all its callous and disinterested regularity. There were no portents in the weather. It promised to be fine and sunny — a day for lounging in parks, not a day for shooting archbishops dead.

MacGregor took me to St Patrick's Cathedral early, so that we could claim a seat in the front pew. The great, cavernous, and ribbed interior, designed to make the spirit fly upwards, had no such effect upon me. I experienced no glorious ascension, only a terrifying and crushing sense of impending havoc. What if Nigella hadn't passed my message on? What if there wasn't a single person who'd been deputised to rescue me?

The cathedral began to fill with people. The front pew was soon fully occupied, with one man giving a little sniff of displeasure at finding two unfamiliar people in what he obviously considered his seats. Before long a low murmur rolled from the congregation towards the altar, and it indicated what in a theatre would have been a full house. My legs had turned to jelly, and when Archbishop Mannix entered and blessed the congregation, the effort required to stand was monumental. I had to clutch at the side of the pew to maintain my balance.

Almost everything from this point on remains a jumble of images and sounds. Mannix was a tall man, and seemed taller than he was because he was so ramrod straight. He looked magnificent in a glittering, gold chasuble that hung about his shoulders like a shield. I could discern his Irish accent through his carefully enunciated Latin. The Vienna Boys' Choir sang, and the congregation stood, knelt and sat, and responded as one with the practised precision of well-drilled church goers, familiar with the arcane demands of the Roman liturgy. I stole a glance to the left and right, but couldn't see Clutterbuck anywhere, and I couldn't see, either, anybody who looked as if he could have been from Army Intelligence.

I don't recall a word of Mannix's sermon. My head was fizzing and pinging with fear. I could hear, or fancied I could hear, the blood rushing up my carotid artery into my head — and for a while, this was all I could hear. This was nothing like stage fright. This was naked terror, primal and unstoppable. I heard myself making small, simpering and gasping sounds and felt tears running down my face. MacGregor nudged me sharply in the ribs. I buried my face in a handkerchief to disguise my distress from those near me.

I'd been told to ready myself when the altar boy tinkled a bell three times and the words 'Sanctus, sanctus, sanctus,' rang out. I missed the bell and the words, but MacGregor was there to warn me that the time was imminent. We were all kneeling, and I looked up and saw that Mannix had faced the altar and was uttering words, audible but not intelligible, and anyway in Latin. He then genuflected and raised a host above his head. The bell rang three times again and I heard Lady Macbeth's bell tolling in my fevered brain. MacGregor rammed his fingers sharply into my armpit and I stood up — for what else could I do?

But where were they? Where were the people who would prevent this from happening? Out of the corner of my eye I saw a movement, in the shadow of a chapel off to the side. A priest in a black cassock stepped forward — only it wasn't a priest, it was Clutterbuck. He raised a rifle to his shoulder, the familiar .30 calibre, semi-automatic, M1 Garand rifle that the Americans favoured. Of course, he wasn't going to leave this up to me. Of course, he wanted the thrill of executing the man he believed was the incarnation of evil. At the end of the pew, a nun rose to her feet and from within the folds of her voluminous habit she produced a pistol, aimed it with absolute assurance, and fired a single shot. Clutterbuck fell to the ground, the clatter of his rifle lost in the echo of the gunshot.

On the other side of MacGregor the man who'd sniffed his displeasure had pressed a pistol to MacGregor's head and slipped a handcuff around one of his wrists. I have to presume that what happened next was chaotic, but my mind and body had by this time had enough, and I slipped into a blessed faint. In keeping with the pattern of my life, at a moment of supreme stress I'd retreated into the relative safety of unconsciousness.

When I woke I found I'd been carried into the small room where I'd met with Trezise and his priest in what now seemed like another life. As the room and the people in it resolved themselves I could make no connections that made sense. There was a flurry of activity in the crowded space and a nun was bending down and asking me if I was all right. She looked vaguely familiar, but the veil and wimple framed her face so closely that I couldn't be sure. I sat up and said, 'I saw a nun shoot Clutterbuck. Nuns don't shoot people, do they?'

'No, Will,' said the nun, 'nuns don't shoot people, but I'm not a nun.'

She turned away and removed her wimple, and when she faced me again I was staring, open-mouthed, at Nigella Fowler.

'Paul Clutterbuck is dead,' she said, 'and all his cronies have been rounded up.'

'But you were going to marry him this afternoon.'

'Unfortunately, I had to kill him this morning. I'm glad it wasn't the other way around, or now I'd be a widow.'

In a fog of bewilderment I heard myself saying, 'I know nothing.'

Nigella leaned down to my ear and whispered, 'Ain't that the truth, Will Power, ain't that the truth.'

I was sitting in Mother's dining room that Sunday afternoon, drinking tea with Nigella Fowler and listening with a mixture of awe and something like love to her telling me that both she and her brother were with Army Intelligence. Mother was upstairs soaking off what she called the 'filth of a filthy home.' She was unharmed, although she complained that conversation with Mary Rose Shingle was more than was required of most in a time of war.

'Paul Clutterbuck wasn't really such a very smart man, Will,' Nigella said. 'His mind wasn't a subtle instrument, which is why I could get so close to him without him suspecting that I was anything more than a potential source of income for him. He believed absolutely in his own magnetism. He believed in the gratitude of a plain girl for the attentions of a handsome man. In many ways he was a dangerous fool.'

'You were magnificent,' I said, and was unashamed of the tears that blurred my vision.

'I was terrified, Will. It wasn't supposed to happen like that, but when James was called away I had to take charge. It was never our intention that I'd be anywhere near the cathedral.'

'Where is James?'

She waggled her finger at me.

'Clutterbuck's group isn't the only one of its kind in the country, Will. More than that, I can't say.'

'There's a man named John Trezise and he's been charged with the murder of a woman named Anna Capshaw. He's innocent.'

All that I knew about Paul Clutterbuck tumbled out in a rush, including the fact that he'd killed Gretel Beech. I saw no reason, however, to reveal that I knew the whereabouts of the body. I judged that there was nothing to be gained by so doing. When I'd finished, Nigella said that John Trezise would be released as soon as was practicable, given that the police would have to be convinced that I was telling the truth. Similarly, the murder investigation against George Beech wouldn't be pursued.

I was conscious of the fact that Nigella must be experiencing strong and confusing emotions, having shot and killed a man, even one as fundamentally loathsome as Paul Clutterbuck. She agreed that the reality of having taken a life hadn't yet hit her, and as soon as she said these words she went quiet and then began to sob. She tried valiantly to control herself, but failed, and when I reached for her she fell into my arms and wept and wept until my shirt front was wet with her tears.

This was how Brian found us when he entered the dining room. He moved stiffly and I could see through his half-buttoned shirt that his abdomen was tightly bandaged.

'Mother's just told me what happened this morning,' he said. 'Christ Almighty.'

Nigella turned her tearful face towards Brian, and in a wild change of emotional gear she threw her head back and laughed.

'You! Ziggy what's-his-name. You're Will's brother! Now I've seen everything, and I mean that literally.'

'Let me explain,' I said firmly.

*

The next day, on our way to meet with James and Nigella Fowler in James' tiny office in the Victoria Barracks, I asked Brian who he thought had attacked him on the train on the way back from Maryborough.

'Sarah Goodenough, of course. She's crazy. You don't believe any of that guff she gave the police about me being obsessed with her, do you?'

'Are you going to have her charged with anything? She shouldn't just get away with it.'

'Are you kidding? I want to forget the whole thing. I'll put it down to experience, and remind myself never to get involved with a lunatic again. It just ends in tears.'

James Fowler wasn't altogether happy with Brian's

unauthorised role in infiltrating the Order of the Shining Knights, even though Brian and I had agreed to downplay it, but he was so pleased by the outcome that his displeasure was expressed in the mildest of terms.

'Archbishop Mannix has officially expressed his gratitude to Intelligence and he's included a note of thanks to be given directly to you, Will.'

He passed a piece of thick, embossed paper to me.

'Privately, he's let us know that shooting people dead in his cathedral is not the purpose for which it was built. He also said that he didn't think his homilies were so boring that they'd benefit from the interest added by gunfire. At least he's got a sense of humour about it.'

Fowler went on to explain that it was in the nature of Intelligence work that there could be no public recognition for a job well done. We'd have to be content with knowing that the relevant authorities were silently grateful.

'Which brings me to the point of this meeting. Nigella? If you'd like to take over from here?'

Nigella cleared her throat.

'Since the beginning of this war the forces have been using civilian entertainers to keep the troops happy. I don't know if you're aware of it, but whole Tivoli shows have been staged at various bases — costumes, music, the lot. Obviously these groups can't be sent forward into combat areas, so LHQ — that's Land Headquarters to the uninitiated — here in Melbourne have decided to set up small concert parties to go into dodgy areas, do their act, and get out again quickly.'

I interrupted.

'And you're looking for performers.'

My heart was beating with excitement. I am, after all, an actor above all else. Whatever skills I bring to other areas of my life, they are underpinned by those peculiar gifts which good performers possess. We're a rare and happy breed, sometimes despised, but always, I suspect, envied. We can throw off the shackles of the drab and everyday, and rule whole kingdoms, fall grandly in love, and die heroically, and we can do all these things in the course of a single evening. Nigella, who'd glimpsed a little of my talent in her brief exposure to it, was about to soothe the awful ache of withdrawal that all actors feel when away from the stage, with the offer of work. If I didn't love her before, what I now felt was unmistakably that emotion.

Nigella looked at her brother, who continued what she'd begun.

'It's a little more complicated than that. What we're looking for are performers whose real job is something else entirely. We have a problem in Darwin. Your brother Fulton has been doing superb work in a unit that very few people know anything about. It's called the Northern Australia Observer Unit, and it's a bit of a guerrilla outfit. These are tough men. Someone doesn't like what they're doing, and we suspect it's either someone inside the unit or certainly someone inside the armed forces. Three of these men have been found dead, and they didn't die of old age. We want to send you two up there as part of a concert party, and we want you to make contact with your brother and find out as much as you can. We're hopeful that this can be sorted out in a matter of weeks. Nobody, and I do mean nobody, up there will know that you're working for us. You'll be on your own.'

'What sort of entertainment do these concert parties put on?' I asked.

'We'll put you in touch with the right people down here who'll give you a crash course, but my understanding is that you pretty much do what you like. If you're willing to slip on a dress, apparently that goes down a treat.'

'And when would this happen?' Brian asked.

'Immediately,' Nigella said. 'Do you need time to discuss it?'

'No,' I said, and looked at Brian who nodded his agreement. 'We'll do whatever we have to do. I'm sure Brian will shave his legs if it's for the good of the country.'

'I can't overstate how dangerous this is, Will. You'll have to watch each other's back like hawks. Trust no one.'

I only half-heard those last words. My head was swimming with the glorious prospect of bringing *Timon of Athens* to Shakespeare-starved troops. All I could hear at that moment was thunderous applause.